There was a shadow on the water

A shadow that was darker than those cast by the trees. As they came closer, Kate saw that the shadow was a man in a dark suit, lying facedown in the shallow river. The back of his head was above the surface. There was a blackish stain on his fair hair, just behind his right ear. Lines of the same color had run down to his collar.

For a moment, horror rooted them to the spot as if they were paralyzed, then Andrew yelled, "Grab an arm. He might still be alive." There was such command in his voice that Kate didn't hesitate. Splashing into the water, she reached down to take hold of one of the man's arms as Andrew grasped the other.

The moment her fingers touched the man she knew he was beyond all mortal help. His body was rigid. Gritting her teeth, Kate forced back the nausea that was threatening to render her powerless.

ABOUT THE AUTHOR

Margaret Chittenden is a multitalented
author who started writing children's books
in 1972 and then became interested in
romantic suspense, no doubt because of her
English background. She has over twenty
books and one hundred articles and short
stories to her credit. Margaret loves to relax
at the beach when she has the time. She and
her husband make their home in the state of
Washington. This is her first book for
Harlequin Intrigue.

The Wainwright Secret

Margaret Chittenden

Harlequin Books

TORONTO • NEW YORK • LONDON
AMSTERDAM • PARIS • SYDNEY • HAMBURG
STOCKHOLM • ATHENS • TOKYO • MILAN
MADRID • WARSAW • BUDAPEST • AUCKLAND

For my dear friend, Stella Cameron,
who writes a nifty mystery herself

Harlequin Intrigue edition published April 1992

ISBN 0-373-22183-5

THE WAINWRIGHT SECRET

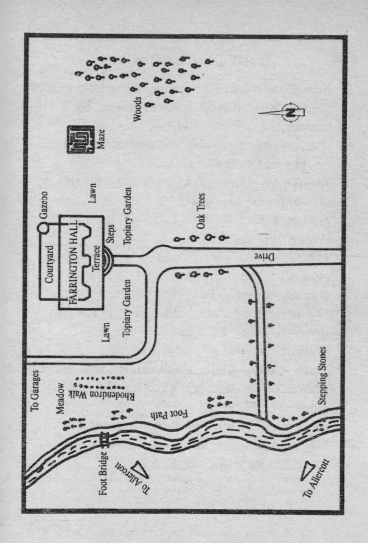

CAST OF CHARACTERS

Kate Wainwright—She came to England to meet her relatives; instead, she was greeted by murder.

Andrew Bradford—He knew what was going on, but was sworn to secrecy.

Jocelyn Bradford—Andrew's daughter saw all—before it happened.

Frederick Wainwright—Lord and master of the Wainwright family.

Hilary Wainwright—Frederick's dutiful wife always looked nervous.

Sikander Balraj—His grandfather was a Wainwright who was banished from the family.

Bennett Coby—He was married to a Wainwright who was now dead.

Elaine Coby—Bennett's daughter loved money.

Robbie Coby—Bennett's son loved money even more.

Emory and Lottie Wainwright—They were brother and sister; Jocelyn called them Tweedledum and Tweedledee.

Chapter One

The body lay facedown in the shallow river. Minnows, darting between the reeds like quicksilver, played hide-and-seek among floating strands of the intruder's blond hair, brushing against his well-manicured fingers and the excellent fabric of his tailored suit. The mist over the water was thick now, sometimes billowing in the slight breeze, making the body appear to be moving. But it wasn't moving. It would never move again.

During the explosive argument the birds in the nearby beech trees had stilled their voices, but now that the other intruder had returned to the big house across the meadow they ventured an occasional trill or twitter. In another hour or so darkness would fall and they would be silent again. As silent as the body in the river.

DRIVING HER RENTED CAR slowly up a driveway lined with oak trees, Kate Wainwright gazed in awe at the imposing bulk of Farrington Hall. The house, built of weathered stone that gleamed darkly under the overcast afternoon sky, was even larger than its name had led her to expect.

She parked the car where the driveway swept to the left around a formal garden in which bushes had been clipped and tortured into shapes resembling art-deco chess pieces.

Emerging, she shivered slightly in the cool damp air. Evidently a May afternoon in England could be just as chilly as a May afternoon in Washington State.

On the east side of the house, in the middle of an incredibly green lawn, stood an unnaturally square collection of high hedges. The maze her grandfather had told her about? Beyond the grass the land was heavily wooded. To the west, beyond another lawn and a double row of tall rhododendron bushes just coming into bloom, a daisy-starred meadow sloped gently down into the distance, where a winding river glinted like molten steel between clumps of trees.

Silence hung over the land and the house, broken only by the occcasional twittering of the birds that hopped around in the oak trees. In the stillness Kate felt an uneasiness that had no real explanation. For the first time she wondered if it had been such a good idea for her to come to England. Maybe she should have stayed home in Seattle.

Abandoning her luggage and camera gear for now, she walked through the topiary garden, up semicircular steps to a wide terrace and an imposing portico. The massive front door stood open and Kate hesitantly entered a large shadowy vestibule, where Grecian-looking statues stood guard in several alcoves. Still feeling chilled, rubbing her forearms, Kate reflected that in such elegant surroundings she should probably be wearing something dressier than French-cut jeans, a red cotton shirt and white Reeboks.

"Hello," she called tentatively.

Only the faint echo of her own voice answered her.

At the foot of a dramatic staircase a large damask table napkin lay on the gleaming parquet floor. Beside the front door, an umbrella stand had been knocked over, spilling out a motley collection of walking sticks. Why were they just lying there? Should she pick them up?

The top of Kate's head tingled. She was being watched.

Glancing up the staircase, she saw a tough-looking, short-haired gray cat staring down at her. "Hi, cat," she called. "Where is everybody?" The cat yawned, turned away and stalked into the shadows. "Nice to meet you, too," Kate muttered.

Wincing at the squeak of her Reeboks on the parquet, she headed toward an open door to the right of the vestibule. The room was decorated in cluttered Victorian style with a preponderance of old photographs and fanciful clocks. A grand piano dominated one corner. A round table had been placed in front of the empty fireplace and set for tea. From the look of the pushed-back chairs and neglected plates of little cakes, the eight diners had deserted the area in a hurry.

Conscious of the mysterious stillness of the house towering above and around her, she checked the rooms in the halls on either side of the vestibule.

She saw masses of heavy Victorian furniture, a lot of darkly rich oil paintings in ornate gilt frames, enough bric-a-brac to fill a couple of antique stores and mirrors that threw back randomly angled reflections of her own tall sturdy body, long, windblown black hair and questioning brown eyes. Unexpectedly she also found a modern kitchen done in black and white with splashes of red.

There were no people to be seen anywhere.

The last door she opened, on the left side of the vestibule, revealed a dim windowless room lined with books. A sofa and several chairs stood about, including a large blue reclining chair with a quilted comforter flung over it. Once again there were no signs of life.

"This is all very peculiar," Kate said aloud.

The comforter moved abruptly and Kate stopped breathing as a man's face appeared in the shadows of the big chair. Cast into a state of shock by this materialization, Kate grabbed for the doorjamb as the man set aside the comforter, unfolded himself from the chair and switched on a nearby floor lamp.

He was a remarkably handsome man of thirty-five or so, a tall man, very much at ease, muscular, dressed in white twill pants and a dark blue sweater. His hair was honey blond and beautifully cut, his face lightly tanned, his eyes a brilliant slate gray with a slightly ironic look to them.

"Not really peculiar," he drawled, gesturing at the rows of books. "Lots of leather-bound volumes bought more for show than go, but there are some rather nice first editions, and the classics of literature are well represented." He hesitated, his upper lip stretching in a somewhat supercilious smile. "Not that anyone as obviously American as you is likely to be interested in old English writers."

His wonderfully plummy British accent had done such delightful things for the English language that it was a moment before Kate was struck, and irritated, by the patronizing nature of his comments.

"As a matter of fact, I studied English literature in college, so I'm fairly well acquainted with English writers," she said stiffly. "Enough for one of the nineteenth-century poets to come back to me as I drove into the grounds." Straight-faced, she quoted: "'The Stately Homes of England, how beautiful they stand, amidst their tall ancestral trees, o'er all the pleasant land.'"

He studied her for a moment with a very thoughtful expression on his face. "More to you than Kipling's rag and bone and hank of hair, isn't there? But don't lose sight of Virginia Woolf. She wasn't impressed with these old piles. Called them 'those comfortably padded lunatic asylums, which are known, euphemistically, as the stately homes of England.'"

Of all the condescending, sarcastic... "This is a ridiculous conversation, isn't it?" Kate said with a phony smile of her own.

"I'll try to do better from now on." He glanced at the mantel clock. "Lord, I've been asleep for two hours. How dreadfully decadent."

"Are you one of the the Wainwrights?" Kate asked.

"Not even a distant relation," he said quickly, as if the very thought was an insult. "I'm Andrew Bradford," he added, extending a competent-looking hand for her to shake. "I expect you are Kate Wainwright? The Seattle branch of the family?"

She withdrew her hand before his could swallow it up. If he wasn't a relative, who was he? Maybe he was Uncle Frederick's valet. Would a valet be taking a nap in the library at five o'clock in the afternoon?

One blond eyebrow was raised in amusement, she noticed. Had she been staring at him? He probably thought she was mesmerized by his rugged masculine beauty, which she was.

"Grandpa William rarely spcke of his four brothers," she offered as distraction. "I don't know anything about their families. I didn't ever really expect to meet any of them, until I got Uncle Frederick's letter inviting me to the family reunion." She took a breath, aware that she was babbling. "What are the Wainwrights like?"

A closed expression appeared on his strong features. "Not my business to reach such conclusions. You'll have to judge for yourself."

Was he always this rude, or was he just having a bad day? Kate wondered.

"None of the brothers is alive except for Frederick," he went on before she could respond. "George, Charles and Alexander died even before William. Their wives, too."

Kate nodded. "Uncle Frederick said in his letter that he and Aunt Hilary were the last survivors of Grandpa's generation." She glanced around her, still puzzled by the absence of sound in the house. "The various descendants were all invited, weren't they? Haven't they gotten here yet?"

"Oh, yes. They all arrived two days ago. Now that you're here everyone's in place with a smile on his or her face, waiting with bated breath."

"For what?" Kate asked, but he just gave her a reprise of his supercilious smile and walked past her to the doorway. Why on earth was he so hostile?

"Where is everyone?" he asked, looking around the vestibule.

Kate made an exasperated sound. "That's what *I* was trying to find out. I went through every room on this floor and they are all empty."

"That's rum." Hands in pants pockets, jiggling some change, he stared at the spilled walking sticks, the forsaken napkin. "Very rum," he repeated.

"There's an abandoned tea table in that room over there," Kate told him, following him out. "Shades of 'Who's been sitting in my chair?' What do you suppose happened?"

He shrugged. "Haven't the foggiest, Miss Wainwright."

"Well, there must be an explanation." Her voice had risen slightly, out of annoyance.

He raised both eyebrows this time. "Let's not get our knickers in a twist, shall we?" he said languidly. With that, he stepped out through the front door onto the terrace. "Hello, here they come," he said, gesturing toward the east.

Kate joined him, and saw several people straggling into view from the direction of the woods. "Why do you suppose they all took off in the middle of tea?'' she asked, after watching for a couple of minutes.

"I've no idea," Andrew Bradford said. "But they're all there. Except for Fishface. Wonder where she's got to."

" 'Fishface'?" Kate queried, but he didn't answer. "Is that Uncle Frederick in the tweed jacket?" she asked. "He looks exactly like Grandpa Will."

Andrew nodded. "All five Wainwright brothers were fair-haired and blue-eyed, I believe."

"That's Aunt Hilary with Frederick?"

"Yes. You'll like her. Charming lady."

"And the young man with black hair?"

"The Indian branch. Sikander Balraj. Age thirty. Grandson of Alexander Wainwright and his Indian wife, Deva."

The slim bespectacled young man was wearing baggy slacks, a shirt and bow tie and a heavy shawl-collared cardigan knitted in several colors. A real snappy dresser, Kate thought. He was followed by an older man in a black-and-white sweater, accompanied by a slight young man with a large nose and long hair, and a young woman with masses of bright blond curly hair that made her head look too large for her thin body.

"Bennett Coby, his son, Robbie, daughter, Elaine— they're twins by the way. Twenty-two years old. They live in Ontario, Canada. Bennett was married to Jennifer Wainwright, now deceased, daughter of Charles Wainwright."

Even at this distance, Kate could see that the young woman had had the misfortune to inherit the same nose as her brother.

Some distance behind the Cobys, a short plump middle-aged woman leaning on a cane and a man who looked enough like her to be a clone were huffing along at a much slower pace than the rest. They were both wearing glasses with gold rims. "The Australian division," Andrew said. "Emory and Lottie Wainwright. Forty-eight years old. Fishface swears they look like Tweedledee and Tweedledum."

She wasn't going to give him the satisfaction of asking who Fishface was. "Are they twins, too?"

"George Wainwright's offspring."

There was an odd note in his voice. Hostility again?

"There have been twins in most generations of Wainwrights," he added.

"What about the older lady?"

"The housekeeper, Mrs. Hogarth. She runs the place almost single-handedly, though Hilary has imported a handful of dailies from the village of Allercott to help her during the family invasion. I suppose they must have gone home for the day."

"You seem to know a lot about the family," Kate said, but Andrew was walking across the terrace to meet the first arrivals and either didn't hear her or chose to ignore her. Feeling irritated again, Kate followed him.

"Delighted to meet you at last, my dear," Frederick Wainwright said heartily as Andrew introduced them. He appeared far younger than his seventy-three years. Tall and slender and distinguished-looking, he had her grandfather's bright blue eyes, ruddy complexion and silvery hair, a duplicate neatly trimmed silver mustache and that same unmistakable air of an English gentleman.

"Surprised to see you all the same," he added. "Understood we'd be sending a car to Heathrow to fetch you. Had a lad alerted, in fact."

"I rented a car," she explained, gesturing.

Frederick turned to look beyond the topiary garden at the somewhat dilapidated car. "Harrumph," he commented.

He made the sound exactly as Grandpa Will would have done, Kate noted, and probably intended the same meaning. Grandpa Will never approved of independent women, especially if they were *his* women.

Kate's aunt Hilary enfolded her in a hug that was wonderfully soft and fragrant with lavender. She was almost as tall as Kate, but far less substantial, almost frail. Kate could feel her bones as she returned the hug.

Hilary appeared very ladylike but slightly dowdy in a beige sweater and matching cardigan, a tweed skirt and sensible walking shoes. Her bobbed brown hair was just beginning to gray. She looked younger than Frederick, Kate thought—fourteen, fifteen years? Which would put her around fifty-eight. She seemed nervous, picking minuscule bits of fluff off her skirt, tugging slightly at her cardigan, fussing with her hair. Kate wanted to take her hands and hold them warmly while murmuring, "There, there."

The others hesitated as they came up the steps, gathering around to shake hands as Hilary introduced them.

After a minute, Frederick waved them on. "Tea will be getting cold," he said.

"I'm putting the kettle on right away," said the elderly housekeeper, coming up behind everyone else. "Need a fresh pot or two after all that excitement, I shouldn't wonder."

No one needed further urging and they all went on into the house, Kate, Andrew, Frederick and Hilary bringing up the rear. What excitement? Kate wanted to know. Wasn't anyone going to explain what was going on?

"You'll need help with your bags, I suppose," Frederick said. "I'll send over to the garages for one of the lads."

"Now, what's all this?" Hilary said, coming upon the spilled canes. Making *tsk-tsk* sounds, she crouched and began placing the items carefully back in the stand.

"Sorry, Hilary," Lottie Wainwright called from across the hall. "I grabbed for a cane on the way out and knocked the whole things for a loop. Bloody arthritic hip wouldn't let me bend down to pick 'em all up."

"My father collected those walking sticks," Frederick told Kate. "Robert Wainwright. Your great-grandfather." He nodded once, then turned his bright blue eyes onto Andrew. "Sorry to have to tell you this, old man, but you're going to have to speak to that daughter of yours."

So the gorgeous but supercilious Andrew Bradford had a daughter. Which meant he probably had a wife, too. Poor woman.

"Jocelyn? What has she been up to?" Andrew asked.

Frederick gestured vaguely around the vestibule, at the umbrella stand, the place on the floor where the napkin had lain until Elaine Coby had picked it up a minute ago. "She came dashing into the drawing room—we were having tea— and she was all in a tizzy about some body she'd seen under the beech trees. Very convincing, she was—all pale skin and staring eyes, lots of melodrama. Almost gave me a heart attack."

"A body?" Andrew sounded shocked and disbelieving.

Even while she was registering shock herself, Kate was pleased to see that Andrew Bradford could be shaken out of his equanimity.

"*Whose* body?" he exclaimed.

"What I'd like to know, old man," Frederick said. "Off we went to the woods like hounds to the chase and what did we find? Not a blade of grass disturbed. Turned out she hadn't really seen a body—she'd had a vision or some such nonsense."

"Remember your blood pressure, darling," Hilary murmured, tugging away at her cardigan again.

Frederick's face had certainly gone red. "Have a word with that girl, if I were you," he reiterated.

"I'll do that," Andrew said through lips that had tightened considerably. Returning to the entrance, he stepped outside. "Here she is now," he called back over his shoulder.

Curious, Kate joined him on the terrace. Still some distance away, trailing slowly toward the house, was a tall girl wearing a brown-and-white Western-style shirt and blue jeans, her light brown hair done up neatly in a single braid. Everything in the girl's posture—chin tucked down, shoulders hunched, arms clasped across her chest—proclaimed *I do not want to be here. I wish I could disappear.*

"Damn it, Fishface," Andrew muttered. "What the hell am I to do with you?"

JOCELYN BRADFORD WANTED nothing more than to turn herself around and keep walking in the opposite direction until she reached the end of the world and fell off. Her father was furious, obviously; she could tell by the set of his shoulders, the solid placement of his long legs.

There was a woman on the terrace behind him. A very pretty young woman with glossy black hair that hung straight down her back. Jocelyn had no idea who she might be, and was torn between hoping she'd stay put, thus inhibiting Daddy's anger, or leave so Jocelyn wouldn't be embarrassed in front of any more people today.

She hesitated at the foot of the steps, glancing up at her father. His handsome face looked thunderous and he'd folded his arms across his chest. From here he looked ten feet tall.

There was only one thing to do. Crumpling gracelessly onto the bottom step, she buried her face in her hands and burst into tears.

"Oh, for heaven's sake, Fishface, not the waterworks, please." He came down the steps hurriedly and sat down next to her, patting her shoulders and head indiscriminately.

"I'm sorry, Daddy," she said in a muffled voice. "I can't seem to help crying. It was so awfully frightening. And now I feel such a fool."

"Better start at the beginning," he advised.

Blowing her nose on a tissue she'd pulled from her shirt-sleeve, she risked a glance at his face. He still appeared quite stern, but the black look had gone from his forehead. Perhaps it wasn't going to be too bad, after all. She noticed that the young black-haired woman had followed him down and was seating herself on a higher step. She had friendly brown eyes and a smiley sort of face. Jocelyn felt quite encouraged. Maybe the new arrival was going to be on *her* side.

She fixed her gaze on her father's face. "I was sitting right here on this step," she said slowly. "I'd decided to miss tea, even though I was hungry, because . . . well, it's a bit grotty, all those dotty people buttering up the colonel."

Her father shot her a look, then rolled his eyes vaguely in the young woman's direction. "This is Miss Kate Wainwright, from America, Jocelyn. She's a relation of Frederick's, too."

Put her foot in it as usual, had she? "Sorry," she muttered, then hugged her knees to her chest and gazed at them. "I was just sitting here," she said again. "It got really quiet all of a sudden and then I saw one of my fuzzy things."

"Fuzzy things?" Kate Wainwright asked.

Jocelyn nodded. "It's like looking at shadows of things that aren't quite there yet." She glanced apologetically at her father. "Do you remember me telling you this morning that I'd seen a picture in my mind of a body just as I was going to sleep last night? You thought I'd probably dreamed it? Well, while I was sitting here it happened again, still fuzzy, only in more detail—a man lying on his back beneath some beech trees. It was quite clear in my mind that he was dead, and he was definitely under beech trees—I could see the leaves. So it had to be in the woods, I thought. But we tramped all over and we couldn't find a thing." She picked up a small rock that had found its way onto the step and started dropping it from one hand to the other.

"All right," her father said crisply. "You saw a fuzzy picture of a body. What did you do next?"

She dropped the pebble and dusted her hands together. "I searched the house for you, but I couldn't find you. The others were all in having tea, so I sort of burst in and told them what I'd seen. I didn't know they were all going to jump up and hare off to the woods, but I suppose they got excited. They thought I'd seen an actual body. I probably didn't explain very well. I was so frightened."

She looked pleadingly up at her father, but his face didn't soften. She sighed. "When they got to the woods, they hunted all around. Then the colonel started questioning me and I told him about the fuzzy things and he decided I'd probably made it up and they should come back and finish their tea."

" 'The colonel'?" Kate queried.

Jocelyn's father answered her without turning around. "Frederick. He served in the army during the war. The local people always call him 'the colonel.'" His gray eyes were holding Jocelyn's very steadily. "*Did* you make it all up?"

"I didn't. Honestly." She gazed helplessly at him, "I couldn't believe the body wasn't there. I was so sure..."

Kate Wainwright still looked sympathetic. She had jolly nice hair, Jocelyn thought. It was as straight as Jocelyn's own, but with a fringe at the front that went up and over in an interesting spiky sort of way. "You've had this sort of experience before?" she asked.

Jocelyn's father snorted and Kate flashed him an irritated look.

"Ever since I was small," Jocelyn said. "The pictures just sort of appear unexpectedly. I don't make them come. I don't want them." She shuddered, feeling the coldness that always accompanied the pictures, the terrible sense of dread.

"And they've always come true?" Kate persisted.

"Usually." She hesitated. "I suppose you think I'm weird."

Kate shook her head. "No, I think you probably have some kind of extrasensory perception, which is a gift that's given only to special people. Maybe you tuned in on something that happened somewhere else."

Jocelyn began to feel better. At least someone was taking her seriously. "I should probably have gone into the woods to look without telling anyone," she said. "But I didn't really want to go looking for a body by myself."

"Very wise of you," Kate said.

"Do you think so?" Jocelyn said eagerly, then tipped her head to one side. "Are you really a Wainwright? You don't look like one. Sikander doesn't, either, but his mother was Indian."

"I'm a mixture, too," Kate explained. "My mother was Italian and volatile, my father very reserved and English. I look like my mother, but my temperament's half and half.

You can never be sure if I'll adopt a laissez-faire attitude or blow up like Mount Saint Helens.''

Jocelyn decided she liked Kate Wainwright. She didn't talk down to her and there was a sort of good-natured edge to her voice that was very attractive.

"We're getting off the subject," Andrew Bradford said.

Which brought him another exasperated glance from the American woman, Jocelyn noted.

"You really must show some discretion about these experiences, Fishface. You can't go getting people all stirred up."

"Yes, Daddy." Jocelyn felt as if she were going to cry again any minute. She hated it when her father was cross with her.

"Better go bath before dinner," he said more kindly.

Jocelyn made a face. "I don't really want to go in to dinner," she said slowly. "Everyone hates me, Daddy. Perhaps I could just go straight to bed. I do feel awfully tired."

Her father shook his head. "Sorry, old dear, Bradfords aren't allowed to be cowards. My father used to tell me that all the time when bullies picked on me in school. I see no reason why it shouldn't apply to you."

Jocelyn tried to imagine anyone having the nerve to pick on her father, and failed utterly. Reluctantly she got to her feet. "All right," she said gloomily. "I'll do it for the Bradford reputation. Nice to have met you, Miss Wainwright," she added.

"'Kate,'" the young woman said. She smiled encouragingly. "I wouldn't worry about everyone hating you. I would think they'd all be relieved there isn't a body, after all."

Jocelyn smiled at her, then turned around and ran up the steps and across the terrace, slowing when she reached the vestibule. None of the Wainwrights were in sight, which at first relieved her, then frightened her. Farrington Hall was such an old house, full of history. It seemed to Jocelyn that if she listened really hard she'd be able to hear whispering voices from the past.

The vestibule was large and shadowy, with dim niches here and there where white statues gleamed. Jocelyn fancied she could feel their eyes watching her as she went slowly up the stairs. She always felt a need to tiptoe on these stairs so she wouldn't disturb any ghosts.

She was almost to the third floor, when she began to experience a horribly familiar coldness. She hesitated, hoping it would go away, but instead it intensified. And then her vision began to blur. "Please don't let it happen," she murmured.

Hanging on to the banister, she forced her trembling legs to keep climbing. By the time she'd reached her room she could barely see where she was going. Flinging herself onto her bed, she closed her eyes tightly, as though that would help to blot out the picture that was forming inexorably.

She couldn't hold it back. Her teeth were chattering from the cold, her whole body trembling. *Do something,* she scolded herself. *Get up off the bed and move around. Talk out loud. Fight back.* But a dreadful languor held her prisoner and she could not move. Now shadows were forming in the long dark tunnel of her inner vision, gradually becoming trees that sheltered something. Something she didn't want to see, but could not look away from. A man's body, lying on his back. A man in a dark suit. A dead man. How could she be so sure he was dead? Because of the coldness—wave after wave of it washing over her, threatening to drown her.

IT WAS A FEW MINUTES before Andrew spoke. "I'd rather you didn't encourage Jocelyn's fantasies," he said, turning to look up at Kate. "I'm afraid she's just looking for attention."

"Maybe you don't give her enough," Kate suggested, which was a bit of cheek, considering she'd just met the two of them. "She looked to me like a child in need of a hug," she added.

"I prefer to give her space," he said defensively. "She's been the victim of too much attention all her life. I'm quite sure that's why she occasionally has these…episodes. I've had her in therapy—my mother's a psychotherapist—but I can't say it's doing a lot of good. The problem is exacerbated at the moment because Jocelyn's mother died five months ago, of cancer, and Jocelyn hasn't quite adjusted yet."

"I should think not," Kate protested. "Poor little kid, what is she—eleven?"

"Twelve, just. But she's remarkably self-reliant."

"Twelve years old. And lost her mother. I'd think the last thing she needs is space." She looked at him directly. "I'm sorry. I didn't even offer any sympathy, and it must be hard on you, too, losing your wife."

He felt, and probably looked, tremendously embarrassed. "I don't know how to put this tactfully," he said. "Straight out is best, I suppose. Jocelyn's mother and I separated while she was still pregnant with Jocelyn. I haven't seen much of my daughter during the past twelve years apart from holidays."

"You left your wife while she was pregnant?"

Amazing how huffy women could get the minute they imagined one of their own had been mistreated. "I suppose you could put it that way," he said with some stiffness of his own.

She was gazing at him with obvious disapproval. He wouldn't have thought brown eyes could look frosty—one thought of brown eyes as warm and friendly—but at the moment Kate Wainwright's were neither. He'd be damned if he'd explain his situation to her. Let her think what she liked.

"Why are you here?" she asked abruptly.

Feeling mildly put out by this inquisition and thus a little on the devilish side, he decided to misunderstand her. "Better philosophers than I have attempted and failed to answer that question, Miss Wainwright," he said.

A look of astonishment spread over her face, followed by a gurgle of laughter that Andrew had to admit was very melodious. At least this Wainwright relation had a sense of humor. He felt a slight softening going on inside, but quelled it at once. He knew why Kate Wainwright had come to Farrington Hall and he didn't want her thinking he'd be on her side.

"I'm just naturally inquisitive, I guess," she said with a charming smile. "When I was a kid my grandmother used to say I had a bump of curiosity a yard wide. I spent a lot of time examining my body to see if I could find it."

Her tall body was built on fairly generous and curvaceous lines—not an ounce of fat that he could see, but good solid flesh with a hint of muscle behind it. Examining such a body might be—

He put an immediate stop to such lewd thoughts. He would tell a limited version of the truth, he decided. "Frederick invited me down to recuperate," he told her. "I've been ill with pneumonia. Seemed a good chance to get to know Jocelyn a little better, so I took her out of school a bit early and brought her along. She goes to a private school, one for gifted children, so they're relaxed about such things."

Her expression showed sympathy rather nicely, he thought. She had a lovely wide mouth. Anything he hated it was a woman with a stingy mouth. Actually, she was quite striking with that jet black hair and creamy skin and dark eyes. Too bad they hadn't met under more auspicious circumstances. Too bad she was a Wainwright. "I suppose I should go in and try to make peace," he said with a sigh. "I can't imagine what possessed Fishface."

"It's all very peculiar," she murmured.

He raised an eyebrow. "Isn't this where we came in?"

The sound of her laughter really was delightful, he thought. It tempted a man to keep the jocular remarks coming. Which wasn't a good idea given the current Wainwright situation.

Standing, he reached a hand down to help Kate to her feet, then they both turned to go up the steps—and stopped dead. Jocelyn was standing at the top, her face the approximate color of buttermilk.

His heart contracting, Andrew took the steps two at a time. "What's wrong?" he said sharply.

Jocelyn looked up at him in silence for a moment, her mouth working, then she said, "Do you remember the story of the boy who cried wolf, Daddy?"

Kate Wainwright joined them silently. Andrew nodded, putting his hand on his daughter's shoulder. She was trembling uncontrollably. "A shepherd boy, wasn't he?" he said, speaking evenly in an attempt to calm her. "He kept routing the villagers out of bed with false alarms about a wolf attacking the sheep, until they wouldn't believe him anymore. So when a wolf actually came, he couldn't get anyone to help."

Jocelyn's light blue eyes seemed too large for her pinched white face. "I saw it again, Daddy," she said shakily. "The dead man under the beech trees. And I remembered that there are a few beech trees by the river.''

"Are you sure about this, young Jocelyn?" Andrew said sternly, then stopped as her face began to crumple.

"We could at least take a look," Kate suggested quietly.

Exasperated, Andrew glared at her, but she was gazing at Jocelyn with that charmingly sympathetic expression of hers and it disarmed him. She was so tall he could chart her expressions without ducking his head. In the clear cool light, her skin showed no flaw. Remarkable.

"Please, Daddy?" Jocelyn begged. "I know you think I'm crackers, but I'm not making this up, really I'm not."

Andrew sighed, acknowledging defeat. "Go on in and get a cardigan or something," he said finally, adding as she shot away toward the front door, "and tell Hilary we're taking Kate for a walk in the grounds. Don't tell anyone anything about fuzzy things."

"I won't, Daddy," she called back.

"Bodies, indeed," he muttered.

Chapter Two

It was cold by the river. In the past few minutes the sky had darkened and a breeze had come up that had a definite edge to it. Kate was glad of the leather jacket she'd pulled out of her car before they'd started off across the meadow.

This was the strangest arrival she'd ever had anywhere, she decided as they walked along the riverside footpath. Jocelyn had called the Wainwright relatives "dotty"— perhaps Jocelyn, Andrew and Kate were the dotty ones. Were the three of them seriously searching for a body on the strength of a fuzzy image that had appeared to a twelve-year-old girl? Feeling chilled again, she fastened the snaps on the front of her double-breasted jacket and pulled the collar up.

Andrew glanced at her sideways. "Too bad you didn't arrive yesterday," he said without noticeable friendliness. "It was much warmer—quite hot, actually—foggy in the evening, though."

"Daddy," Jocelyn said tensely.

The rising, quivering note of fear in her voice sent a shaft of ice shuddering down Kate's spine even before she saw that Jocelyn was pointing at the water a few yards ahead, just this side of a small footbridge. The river was a wide one, but no more than two or three inches deep at this point. It rippled lazily as the breeze wafted over it.

There was a shadow on the water. A shadow that was darker than the tree shadows. As they came closer, Kate saw that the shadow was a man in a dark suit, lying face-down in the shallow river. The back of his head was above the surface. There was a blackish stain on his fair hair, just behind his right ear. Lines of the same color ran down to his collar.

For a moment, horror rooted them to the spot as if they were paralyzed. Then Andrew yelled, "Grab an arm—he might still be alive."

There was such command in his voice that Kate didn't hesitate. Splashing into the water, she reached down to take hold of one of the man's arms as Andrew grasped the other.

The moment her fingers touched the man she knew he was beyond all mortal help. His body was rigid. Gritting her teeth, Kate forced back the nausea that was threatening to render her powerless. Ignoring muscles that smarted in protest, she helped Andrew haul the man out onto the bank. As gently as possible, they laid him down on his back on top of a drift of bluebells under a beech tree.

His face was a ghastly color, his blue eyes wide open, his jaw hanging loose. He was probably about forty. As Kate looked at him the world tilted on its axis and her stomach threatened to erupt.

"Steady," Andrew murmured.

At first Kate thought he was speaking to her, but the concern in his voice was for his daughter.

Jocelyn was hugging herself tightly, staring at the body, her eyes wide with fear. "That's how I saw him," she whispered. "He was lying just like that. Under the trees."

Andrew put his arms around her and held her close. "I know, Fishface. You were right, after all. I'm sorry I didn't take you seriously."

"I didn't want to be right, Daddy," she wailed against his chest. "I wanted to find out there was nothing here. I wanted you to laugh at me because I'd imagined it all." Her slight body was shaking, her face deathly white. "I didn't know it was *him*," she said in an even louder voice, sounding close to hysteria.

"It's all right," Andrew said crisply, setting her away. "Now listen carefully," he added, pointing to a group of trees farther along the bank. "I want you to go over there and sit down. If you feel faint, put your head between your knees. I'll be with you in a minute."

He glanced at Kate as Jocelyn moved away like a sleep-walker. "Are you all right?"

She nodded automatically, though she still felt nauseated, and distinctly dizzy. Even as she nodded, she swayed. Andrew caught her and held her tightly in arms that felt like iron. How soft his sweater felt against her cheek, Kate thought. It must be cashmere; nothing felt quite as wonderfully soft as cashmere. She was tempted to burrow into the softness, to go on standing in the safe shelter of his arms forever.

"Don't *you* go female on me," he exclaimed.

Anger restored her circulation. She took a deep breath and pulled away from him, ready to chew him out for his lack of sensitivity. But then she noticed that his eyes looked sick and his face had paled under his tan. This wasn't any easier for him than it was for her. And he had been ill recently. "I'm okay now," she said, which was obviously not true; she was shivering uncontrollably, not just because of getting her feet wet. Looking down at the body, she started to say something more, but her voice couldn't seem to make it through her dry throat. "Who is he?" she managed hoarsely at last. "He looks like a younger version of Uncle Frederick."

"He's Harry Wainwright," Andrew said.

There was a hard note in his voice that bothered Kate. "Uncle Frederick's heir?" she asked.

He looked at her oddly, then nodded. "Frederick told you about him when he invited you, I suppose."

"He said he wanted his brothers' descendants to meet one another and he also wanted to introduce us all to his cousin, Harry Wainwright, his heir."

He nodded. "Harry's father, Peter Wainwright, was Frederick's uncle—Robert Wainwright's younger brother. Peter died a few months ago, at the ripe old age of ninety."

Were they really standing there discussing relationships while a man lay dead at their feet? Natural enough, she supposed. She had noticed before that in times of intense stress, people tended to strive hard for normality.

"Looks as if he's been in the river for some time," Andrew said. His mouth looked pinched and there was still a sick look around his eyes. "He was at the house yesterday. He's the only relation not staying with Frederick and Hilary. He lives in Market Ridgeway, the village beyond Allercott, touristy sort of place. He owns an exclusive men's clothing shop there. He decided to walk home after tea, I remember. Said he needed the exercise. He was supposed to come back to dinner this evening."

He turned away abruptly and walked over to where Jocelyn was sitting on the ground, hugging her knees. Kate followed him, her Reeboks squelching, knees threatening to give way. "Are you feeling better, Fishface?" he asked his daughter. "You and I have to run to the house and call the police."

"I don't want to stay here alone," Kate protested.

"Somebody has to," Andrew said.

"Why does anybody have to stay? Harry's not going anywhere." She was getting hysterical. She took a deep breath. "All right, I agree, it doesn't seem decent to run out on him."

"I'll stay with you," Jocelyn said. "My legs are still wobbly, anyway." She looked up at her father. "Why do we have to get the police?"

"Any death that isn't due to natural causes has to be investigated," Andrew replied evasively.

"But the way you said it, are you thinking it's..."

Andrew hesitated a moment more, then said gently, "Yes, love, I'm afraid it looks very much like murder."

Jocelyn flinched, but she didn't take her gaze off her father's face. Brave kid, Kate thought approvingly. "You don't suppose whoever killed him's still around?" she asked, looking nervously over her shoulder.

"More likely to be miles away if he's got any sense at all."

"Couldn't it have been an accident?" Jocelyn asked. "It was really foggy last night. Harry could have stumbled..."

Kate shook her head. "If you stumbled into the river and fell and hit your head on a rock, you'd hit the front of it."

"He could have slipped and fallen backward," Jocelyn suggested.

"And then turned over?" Andrew asked gently.

Kate felt hollow inside. "You'd better go," she said to Andrew, then added, "Hurry back."

He nodded, but then got down on his knees in front of his daughter and put both hands on her shoulders. "I don't want you to tell anyone at all about having another fuzzy thing, all right?" he said.

Understanding jolted through Kate's body, making her shiver. Andrew was afraid Jocelyn's abilities might reach the murderer's ears. If the murderer was still in the area, Jocelyn would be in danger.

"I won't, Daddy," Jocelyn said solemnly.

Andrew stood up, glanced once more at Harry Wainwright's body and started away across the field. As soon as he was out of earshot, Jocelyn began sobbing softly, but there was no hysteria in the sound.

Kate let herself down beside the girl and drew her into her arms. "You go right ahead and let it out," she murmured, close to indulging in a little sobbing of her own.

After a couple of minutes, Jocelyn recovered and pulled gently away, sniffling. Kate found a crumpled tissue in her jacket pocket and handed it to her.

"I'm such a baby," the girl muttered.

"No, you're not. There'd be something wrong with you if you didn't get upset, given the circumstances, especially as you knew him. You did know him?"

"Not really. I met him for the first time when Daddy and I came down from London yesterday morning." She glanced over at the body, then shuddered and turned back to Kate. "The awful thing is I didn't like him much."

"Why not?" It was shameless to pump the girl at a time like this, but what else were they going to talk about?

Jocelyn considered for a while. "He came into the kitchen while I was in there playing with Gray Boy—the cat. He said, 'Oh, so you're Jocelyn, are you?' Then he laughed in a funny sort of way and asked me to give him a kiss. Which I wouldn't do, of course." She hesitated, obviously selecting her words. "I told Daddy about it. He was very cross. I can always tell when Daddy's cross—the back of his neck gets stiff."

It had been stiff ever since she'd met him, Kate thought. "Your father met Harry for the first time yesterday morning, too?" she asked.

"Oh, no, Daddy's known him for a long time. He'd never mentioned him to me, but later on I heard them having a big fight on the stairs and I gathered they'd had some kind of problem in the past."

"What kind of problem was it?" Kate asked, making her voice casual.

A wary expression crossed the girl's face. "I couldn't make out what they were shouting about."

She was lying, Kate was pretty sure. If Andrew Bradford had quarreled with Harry Wainwright just before his death... "How did the other relatives get along with Harry?" she asked.

"Well, he and Lottie had a go-round yesterday, as well. I don't know about anyone else." She pondered for a minute, then said, "I don't think *anyone* liked him—except the colonel. He kept trying to tell everyone Harry was a good person, saying that he sold really good suits and things and that he had given his sister a home when her husband had died. But it didn't do any good. When Harry came in for tea it was as if everybody except the colonel had banded together against him." She frowned, then added, "Because he was the heir, I suppose. It stands to reason, doesn't it? There they all were, direct descendants of Wainwright brothers, all hoping to inherit from the colonel, and the colonel had brought Harry on the scene."

Did she realize she'd just given a whole lot of people a motive for murder? Kate wondered, then looked at Jocelyn's innocent face and knew she didn't. "How do you know they all want to inherit?" she asked.

"Daddy says there's no other reason they'd come all this way," Jocelyn explained. "I mean, after all, Australia, Canada, India, the U—" She broke off hurriedly.

Kate stiffened. Andrew's hostile attitude toward her was explained. He thought *she* was after Frederick's money. Of all the... "What's it got to do with your father, anyway?" she asked Jocelyn.

"He's the Wainwrights' solicitor." The girl's face was crimson with embarrassment. "I forgot you were one of the relations," she said apologetically. "Mummy always said I couldn't open my mouth without putting my foot in it. She teased me a lot about that." An expression of pain crossed her mobile face.

Andrew Bradford was hopelessly miscast as a solicitor, Kate decided. In English mystery novels the solicitor was usually a little dry-as-dust man with a bald head and rimless spectacles. How would she cast him? Perhaps as one of the Viking rovers whose raids and conquests were famous in English history. He had a certain sea-warrior look about him.

Jocelyn still appeared embarrassed.

"I'm sorry about your mother," Kate said. "Would you like to talk about her, or would you prefer not to?"

Jocelyn looked at her directly. How wonderfully clear-eyed she was. "I do like the way you put that," she said, "straight out without getting maudlin about it. I've been clutched to an awful lot of maternal bosoms lately. It never seems possible to talk about Mummy to people like that." She sighed. "I miss Mummy awfully. She was a jolly nice mother. Beautiful, too. The sort of woman men turned round to look at. But she wasn't selfish the way some beautiful women get. She always had time for me. We used to have long talks, and we used to laugh a lot. She could always make me laugh."

"She sounds wonderful," Kate said.

"She was."

"I understand you don't know your father too well," Kate said, without attempting to keep disapproval out of her voice.

"You mustn't blame Daddy for that," Jocelyn said. "Mummy loved traveling, you see. Cannes, Biarritz—even Bermuda and the Bahamas. She always took me with her—I've been in more schools than you could imagine—but Daddy always had his work, you see."

"All the same, Joss, your father could have—" She broke off. It wasn't too tactful to criticize Andrew to his daughter. In any case, Jocelyn had glanced across at the body lying under the trees a few yards away and was looking distinctly pale again. It was time to switch to a lighter subject. Trouble was, in the circumstances, nothing light would come to mind.

"What did you call me?" Jocelyn asked.

"'Joss'?" Kate gave her an apologetic glance. "Sorry, it's a terrible American habit, shortening people's names."

"But I like it. 'Joss' sounds much jollier than 'Jocelyn.'"

"Better than 'Fishface,' anyway," Kate said.

Jocelyn looked at her ingenuously. "I like being called 'Fishface,' too," she said. "Daddy told me when I was born I had fat cheeks and looked just like a little fish. That's where he got the idea for my nickname."

Something didn't add up here. Andrew had left his wife while she was pregnant, but he had evidently been around for the birth—then absent for most of the following years.

"'Jocelyn' is sometimes a man's name, you know," the girl added.

"No, I didn't know," Kate said, making a mental note to look into Jocelyn's relationship with her father at a less stressful time. "I've never run into it before. I think it's a great name. Musical."

Jocelyn's mouth twitched into what might have become a smile under other circumstances. "I like you, Kate," she said warmly. "Will you be my friend?"

Kate put an arm around her shoulders and hugged her, then noticed that several people were coming along the footpath—Andrew, Frederick Wainwright, a stocky man in a brown jacket, some other people in police uniform. She had a distinct feeling of unreality as she watched them approach. Not only was she suffering from shock, coupled with jet lag, so that she felt out of sync with everything around her, but in one afternoon she'd managed to acquire a group of apparently greedy relatives left out of their wealthy uncle's will, plus a dead potential heir. All this together with an English country house Hercule Poirot would have felt quite at home in. Somehow she'd managed to walk right into the middle of an old-fashioned English mystery story. She had a sinking suspicion that she wasn't going to be able to walk right out of it again.

Chapter Three

"I can't believe we're just sitting here as if nothing has happened," the Canadian, Bennett Coby said from his end of the long, linen-draped dining table. At the slight tremor in his voice, Hilary put a slender white hand on his arm.

It seemed astonishing to Kate, too, that while half a mile away a dead man lay staring sightlessly up at the sky, his relatives were calmly eating dinner, all dressed to the teeth: the men in suits; Hilary in a gray-green dress of shot silk; Lottie encased in burgundy; Elaine Coby in a poorly cut black sheath that made her look thinner than ever; Kate herself in a loden green silk jumpsuit, the drabbest thing she'd brought with her; Jocelyn in a neat blue dress with a white collar.

Jocelyn had been very subdued since they'd returned to the house. Which wasn't too surprising. Ever since they'd heard that Jocelyn's "vision" had proved true, the others kept giving her furtive glances as though they expected her to go off in a trance.

"What else would you suggest?" Frederick asked Bennett.

He was presiding at the head of the table, looking very distinguished in a well-cut dark suit. He seemed rather pale, Kate thought, though that might be the effect of the elaborate glass chandelier that was too far above their heads to chase the shadows from the room, which was the size of a ducal hall.

"Naturally, we are all upset about poor Harry," Frederick continued. He paused, pressing his fingers to his eyes momentarily. "It does no good to give way to hysteria," he said briskly. "Business as usual—that's the ticket to civilized behavior."

Kate could almost hear trumpets sounding out "God Save the Queen."

"I'm sure Detective Inspector Erskine will take care of everything," Hilary added soothingly.

The inspector, a somewhat dour Scot in a brown tweed jacket and baggy cords, had come back to the house and taken what he'd called preliminary statements from Kate, Andrew and Jocelyn, promising—threatening?—that he'd go into more detail later. He and his colleagues were still working around the body. Kate's mind flashed an image of the beech trees by the river, now guarded by yards of white crime scene tape. She shivered and wrenched her thoughts away from the accompanying image of that dead bloodless face.

"Why should we be civilized?" Lottie Wainwright, the Australian woman, asked. "Seems to me we might do a bit of sleuthin' before the wallopers get here."

"'Wallopers'?" Andrew queried.

"P-p-police officers," her twin brother, Emory, translated.

He hadn't said enough earlier for Kate to realize he had such a pronounced stammer.

"We might start with you, Elaine," Lottie suggested. "You were getting real cozy with Harry yesterday."

A wave of scarlet rose from Elaine's low neckline all the way up to her teased blond hair. "I don't know what you mean," she said primly.

Lottie pointed her fork at the girl. "I *saw* you. Flirting with Harry. In the vestibule. Yesterday afternoon. Wasn't having any, was he?"

Elaine jumped to her feet, flinging down her napkin. "That's an absolute lie," she shouted.

Andrew, sitting next to Lottie, murmured something to her that sounded disapproving. The plump woman looked at him in a very arch manner, showing all her rather large teeth. "You're a corker you are, cobber," she said, then grinned cheerfully at Elaine. "Well, what about it, then?" she persisted. "What *did* you talk to Harry about?"

"Really, Lottie," Hilary protested as Elaine slumped back into her seat and seemed about to burst into tears. "This isn't any of our business."

"Harry's been murdered," Lottie pointed out. "Anything that happened yesterday is our business."

Including the argument she'd had with Harry herself? Kate wondered. Jocelyn was gazing at the Australian woman, obviously thinking the same thing.

"Sikander's the one who was really mad at Harry," Elaine blurted out, obviously deflecting attention from herself.

"Too right," Lottie agreed, evidently willing to be diverted. "What was it he called you at tea yesterday? A 'raghead'?"

Sikander appeared to take the comment calmly. But his hands, Kate noticed, were gripping his knife and fork so tightly his knuckles gleamed. He was a very good-looking young man, with bronze skin, very white teeth, black hair and dark eyes. They had a bond, she and Sikander; neither of them looked anything like the other blue-eyed blond Wainwrights.

"What does that mean?" Jocelyn asked.

"Many Indians wear turbans," Sikander explained, hands clenching tighter, the pupils behind his magnifying spectacles contracting visibly. "I do not wear a turban, but that is not the point. The remark was intended as a great insult and that is how I took it."

Andrew made a grimace of distaste. "Not a very nice chap, our Harry," he said quietly.

What about *his* quarrel with Harry? Kate wondered. Lottie mustn't have witnessed that one. The dead man had obviously had a busy day yesterday—three arguments and one insulting remark. Who else had he quarreled with? The murderer?

"How about you, Hilary?" Lottie asked. Was there no stopping the woman? "How did you get on with old Harry?"

Hilary's slender hands fluttered like distress signals and finally settled at her throat. "Please, let's not do this," she begged. Looking pleadingly down the table at Andrew, she added, "Surely we shouldn't discuss this dreadful affair until the police have finished gathering their evidence?"

Andrew gave her a sympathetic smile, but shook his head. "Actually, it's probably a good idea to talk about it, Hilary. Inspector Erskine will be asking us all questions, I expect."

"What kind of questions?" Elaine asked.

"The usual routine, I suppose. Where we all were at the time of the murder, which would seem to be between the hours of five and eight p.m. yesterday. When we last saw Harry. What sort of man he was."

There was a silence, then Lottie said, "Emory and I were probably the last to see Harry alive."

"A-p-part from the m-murderer," Emory added hastily.

Lottie nodded solemnly. "Too right." She frowned. "Last we saw of him, he was just starting off across the meadow toward the river."

"What time was that?" Andrew asked.

"Five past five. Right after tea. We were in a hurry to get to Allercott to buy postcards before the shops closed. We borrowed Hilary's car, the Austin. While we were waiting for the lad to bring it over from the garage, Harry came out of the house. I offered him a lift, but he said he'd rather walk." There was a look in her prominent blue Wainwright eyes that made Kate think Harry's voice might have lent a more meaningful emphasis to the statement.

Lottie shook her head. "Poor bugger. Probably would still be alive if he'd let us take him home."

"He was alone?" Frederick asked.

Lottie nodded eagerly, her spectacle frames glittering.

"What time did you come back to the house?" Andrew asked.

Lottie shrugged. "Half past six? I didn't notice. I drove back slowly because of the fog. It was all right going, but coming back was a bit chancy."

"Did you like Harry?" Andrew asked.

Lottie showed all her large teeth. "He seemed jake enough, didn't you think, Emory?"

Jocelyn fidgeted a little next to Kate. Kate exchanged a glance with her. Obviously Lottie wasn't going to admit quarreling with Harry.

"Did you notice anything special about Harry at that time?" Andrew asked. "Any small detail that might not seem significant, but just might be helpful?"

Emory stirred and said, "Didn't he have a . . ."

"A coat on," Lottie finished for him. "Yes, he did. Good on you, Emory. What was it, a suit jacket? And it had been hot all day. But, then, Brits do like to be dressed properly. I remember our dad wearing a tweed suit on Christmas—and Christmas Day in Australia is hot as Hades. 'Course it *was* getting colder—the fog was just starting to come up."

Emory was staring at Lottie with a puzzled expression. Kate glanced at her in time to see her move her head slightly. It was an infinitesimal movement, but definitely negative. Apparently only Kate and Emory saw it. What was that all about? she wondered.

Bennett suddenly spoke up again. "I took a long walk after tea on Wednesday," he said. "Not toward the river," he added hastily. "Through the woods."

"In the fog?" Frederick asked.

"It wasn't all that bad in the woods," Bennett said. "I was alone," he added with what seemed unnecessary emphasis.

"Perhaps we should all tell where we were between five and eight that day," Frederick said.

Hilary couldn't remember. "I was probably writing up lists of things to do," she said, fluttering her hands about.

Frederick said it was his habit to spend the hours between tea and dinner writing in his study. "I'm working on my political memoirs," he revealed. "Robbie was playing the piano," he added. "I could hear the sound clearly in my study."

Robbie confirmed that he had played for most of that time. "I'm a concert pianist," he told Kate, his blue eyes brimming with self-satisfaction.

He did look fairly arty, she supposed, though it was her private opinion that shoulder-length tresses looked decidedly odd on a man in a suit. He wasn't quite as thin as his sister, but he needed to fill out a bit in order to lessen the impact of his prominent nose.

Elaine had been painting her fingernails in her room, reading a movie magazine.

"I was practicing yoga in the courtyard behind the house," Sikander said.

"Did any of you notice anything out of the ordinary during that period of time?" Andrew asked.

Everyone shook their heads, including Sikander. But Sikander also pushed up his spectacles and pulled at his nose with the long brown fingers of one hand. Kate was suddenly alert. She had seen people rub their noses like that when they weren't telling the truth.

She sat forward. "Where were *you* between five and eight on Wednesday?" she asked Andrew Bradford.

His mouth curved at one corner in a cynical, but surprisingly appreciative smile. "Well done, Kate," he said. "Let me think about that."

Lottie had been right about one thing, Kate decided; he *was* a corker. He was certainly remarkably good-looking, sitting there in his gray suit, immaculate white shirt and blue striped tie, his thick blond hair shining in the dim light. She had a sudden flash of how it had felt to be held in his magnificently strong arms for that brief moment by the river.

"I was in my room," he said after a minute's silence. "I'm supposed to rest a couple of hours every day for health reasons. I read *The Times*—hadn't had a chance what with driving down in the morning. Interesting article about Argentina and the Falkland Islands."

In other words, Kate thought, Andrew Bradford did not have an alibi for the time in question.

"I watched television with Mrs. Hogarth in the kitchen for a while," Jocelyn offered. "*BBC-1*, something about bats. I went to my room about seven to bath and change for dinner."

Silence reigned for a minute, but it wasn't a comfortable one. It seemed to Kate that each person was glancing at his or her neighbor, perhaps wondering if that person had had any dealings with Harry Wainwright that he or she hadn't revealed.

"Do let's change the subject, shall we?" Frederick suggested. "If Harry left here alone at five o'clock, then I'm sure once the police finish gathering their evidence, they'll find Harry's death has an explanation that has nothing to do with this household."

Andrew looked as if he doubted that, but he didn't comment, and after a few seconds conversation became general.

"You sure are an improvement on the rest of the relatives," Robert Coby said to Kate in a confiding voice. "I was beginning to wonder yesterday if I could stand to stay here a whole month. Now I *know* I can."

Kate groaned under her breath. In her current mood, in any mood, she had no need of a twenty-two-year-old admirer.

"We're—what are we—cousins?" he murmured.

He was leaning far too close to Kate, invading her space. One more inch and she was going to slap him. "Fairly well removed," she said flatly.

He leered at her—there was no other word for it.

"I guess that makes us kissing cousins, eh?"

She was suddenly aware that Andrew Bradford had been an interested observer of this exchange and was glancing from her to Robbie with one blond eyebrow canted in a quizzical way that spoke volumes. Kate looked at him coldly, and he resumed talking to Elaine, who had apparently recovered from her earlier embarrassment. She was giving Andrew the identical smoldering-eyed attention her twin brother had turned on Kate. Evidently they both suffered from an excess of hormones.

"Exercise reduces stress considerably," Sikander was saying to Jocelyn in his singsong, very pleasant voice.

"I get lots of exercise in school," Jocelyn said. "I'm on the first eleven in field hockey—right wing."

"But that is tremendously wonderful," Sikander said with great enthusiasm.

Everyone laughed and he immediately looked offended. Touchy type, Kate decided.

On Kate's other side, beyond Robbie, Emory Wainwright was tucking with gusto into his second helping of roast lamb. Hilary was having a low-voiced conversation with Bennett Coby at the other end of the table. Bennett was a fairly attractive-looking man, Kate decided. He was tall and slender and he had nice features, even if his chin was rather weak. Obviously the twins had inherited their noses from some other relative.

Hilary's nervous little tuggings weren't in evidence when she was talking with Bennett, Kate noticed. For his part, Bennett hardly took his gaze from his hostess's face. A very pretty face tonight. Hilary's gray-green dress was a little on the matronly side, but it suited her pink-and-white coloring and accentuated the green flashes in her eyes. There was a liveliness about her now that hadn't been present earlier. Was something going on between Hilary and Bennett? Kate wondered. Surely not.

As her gaze returned to Frederick's end of the table, she glanced idly at the sideboard, where Mrs. Hogarth had laid out the food. Her breath caught in her throat. Lying beyond the meat platter and an empty potato dish was a handgun—an ugly-looking thing.

Surely it wasn't very wise to leave a weapon out like that. What if Mrs. Hogarth were to pick it up out of curiosity? Or Jocelyn.

Catching Andrew's eyes, Kate tilted her head, then looked meaningfully in the direction of the sideboard. He raised his eyebrows as if he were startled. He probably thought she was flirting with him. As if she would.

She disliked Andrew Bradford, she decided. She didn't like the cynical way he looked at her, she didn't approve of the way he'd treated his daughter or his wife and she sure as hell didn't like the way he'd taken it for granted that she was after Frederick's money. All the same, she wanted to communicate her unease to him about the gun. She tried shifting her gaze again and this time he turned his head to follow her movement.

"Are you planning on taking potshots at someone?" he asked Frederick, gesturing to the gun.

All heads turned. All conversation ended abruptly.

Frederick looked rather sheepish. "There *is* a murderer at large, old man. I take my duties as a host seriously—I must protect my guests as well as entertain them." He smiled reassuringly around the table. "It's only an old Mauser I picked up in Germany at the end of the war," he said in a soothing tone of voice. "Souvenir, you know. Bit of a relic now—probably doesn't even work."

Everyone except Andrew started talking again. Andrew was looking down at his teacup as if he were reading the leaves. The sight of the gun had obviously bothered him. He looked tired, Kate thought. It had been a severe bout of pneumonia, Jocelyn had explained. That was why he still had to rest most afternoons.

Sikander had managed to tear his gaze away from the gun. "You should study yoga," he told Jocelyn. "Yoga will help you tune in to the harmony of your mind and body and will relieve you of the distress connected with your psychic ability." Reaching into his inside jacket pocket, he pulled out a small notebook and jotted something down. "Here is a title of a book for you to read. It will teach you much about yoga."

Curious, Kate looked at the note as Jocelyn studied it. Sikander had unusual handwriting—spiky with many flourishes. Sikander wasn't so harmonized himself, she decided.

"That's the first bloody mention I've heard of young Jocelyn seeing Harry's body in her mind before it showed up in the river," Lottie said, suddenly surfacing again. "Don't any of you think that was bloody spooky? I certainly do."

Once again there was a complete silence. Jocelyn gazed miserably at the Australian woman. "Got to admit my first thought was that the kiddie had kangaroos in her top paddock," Lottie went on. "But she was bloody right, wasn't she?" She glanced slyly at Andrew. "*Is* she some sort of psychic?"

"She's never had an experience like that before," Andrew lied without hesitation. "It didn't amount to much, anyway, just vague outlines. I'm sure it'll never happen again."

Good for Andrew, Kate thought. Jocelyn looked at him gratefully.

Lottie wouldn't leave it alone, though. "Reminds me of an old rhyme," she said with a laugh. " 'As I was going up the stair, I met a man who wasn't there. He wasn't there again today. I wish, I wish he'd stay away.' "

Jocelyn got to her feet and fled from the room. Kate half rose to follow her, but Andrew waved her back. "I'll go," he said, getting to his feet.

Frederick looked at him in a worried way. "You will come back? I've decided to go ahead with it tonight."

The two men exchanged a steady glance. "Against my advice?" Andrew murmured.

"It seems more necessary than ever," Frederick said in an apologetic way.

Andrew sighed. "I'll come back." He looked daggers at Lottie, then turned on his heel and left the room.

It was obviously no easy task to make Lottie feel uncomfortable. She simply laughed again and started talking across the table to Sikander. Kate mulled over the exchange between Andrew and Frederick. Whatever Frederick had planned, Andrew was obviously against it.

Lottie was telling Sikander that Frederick and Hilary were coming up on their fortieth wedding anniversary. "I was married for five years once," she added, beaming around the table, her spectacles glittering. "Divorced, thank heavens. Took my own name back. Good name, Wainwright, isn't it, Frederick?"

"I've always thought so," Frederick said dryly.

"Emory agrees, don't you, dear?" She looked down the table at her twin brother, who seemed to be off in a world of his own, gazing up at the chandelier through his gold-rimmed spectacles. "Emory," she said sharply. "Pay attention, mate."

For a moment he looked too embarrassed to speak, then he said, "N-n-name. G-good name. Yes."

"Is Jocelyn all right?" Hilary asked worriedly as Andrew came back into the room.

"She will be," he said, then flashed a hostile glance at the cause of the problem.

Lottie met his gaze without flinching, a beaming smile on her round face. "No worries," she said. "I'm always yabbering when I shouldn't."

"Who are the portraits of, Uncle Frederick?" Kate asked as a diversionary tactic, indicating two large oils on the wall behind the sideboard.

"I'm glad you asked, my dear," Frederick replied. "A little family history might be a good way to take our minds off... the tragedy."

It seemed to Kate that almost everyone in the room leaned forward at that moment. She received the distinct impression that this was something they were all very interested in.

"The rather tough-looking bearded gentleman on the left is my grandfather, James Wainwright," Frederick said, walking over to the sideboard. "James started out in life as a coal miner in Northumberland. But in his teens he went out to South Africa, where he accumulated a vast fortune in gold and diamonds."

Kate sensed tension among the listeners. Was the story of interest to them, or the mention of that vast fortune?

"When he came back to England," Frederick continued, "he bought Farrington Hall from Lord Farrington, an impoverished aristocrat." He tugged slightly at his mustache. "James spent a great deal of money founding a hospital hereabouts, as well as an orphanage and a group of senior citizens' homes. Some people accused James of trying to buy a knighthood with all his charitable works." He smiled ruefully. "The accusation was true. James admitted it in his diary."

Frederick's smile faded as he turned to look at the other portrait. This man did not have a beard, but he did have a full mustache and side whiskers. He was wearing a heavily braided dress uniform complete with several medals. Kate gazed at the portrait a little longer before concentrating on what Uncle Frederick was saying.

"This equally tough-looking gentleman is my father, Robert Wainwright," Frederick said. "He served valiantly in the Boer War. I'm afraid he and my mother, Elizabeth, weren't quite as philanthropic as James. Instead of donating to charity, they gave lavish entertainments for everyone who was anyone, hoping for general acceptance into the gentry. Robert also had his eye on a title, but like his father, he never managed to pull it off."

He smiled. "This might be a good time to tell you all that I appear to be succeeding where my father and grandfather failed. The prime minister has informed me that my name has been placed on the queen's New Year's honors list. If all goes well, the title James and Robert Wainwright sought so assiduously will be mine, as a reward for my work in politics."

As everyone murmured congratulations, he waved one hand in a politely dismissive way. "When my father was repeatedly denied the title he sought, he was a bitterly disappointed man. Eventually he became something of a tyrant, I'm afraid. When my brothers displeased him in 1933, he packed them off with a fairly generous portion and a warning to stay away. As you all know, William went to the United States, Charles to Canada, Alexander joined the army and was posted to India. George elected to emigrate to Australia."

Kate jumped in with the question she'd had in mind ever since she'd received Frederick's invitation. "Why did your brothers leave home?" she asked her great-uncle. "Grandpa told me Robert threw them out, but he would never tell me why."

Frederick's mouth tightened. "They were always fighting with Father and one another," he said. "Father simply got fed up. He'd probably have thrown me out, too, once I was old enough, but he had a stroke in 1935 and needed my help in managing his affairs."

It wasn't a satisfying answer, but before Kate could frame another question, he went on, "As all of you know, when my father died, I inherited the remainder of the estate. Some of you have the opinion that this was unfair." His glance touched lightly on Lottie. "Unfair or not, it was legally mine to do with as I wished. I invested my inheritance in various ways, and I'm happy to say I have succeeded in increasing the value of *my* portion quite remarkably."

Andrew, Hilary and Kate were the only ones who were not literally sitting on the edges of their seats.

Frederick returned to his position at the head of the table. "Apparently my four brothers weren't as careful with their portions. Profligate, would you say?" He looked around the table in an amused way as various protesting noises were made. Kate kept silent. Whatever her grandfather's "portion" had been it had disappeared before she was born. William and Sarah Wainwright had lived in comfortable, but modest circumstances.

"Well, that's enough ancient history," Frederick said after a moment. Then he paused, before going on. "It seems to me that it is difficult for us to make small talk while we await word on the...disposition of poor Harry," he said. "In the meantime, perhaps we should remember that Kate just arrived a short time ago and hasn't really had a chance to get to know us. We told a little about ourselves last night at dinner, Kate," he said directly to her, "but I'm sure no one will mind repeating themselves." He smiled around the table. "Who knows, we may even remember details we forgot to share. We mustn't hold back out of shyness, must we? Perhaps we can ask Sikander to begin. My boy?"

Sikander got awkwardly to his feet, looking rather embarrassed to be singled out. "I am Sikander Balraj," he said in his singsong way. "I am thirty years old. My grandfather Alexander went with the army to India, as you have heard, when he was twenty years old. He married Deva, my grandmother, and they had a daughter, Devi, who married Mr. Balraj and became my mother. All dead now." He paused, hanging his head, then went on. "I'm afraid my grandfather, Alexander, drank more than was wise. In his later years he suffered greatly from gout." He hesitated. "For myself, there is not much to tell. Since graduating from university I have worked as an accountant for a Japanese manufacturer of fertilizer in Delhi."

"Thank you, Sikander," Frederick said when it became apparent the young man had no more to tell. He looked down the table. "Perhaps you'd like to fill Kate in on your branch of the family, Bennett."

Bennett stood up with obvious reluctance. This was all a little juvenile, Kate thought. Show and tell. But good distraction. Everyone seemed much more relaxed now.

"I was married to Jennifer Wainwright, daughter of Frederick's brother Charles—the one who emigrated to Canada," Bennett said. "I work in insurance. Rather dull sort of person, I'm afraid," he added with a glance at Hilary. "I brought Jennifer and my kids to visit Farrington Hall ten years ago, so I'm at an advantage, having met Frederick and Hilary before." He paused. "And Harry, also."

He didn't seem too enthusiastic about that, Kate thought.

"Unfortunately my dear wife died two years ago, so this time there's just me and Robbie and Elaine. They can tell you about themselves, I'm sure." About to sit down, he hesitated. "I must say I was glad to have the chance to return," he added, glancing again at Hilary before taking his seat.

Uh-huh, Kate thought, then looked around to see if anyone else had noticed these meaningful glances of Bennett's. Apparently no one had. Her gaze met Andrew's and she realized he was watching her with sardonic interest, obviously aware that she was forming conclusions.

Hastily she averted her eyes and forced herself to pay attention to Robbie, who was talking about his career in fairly glowing terms. Lack of confidence was not one of the young Canadian's problems.

Elaine announced herself as a professional beauty consultant. Then it was Emory's and Lottie's turn.

"Our father was George Wainwright," Lottie began. "He went out to Australia when Robert gave him the boot."

She glanced at Frederick with a smile that wasn't quite friendly—there were undercurrents here, Kate realized.

But a second later, Lottie went on, looking all cheery and twinkly again, plump as a partridge in her navy blue dress. "Emory and I own a winery in the Barossa Valley, the one our dad started with the money his dad gave him." Again another glance at Frederick. "Very good it is, too, especially our Chardonnay. I should know—I'm a real wine lover."

Kate had already noticed that.

"We brought along a bottle for everybody," Lottie continued. "I'll see you get it in the next day or so. Emory hasn't uncrated it yet, have you, Emory?"

Once again Emory was caught being inattentive. He started and looked blankly at Lottie. Then he smiled tentatively. "Everyth-thing Lottie s-s-says goes double for m-m-me."

His hair was dyed, Kate suddenly noticed. It was as blond as Lottie's, but it had dark roots and it didn't have any gray mixed in with it, as Lottie's had. How very odd.

"Kate?" Frederick said.

Oh, Lord, of course she'd have to do her bit. *Okay, keep it short and sweet, just like everyone else,* she decided. "Kate Wainwright," she said. "My grandfather was Uncle Frederick's brother William. The reason I don't look like a Wainwright is that my father married a woman named Helena Giovanni, who was fresh out of Italy. Unfortunately they died in a fire in our home when I was four. Grandpa Will and Grandma Sarah raised me. Grandpa died seven years ago, and Grandma died a month after I graduated from the University of Washington. Since then I've been working as entertainment director for the Sky High Resort in the Cascade Mountains." She hesitated, but decided no one needed to know anything more.

There was a short silence, then Frederick stood up again and, surprisingly, quoted from a poem by Robert Burns: "'Oh wad some power the giftie gie us to see oursels as others see us!'"

"What's that supposed to mean?" Lottie asked, thrusting her jaw forward.

Kate noticed that Andrew was looking distinctly uncomfortable all of a sudden. Why? she wondered.

In spite of Lottie's rude tone, Frederick smiled at her in a fairly friendly manner. "It means that you all appear to see yourselves in rather flattering terms," he said lightly. "It means that you haven't been quite honest."

He seemed quite composed during the general protest that ensued. Kate felt fairly composed herself. *She* hadn't lied.

"I'm still not sure this is a good idea," Andrew said to Frederick.

The angle of his neck looked very stiff, Kate thought, remembering what Jocelyn had said about that.

"Private consultations would be better. They don't even know—"

"I should explain your purpose here, of course," Frederick interrupted. Again he gave one of those all-encompassing glances around the table. "While it is true that Andrew is recuperating from his recent illness," he went on, "he is also here in his role as my solicitor. Andrew and his father and grandfather before him have always handled Wainwright legal affairs. In the past few months, Andrew has also checked into the activities of the entire Wainwright family."

Once it had sunk in, that statement brought forth another babble of sound. "Are you saying that Andrew Bradford spied on us?" Kate asked, beginning to feel furious. "Couldn't he have done it openly? Couldn't he have asked straight out how we were doing, what our lives were like?"

Frederick answered her before Andrew could. "As I told you earlier, my dear, the Wainwright family squabbled constantly. None of my brothers wanted to keep in touch. I was afraid none of you would wish to do so, either. But I certainly wouldn't call my benign interest 'spying.'"

He made it all sound very reasonable, but Kate was still unhappy with the idea of someone checking up on her without her knowledge. All the liking and respect she'd begun to feel for Frederick was in danger of being swept away.

Andrew Bradford, she saw, was now taking folded papers from his inside jacket pocket, smoothing them out on the tablecloth in front of him.

"Proceed, Andrew," Frederick said.

There was an immediate silence as all eyes fixed on Andrew. Hostility pervaded the air.

And then Mrs. Hogarth came into the dining room, still wearing an apron over her print dress, her hands clasped tightly in front of her ample girth. Going over to Frederick, she murmured something only he could hear.

Frederick's mouth tightened, then he glanced around the table. "It seems Inspector Erskine is ready to have a word with us," he said.

Chapter Four

For a full minute nobody moved or spoke, then everyone spoke at once. Mrs. Hogarth left the room, presumably to show the inspector in. Only Kate and Frederick seemed to notice when Andrew stood up and went over to the sideboard, where he dropped his napkin over Frederick's gun.

"I'm sorry to disturb your dinner," the inspector said from the doorway a couple of minutes later.

He rolled every *r,* Kate noticed, which gave his speech a genial sound. But he didn't look genial. He looked decidedly grim. The bottoms of his baggy gray cords were wet. Had he gone wading in the river as she and Andrew had? What had he been looking for?

"It's my unpleasant duty to inform you that Mr. Harry Wainwright was assuredly murdered," he said solemnly. "There will of course be a complete investigation."

"How was he killed?" Robbie Coby asked.

The eager way in which he phrased the question struck Kate as entirely inappropriate.

The inspector regarded him sternly for a moment, then said, "I'm not prepared to say at this moment. We must wait for the results of the postmortem."

Robbie looked disappointed.

Ghoulish kid, Kate thought.

The inspector ran a hand over his wiry pepper-and-salt hair, his glance traveling the faces of the diners. Then his hazel eyes blinked, and Kate thought of a camera, recording everything before its shutter closed.

"I'm afraid I must ask you to remain in this room while my men search the house."

That brought a silence, into which Robbie said, "The murder weapon, I'll bet. What was it? A gun? A knife?"

Ignoring him, the inspector spoke directly to Andrew. "I've a search warrant, of course."

"I didn't doubt it for a moment," Andrew murmured.

The inspector nodded. "I will be asking all of you for some assistance in this matter," he said. "I will begin my inquiries here at ten o'clock tomorrow morning, if that is convenient for you, Colonel Wainwright?"

"I'll put the library at your disposal," Frederick said.

"That would be verra kind."

"You surely don't imagine one of us is involved," Bennett blurted out.

The inspector studied him in the same suspicious way he'd looked at Robbie, then blinked again. "You are?"

"Bennett Coby. Colonel Wainwright's nephew by marriage."

Erskine's grizzled eyebrows drew together. "It will be necessary to establish Mr. Harry Wainwright's movements prior to his death. At present we have no suspects. Do you have a suggestion of one?"

"I thought—well, naturally I assumed—that someone had accosted Harry by the river. A robber, perhaps, or an irate husband—Harry was something of a womanizer, I've heard."

"Will you be talking to Harry's sister?" Frederick asked.

"She's a widow, lives with Harry. I rang her up, of course.

Asked if she'd need any help. But she said no. Capable sort of woman, but not always pleasant."

The inspector nodded, then turned back to Bennett Coby. "Did you have any more questions, sir?"

Bennett obviously regretted opening his mouth at all. There was a sheen of perspiration on his upper lip, a slight twitch at the corner of one eye. Mutely he shook his head.

Looking at Frederick, the inspector said, "Due to the lateness of the hour, I'm no wanting to discuss the situation at this time." His glance swept the entire company. "I will ask that none of you leave the premises before I've had an opportunity to speak with you. I'm leaving an officer on duty outside this door while we go about our search."

With a slight inclination of his head, he strode from the room, leaving another heavy silence in his wake.

Not the type to put up with any nonsense, Kate thought. Harry's murder investigation was in competent if unfriendly hands.

"Is that bloody walloper saying we are all under house arrest?" Lottie demanded.

"I'm sure he didn't intend anything of the sort," Frederick said calmly. "I imagine Robbie is correct in his assumption that the inspector is looking for the murder weapon. I really don't see any purpose in agitating ourselves prematurely. I expect the circumstances of poor Harry's death will be made clear tomorrow. In the meantime, we shall carry on with our planned discussion."

"Frederick, please," Hilary protested.

She had gone quite white, Kate noticed, and she was twisting her wedding band around her finger quite violently.

He sighed. "Very well, I will at least explain the reason for Andrew's report. As I told you in my invitation, I am not in good health. At my recent annual physical examination, my physician, Dr. Carlton, informed me that my blood pressure is dangerously high and my heart is in a weakened state. I am not, unfortunately, a candidate for heart surgery. And I am not expected to live more than another year or so."

Compassion made Kate's stomach tighten and dissipated her anger. "I'm sorry, Uncle Frederick," she murmured.

Frederick shrugged. "I have lived well, my dear. And as long as the knighthood is bestowed upon me, I will have no regrets." His eyes crinkled. "I've always believed a man should relinquish command while he's still compos mentis."

He looked all around the table. "I'm sure you'll understand my wish to settle my mind on the question of what to do with the assets I have acquired. Hilary will of course inherit this house. After her death it will be handed over to the National Trust to do with as they wish, along with a goodly sum to maintain it. Hilary will be amply provided for, but unfortunately she and I were not blessed with children."

Hilary flushed and lowered her gaze to her clasped hands.

"To put it bluntly," Frederick said tersely, "I invited you here because I wanted to look at you all and decide whether to leave any of my money to you. As I also told you in my invitation, Harry was my official heir. I had felt that an English Wainwright should inherit the bulk of the Wainwright fortune, you see. But lately I've found myself wondering if that was quite fair, considering that you are all Robert's descendants. Now, of course, because of Harry's demise, I will definitely have to rethink my position."

Again he seemed lost in thought.

"What I have to decide now is this. Should I divide my assets equally among you, or is one of you more deserving than the rest? To that end, I think it is important that absolute truth should prevail. Which is where Andrew comes in."

Andrew stood up, wishing devoutly he was anywhere but here. Kate looked angry again, he noticed. Americans did so hate to have their privacy tampered with. Well, they'd all asked for this, rushing to England to see what they could get out of Frederick.

"Sikander Balraj," he said, assuming the dry voice he thought of as his business voice, one totally lacking in emotion. "Sikander omitted this from his biography. Two years ago he was dismissed from his post as an accountant when it was discovered that the company's bank account was going down while his was going up. He was also sentenced to eighteen months in prison, which he subsequently served."

"I have paid my debt to society," Sikander said despondently, without looking up.

Kate glanced at Andrew with a look that should have turned him into a pillar of salt. Obviously he was going to end up the villain of this piece.

"Bennett Coby," he said.

"Damn it, Bradford," Coby protested, bristling. "I've done nothing wrong."

Andrew nodded. "This report deals with your late wife."

Bennett subsided. "Oh, I see."

"Jennifer Coby was an alcoholic during most of her married life," Andrew said evenly. "As well, she spent a great deal of time in Las Vegas, which left her family in straitened circumstances when she died two years ago of a liver ailment."

"That's all a bunch of lies," Elaine said, jumping up as she had earlier.

"Knock it off, Elaine," Robbie said. "It was one thing to protect Mother's reputation while she was alive—it doesn't matter now. Uncle Frederick knows all about Mother, anyway—on our last visit here she was rip-roaring drunk most of the time and she kept going up to some club in London to gamble."

Somewhat sheepishly, Elaine nodded and sat down again.

Might as well get the Cobys out of the way altogether, Andrew decided. "Robert Coby," he said. "Not quite the complete concert pianist yet. Most reviews say he is technically proficient but his playing lacks passion. Lately he has been reduced to playing in department stores."

"Temporarily," Robbie interjected.

Andrew inclined his head. Not for him to get into any arguments. Just state the facts, Frederick had said. Nothing more, nothing less. What Frederick didn't know was that in some cases, this report was considerably less. There were limits to what Andrew Bradford would do for a client.

"Elaine Coby," he continued. "Elaine isn't the beauty consultant she declared herself to be, but she certainly does work at a beauty parlor, where she is a hairdresser and manicurist." Elaine smiled at him gratefully, probably because she knew he was holding back certain information. Namely, that she'd been fired from six beauty parlors in four years.

Emory and Lottie Wainwright were next on the list. Here again Andrew was going to hold back, mainly because he didn't have documentary proof of the deception that was being played out. So all he told was that George Wainwright had spent much of his life in Australia sitting in public houses, complaining that he had been cheated out of his inheritance by his little brother. As for the winery, while many Australian wines were among the finest in the world, the Wainwright label had sunk low in estimation due to inefficient methods of production and problems with too much oak in the wine. The winery was now on the verge of bankruptcy.

Predictably, Lottie started blustering straightaway.

"You've come a gutser there, mate," she said, her face purpling.

He had to admire her colorful language, which he took to mean he'd made a mistake—which he hadn't. In any case, it wasn't his imagination that under the bluster she looked relieved that he hadn't revealed anything more.

"Kate Wainwright." Andrew paused as Kate's brown eyes came up in a startled way. It was too bad he'd had to investigate this particular Wainwright. It had become clear to him that she was a very special sort of woman. Intelligent. Straightforward. Attractive. He had watched her watching the others like a visiting anthropoligist, had almost been able to hear the clicking of her mind as she sorted them all into slots. He would have enjoyed getting to know her if he hadn't known too much about her already. Half of which he was not going to reveal.

"Kate didn't quite level with us, as they say in her country," he said, striving for a lighter tone. "Nothing serious, just that she's out of work at the moment and apparently without any means of support, which is no doubt why she responded to Frederick's invitation so promptly."

There was no gratitude on her face for the information he had concealed. She was obviously furious, which gave a deep burning glow to her brown eyes and a color to her high cheekbones that enhanced her already formidable beauty.

"I quit my job," she said hotly, "because as entertainment director I was responsible for keeping Sky High's guests completely happy and I got burned out on smiling. Frederick's invitation may have been the catalyst that made me decide to quit, but it wasn't the reason."

Glaring at Frederick, she went on, "I am not without means of support—I have some savings including a small inheritance from Grandpa William, who was a fairly successful real estate agent, as I'm sure your spy has told you. On my return to the U.S. I intend looking for work as a photographer. I might even open my own studio. Among my many other duties for Sky High I was also resident photographer, and I took several photographic courses in college. I am perfectly capable of earning my own living. I assure you I am not sitting here with my hand out."

A magnificent performance, Andrew thought. But was it only a performance? Certainly she had managed to captivate Frederick. He was gazing at her with obvious admiration.

"I'm delighted to hear you have goals of your own, Kate," he said. Smiling in his rather tight way at everyone, he added, "I realize I've offended you. Please put the blame on my head, not Andrew's. It was necessary for me to check on all of you. There is a considerable amount of money involved."

They were all murmuring to one another excitedly, Andrew noted cynically. No, not all. Kate was still glaring at her uncle, her hands clenched into fists on the tablecloth. As he admired the clean strong line of her jaw in profile, she turned her laser glare on him and he felt . . . shriveled. "Sorry," he murmured, but she was obviously beyond hearing him. He was glad there wasn't a rolling pin within reach; he was quite sure she'd have crowned him *and* Frederick if there had been.

"And how do you propose going about this elimination process?" Kate asked Frederick in clear ringing tones that rose above the general hubbub. "How do you decide who gets the grand prize? Are you going to have the inspector keep us locked in this room and wait until we kill one another off?"

Everyone was shocked into silence except Frederick, who again had a look of admiration on his face when he met Kate's scathing glance. "I can't imagine what you mean, my dear."

"Maybe you haven't read as many old mystery novels as I have," Kate said. "It seems to me you are setting your relatives against one another exactly as you set them all against Harry by telling them he was your intended heir." She paused, looking from one shocked face to another, looking at Andrew last with a glance that pierced him to the heart. "We all know what happened to Harry, don't we?" she concluded.

Chapter Five

Fortunately Kate hadn't had time to unpack more than a few of her clothes before dinner the previous night, and by the time the inspector had released the family she'd already decided not to finish the job. It wasn't going to take her long to pack them again, even with the cat's help. Gray Boy had come to visit her this morning, and every time she turned around she had to evict him from her suitcase. She was folding lingerie into the case, when someone knocked on her door.

"Come in," she called, and Andrew Bradford walked in, macho in jeans and a pale gray sweater. Cashmere again? Kate wondered, and could almost feel the softness against her cheek, the iron-hard arms holding her intimately.

The man was a paid spy, Kate reminded herself.

"I don't suppose you want me interrupting your unpacking, but it can't be helped," Andrew said. "Detective Inspector Erskine has arrived. He's talking to Frederick at the moment, but he'll want to chat with us soon."

"I'm not *un*packing," Kate said flatly, lifting the cat out of her suitcase one more time. "I'm packing. I'm leaving Farrington Hall."

His eyebrows rose. "Why?"

Andrew's mother had often complained, lovingly, that he was as insensitive as his father, but even he could tell that Kate Wainwright was infuriated by his question.

"It should be perfectly obvious why I'm leaving," she said tightly.

"You've decided you won't qualify as one of the heirs?" Andrew suggested.

Drawing herself up to her full height, she gave him another searing blast of her dark eyes. She was wearing a purple silk blouse and white jeans that might have been tailor-made for her shapely figure. Her long hair was brushed behind her ears to flow like black satin down her back. She looked tired but beautiful, Andrew thought.

"There was no thought of any inheritance in my mind when I came here," she said, biting off every word. "How dare you insinuate that I had mercenary motives. You had no right to spy on me, no right to draw erroneous conclusions and you have no right in my room." Turning her back on him, she hefted the suitcase off the bed, setting it down on the floor with a thud.

"I'd have thought you'd be grateful that I didn't tell about Paul Milton," Andrew said mildly.

Her skin tightened across her cheekbones. "What about Paul?" she asked between clenched teeth.

"There was more than friendship between you."

"So?"

"How did his invalid wife feel about that?"

The anger left her face abruptly. She closed her eyes momentarily, then opened them again. Andrew felt a twist of compassion; there was so much pain in her expression all at once. Paul Milton had made her suffer.

"I didn't know," she whispered.

"You didn't know I knew about your affair with your boss?"

"I didn't know he was married. His wife lived in Phoenix, Arizona—she didn't like cold weather. I knew he flew to Phoenix once a month, but he told me he had an invalid mother in a nursing home. I was stupid enough to believe him."

There was a hurt, bewildered note in her voice that moved Andrew tremendously.

Sitting down on the edge of the bed, she picked up the cat and began rubbing his ears. "As soon as I did find out, I left Sky High. Uncle Frederick's invitation arrived about the same time." All the fire had gone out of her now. "I didn't lie last night," she added. "I really was burned out on smiling. But finding out about Paul's wife was the last straw."

Andrew believed everything she had told him. There was something very straight and open about Kate Wainwright. It was obvious that finding out her lover was married had devastated her. Which meant she must have loved him.

Her fingers were still rhythmically stroking the cat. "I really don't like being thought a gold digger," she said. "So for the record—and do please add this to your report—Uncle Frederick might appreciate the irony—I came because I wanted a family. My parents died when I was little, remember, and I was raised by elderly grandparents, who are both dead now, as well. They did their best for me and by me, but neither of them...was demonstrative. I was often lonely. I spent most of my life wishing I had a real family."

Her eyes shone with moisture and Andrew had to swallow against a sudden constriction in his throat. "I seem to have misjudged you entirely," he said softly. "Please forgive me."

Her eyes met his in a startled way. For a moment there was a silence between them, then her head drooped, her long dark hair curtaining her face.

Don't go, Andrew wanted to say to her. *Stay. Let me get to know you.* Not only had he misjudged this young woman, he was strongly drawn to her. He wanted to walk over to her and pull her to her feet and take her in his arms. He wanted to brush the dark hair away from her face and lift her chin to its usual proud position. He wanted to kiss her. He wanted to—

Alarm bells sounded in his mind. The Wainwright affair was complicated enough already. "I doubt you can leave, even if you want to," he said. "I imagine Inspector Erskine will want us all to stay here until he pins down the murderer."

His brisk tone helped her gather herself together. "I'm aware of that," she said. Setting the cat down on the floor, she stood up, went over to the triple-mirrored dressing table and started putting toilet articles in her carry-on bag. The cat immediately bounded onto her bed and settled down to sleep. "Once the inspector has talked to me I'm sure he'll release me right away," she said. "I want to be ready to leave."

"Frederick will be upset..."

"He had no business hiring you to spy on any of us," Kate said hotly. "If the rest of them have any pride they'll all be leaving, too." She glared at Andrew. "I hate when people think money is the answer, the motive and the reason for everything. People who believe that are shallow and immature."

Andrew winced and raked a hand through his hair, feeling unusually sheepish. "One does get rather cynical in my business, I'm afraid." He hesitated, then added, "If you really do want a family, there's no reason you can't stay on and get to know this one.''

She shot him a mocking glance. "After all you've learned about this family, you can recommend that?''

"Well, at least Frederick and Hilary..."

She laughed shortly as she zipped up the carry-on bag. "Hilary and Frederick's marriage is not too stable. I wouldn't be surprised if it falls apart in the very near future.''

"Where on earth did you get an idea like that?''

"I watch people. Most people give away their inner feelings with their body language. For one thing, Hilary keeps twisting her wedding ring around, as if she wants to twist it off.'' She hesitated, then shrugged. "I think it's entirely possible Hilary's in love with Bennett.''

Once again, Andrew was completely taken aback. "Good Lord, you do have a vivid imagination.''

"I'm not basing my conclusions on imagination.''

He frowned, but decided not to pursue the subject. The marriage seemed fine to him, and body language struck him as a load of nonsense, but he didn't want to get into any more arguments with Kate Wainwright. He wanted to persuade her to stay. Why, he wasn't sure, but it did seem important to him.

Kate was shaking her head. "Under the circumstances, I'm not sure this is a family I want to become a part of.''

"You think it had to be one of the family who killed Harry?''

She looked at him very directly. "One of them, or you,'' she said. There were only a couple of steps between them at the moment. He could see the long separate lashes fringing her eyes, the dark pupils surrounded by irises that were almost as dark, the pristine whites that indicated good health and clean habits. "Anything else seems like too much coincidence," she continued. "According to Joss, everyone except Frederick hated Harry. Hatred's a motive for murder. So is greed. As Uncle Frederick said, now Harry's dead, he has to choose a new heir."

"As he's unlikely to choose me, why should *I* kill Harry?"

"Joss said you had a fight with him on Wednesday."

"She said what?" She'd really bowled him over with that statement. He'd had no idea Jocelyn was even in the vicinity. Without stopping to think, he stepped forward and seized Kate by the shoulders, not caring when she flinched. Sensing trouble, the cat shot off the bed and out of the room. "Did she hear what the fight was about?" Andrew asked frantically.

Her body stiffened, but she didn't pull away. "Take your hands off me," she said through clenched teeth.

He took a firmer grip. "Not till you answer me."

"She *said* she didn't know what it was about, but—"

"But what? Answer me, Kate." If she didn't answer he didn't know what he was going to do.

"I had the feeling she did know," she said.

Her expression showed no fear, only curiosity tinged with suspicion. She was obviously getting the wrong idea, but he didn't care. If Jocelyn had heard, it could destroy everything.

Letting go of her abruptly, he took a step backward. "I'm sorry," he said lamely. "I feel strongly about privacy. I'm going to have to speak to Jocelyn about eavesdropping."

He had to talk to Jocelyn straightaway. If she'd heard what Harry had said to him, what he had said to Harry...

"Don't go anywhere," he said tersely, and strode from the room, barely noticing that Kate immediately sank down onto the bed, her eyes full of questions.

"MAY I COME IN?" Hilary asked, poking her head around the door Andrew had left open.

Still sitting on her bed, having spent the past fifteen minutes trying to sift meaning from the scene with Andrew, Kate managed to produce a welcoming smile. She should have kept quiet about her plans, she thought with a sigh.

Hilary was wearing another pullover-and-cardigan set—pale lavender this time, with the same tweed skirt and sensible shoes she'd worn yesterday afternoon. The outfit seemed to require just as much tugging into place.

"Andrew says you're planning on leaving," she said, perching on the edge of a straight-backed chair.

Kate nodded.

Hilary sighed and began fiddling with her hair. "I can't blame you of course. I felt like running off myself this morning when I woke up. Can't do it, though. Have to stay and face the music, whatever it turns out to be."

"Do *you* think one of the family killed Harry?" Kate asked.

She would have expected Hilary to deny any such possibility, but instead the older woman shrugged. "I don't know," she said. "All I'm sure of is that *I* didn't kill him."

"Did you like him?"

"Heavens no." She flushed and put her hand to her mouth. "I suppose one shouldn't say that about a dead person, but Harry had a very abrasive personality."

"I guess Uncle Frederick liked him, though."

Hilary looked thoughtful. "You know, my dear, I really don't think he did. Frederick has a strong sense of propriety and I think he felt Harry was the proper choice. I can't think why else he'd name him his heir, frankly. Harry was such a fool. Very self-important and conceited. And completely—"

To Kate's surprise, Hilary's fair complexion had darkened and her voice had hardened as she spoke. Now, evidently realizing that she was saying too much, she broke off and began a new assault on the ribbed hem of her cardigan.

"I really do want you to stay," she said in a surprisingly firm voice.

"I'm sorry, Aunt Hilary," Kate began.

Hilary held up a hand as though she were stopping traffic, her cheeks suddenly pinker than usual. "I'm frightened, Kate, really frightened," she said.

Kate stared at her. "Of what?" she asked.

Hilary shook her head, looking miserable. "That's just it. I don't really—" She stopped as running footsteps clattered in the hall and Jocelyn burst into the room.

"What's all this about you leaving?" she blurted out. "You can't possibly leave. You're the only one on my side. We were going to be friends. You said so, you promised—" Noticing Hilary, she flushed. "I'm sorry, Mrs. Wainwright. I didn't see you. That was very rude of me, barging in." Obviously embarrassed, she began backing out of the room.

Kate called her back, and patted the bed beside her, putting an arm around the girl as she sat down. "It's okay, Joss," she said. "It's nice you want me to stay. Thank you. You, too, Aunt Hilary," she added.

Hilary smiled warmly and the knot that had formed in Kate's stomach during Andrew's onslaught began to relax. Smiling herself now, she said, "I guess I overreacted. I do that sometimes. I'll stick around, of course. It was just that finding Harry's body and then learning that Uncle Frederick had—" She could hardly talk in front of Jocelyn about Andrew's spying. The girl was just getting to know her father. It wasn't up to Kate to turn her off him. "I take it your father found you," she said, releasing Jocelyn.

The girl bit her lower lip. "Yes. He was really..." She shook her head. "It's all right now," she said ambiguously.

Before Kate could question her, she added, "I almost forgot. Detective Inspector Erskine wants to see you in the library right away."

Kate's stomach did a somersault. She'd never had much to do with the police. Like most honest citizens, she had a healthy respect for them that was mixed with a certain amount of fear.

"Does he want me, too?" Hilary asked, nervously tugging at the front welt of her cardigan.

Jocelyn shook her head. "He wants me and Daddy and Kate together, because we found the body."

Kate's insides had tied themselves into a knot again. This time she wasn't sure it would ever come undone.

FREDERICK WAINWRIGHT LEFT the library as Kate and Jocelyn approached it. He wore a different jacket this morning—a tan corduroy—and Kate wondered if he had transferred the gun to his pocket. After dinner the night before, he had slipped it into the pocket of his suit jacket, pressing his hand over it as though glad of its protection. Did he really think they were all in danger? Or did he think one of his potential heirs, having bumped Harry off, would decide to hasten *his* demise. That wouldn't make sense— not until he changed his will, anyway, which he'd be pretty foolish to do, considering the circumstances.

Gun or no gun, he looked as soldierly and composed as before. He gave Kate an affectionate smile as he passed her. Evidently he had forgiven her rudeness the previous night. Kate wasn't sure she'd forgiven him for playing the relatives off against one another, but she had weightier matters on her mind at the moment.

Andrew was seated on a straight-backed chair, long legs stretched out in front of him. Inspector Erskine sat behind an impressive desk that had been moved to the middle of the floor. Seated at the end of the desk, Constable Taylor, the young pink-cheeked officer who had accompanied the inspector to the river the previous day, held a pencil in his left hand, poised over a notepad.

"Sit ye down," the inspector said, waving Kate and Jocelyn to two chairs next to Andrew's.

Andrew jumped up and held a chair for Kate, giving her the benefit of his slow smile. "Sorry," he murmured.

He truly did look penitent. How would he look, she wondered, if she were to tell him she'd felt a shock of sexual response go through her body when he'd seized her by the shoulders earlier? Smug, probably.

"Now," the inspector said ponderously, "I should be glad to hear exactly what occurred on Thursday afternoon, starting with Miss Jocelyn, who, I believe, was the first to... shall we say... *learn* of the body's existence."

Jocelyn gave a very intelligent account of the finding of Harry's body, then hesitated, looking at her father.

"It's all right to tell the inspector about your fuzzy thing," Andrew said.

Which she did, first explaining the false alarm that had been played out with the other members of the Wainwright family.

"I've cautioned Jocelyn to keep quiet about her experiences," Andrew said.

The inspector nodded thoughtfully. "Do you have anything to add?" he asked Andrew.

"Only that Kate and I moved the body out of the river in case Harry might still be alive. I hope we didn't damage any evidence."

"There is inevitably some tearing of the muscle tissue when a body is moved after the process of rigor mortis is complete," the inspector told him. Nausea contracted Kate's stomach, making her shiver. "However," the man continued, "in this case, no particular harm was done by your action."

"Was the head injury the cause of death?" Andrew asked.

The inspector hesitated. "The police surgeon is confident the blow knocked the victim out but did not kill him. It would appear he was struck with a blunt instrument, then dragged down the bank into the river and left to drown. As the police surgeon estimated yesterday, he had been dead about twenty-four hours when we were called in."

"Which means he was killed soon after he left this house on Wednesday," Andrew put in.

"I believe you told me yesterday that he was here most of the day on Wednesday and left about five o'clock. Dinner was served at eight, I understand, and everyone who was present at tea was at dinner, except for Harry Wainwright himself."

Andrew nodded. "We didn't miss Harry because he wasn't expected back until Thursday evening, to meet Kate. I imagine his sister thought he'd decided to stop over."

"Dinner on Wednesday lasted how long?"

"A couple of hours. Then we all sat in the drawing room for a while." He raised his eyebrows. "I take it then that my assumption was right? Harry was killed between five and eight p.m.?"

"It would seem so," the inspector said. He looked at Jocelyn. "I'll be asking everyone where they were between tea and dinner on Wednesday, lassie."

"I wandered around in the maze for a bit," Jocelyn said, which was more than she'd said the previous night. Her next words explained the omission. "The atmosphere in the house felt funny and I wanted to stay outside for a while, but then it got foggy, so I came in and watched television in the kitchen."

The inspector blinked. "The atmosphere felt funny?"

Jocelyn bit her lower lip. "As if everybody was on edge."

"What did you think of Harry Wainwright?" the inspector asked abruptly.

"He was smarmy," Jocelyn said without hesitation.

"I beg your pardon, miss?" the young constable said.

"Smarmy," the inspector said, rolling the r. After studying Jocelyn's face a moment longer, he asked, "Is that everything you have to tell me, Miss Jocelyn?"

Jocelyn glanced at her father, then nodded. Obviously Andrew had warned her against telling the inspector about his quarrel with Harry.

"I was in my room, reading *The Times*," Andrew offered.

"Did you see any of the other guests during that time?" Erskine asked.

Andrew shook his head.

"How well do you know the other guests?"

Kate stiffened. Would Andrew reveal the reports he'd made for Frederick?

"I know them only in my position as Frederick's solicitor," he said carefully. "I met most of them for the first time on Wednesday. I've known Frederick and Hilary for years, of course. Harry I'd met on a few occasions when I was down here on business."

"What can you tell me about him?"

Andrew paused for a minute, then said, "He had a bit of a limp that he seemed to exaggerate from time to time. He was always quick to explain that he'd sustained a knee injury playing rugby at school.

"After that he'd just happen to mention that he'd gone to Harrow and Cambridge," Andrew continued. "He wanted to be sure people understood he'd attended public school, you see."

"A bit conceited, you might say."

Andrew laughed shortly. "The word *blowhard* comes to mind."

The inspector darted a shrewd glance at him. "Attended public school yourself, didn't you, sir?"

No flies on the inspector, Kate thought.

"I did," Andrew said tightly. "I don't make a career out of saying so however."

"I never did meet the gentleman myself," the inspector said. "I wonder, though, with all I've heard about Harry Wainwright around the county and what you and your daughter have told me why would the colonel select him as his heir?"

Andrew hesitated. "I must admit, Inspector, I was more than a little surprised—" He broke off. "Frederick is very old school tie himself, you understand, though he's not obnoxious about it. And Harry looked enough like him to be the son he'd never had. And with all his faults, Harry was English through and through. As well, he had the advantage of being here, whereas the other relations were unknown."

He wasn't going to mention his quarrel with Harry, Kate realized with a thrill of nervousness. If he was as innocent as he'd proclaimed to her, why was he keeping the information back?

"Everyone showed up on time for dinner on Wednesday," he went on blandly. "I must say, nobody looked as if they had just committed a murder."

"It doesna always show," the inspector commented.

"Kate wasn't at that dinner, of course," Andrew went on, as if the inspector hadn't spoken. "She hadn't arrived yet."

A neat way to shift attention to someone else, Kate thought, shooting an irritated glance his way. To her further annoyance, the inspector fell for it.

Turning to Kate, he said, "I understand you arrived at Farrington Hall at five o'clock yesterday."

When a sentence had a number of r's in it, his Scottish accent was almost impenetrable. "That is correct," she said as soon as she'd figured out the question.

"At what time did your plane arrive at Heathrow?"

She told him.

"And that was also on Thursday? You didn't happen to arrive a day early to do a little sight-seeing?"

"You're surely not suggesting I might have dashed down here, raced out to the river, killed Harry Wainwright and dashed away again?" she demanded. "I'd never even met him."

"So I understand. You'll forgive me, Miss Kate. The question had to be asked." He surprised her by giving her a shy smile, then he looked over at the constable, who was writing laboriously in his notebook, his left hand curled around his pencil. "Are you keeping up, Taylor?" he asked.

The constable blushed. "Yes, sir."

"I feel I have the right to know if you suspect any of us, or have any evidence against one of us," Andrew said. "I am the family's solicitor, after all."

"Verra well," the inspector said with a sigh. "Mr. Harry Wainwright's sister, Mrs. Sanderham, has informed me that Harry was afraid the other relations would resent him for being named heir. He begged Colonel Wainwright not to invite them. All of which the colonel confirmed when I spoke to him just now. According to Mrs. Sanderham, Harry was afraid one of the relations would take a notion to do him in. The lady is fairly convinced that is what happened. I've no absolute proof of it, but my instincts tell me she may be correct. I learned a long while ago that the likeliest explanation is usually the correct one." He paused. "Also, there is certain physical evidence, which I'll keep to myself for the time being, that points to the murderer being connected to this house."

"Where was Mrs. Sanderham when Harry was killed?" Kate asked.

He smiled approvingly at her. "In London on a buying trip for the shop, she says. We're checking, of course."

He glanced at Jocelyn. "You may go now, lassie." He hesitated before adding, "Your father was right to advise against talking about your... fuzzy things. As for the episodes themselves," he continued, speaking directly to the girl in a grown-up fashion that Jocelyn obviously appreciated, "well, I'm not as inclined to scoff at psychic phenomena as some. My own grandmother had the... well, that's neither here nor there. Mum's the word, all right?"

As soon as the door closed behind Jocelyn, the inspector leaned forward, looking directly at Andrew. "I'm sure you realize the danger she could be in."

"I do," Andrew said grimly.

"Aye. As well, we must be verra careful not to let the newspapers get a whiff of the girl's talent, else we'll be up to our eyebrows in reporters and television cameras."

He kept his gaze fixed on Andrew's face. "The colonel is anxious for me to keep this whole matter quiet," he said. "Which suits me fine. However, that doesn't mean I'll tread softly for fear of stepping on anyone's coat of arms. The fact that the colonel is up for a title or that the name Wainwright has been known in this county for over a hundred years will make no difference to my investigation. You might make sure the colonel understands that." He glanced at each of them in turn. "Is there anything more either of you can tell me?" he asked.

Kate looked at Andrew. He shook his head. Taking her cue from him, Kate did likewise, feeling somewhat guilty. But all she had was hearsay from Jocelyn and a few body language clues. She could hardly offer those as evidence.

The inspector looked down at a notebook. "You might find Emory and Lottie Wainwright for me and send them in," he said to Andrew.

"I'll come with them," Andrew said firmly. "In my role as family solicitor," he added as the inspector seemed about to protest.

The inspector nodded resignedly and Andrew left the room.

"In any investigation it's always difficult to get people to tell all they know at the start," the inspector said as Kate stood up. "It wastes a lot of time, and to quote an old cliché—the truth will out eventually." He hesitated, then his shy but surprisingly warm smile surfaced once more. "Ah, well, I'm inclined to keep things under my own hat," he admitted.

Kate smiled back at him, feeling relieved that the interview was ending on a pleasant note, and he stood up and shook her hand, holding on to it for a moment longer than was necessary. Could he possibly be flirting with her? she wondered. Surely not.

"You seem to have a few doubts about yon Mr. Bradford," he said as he walked with her to the door.

She must be more careful with her own body language, she told herself. No matter that this man had unexpectedly revealed a certain amount of charm; she mustn't forget he was a policeman investigating a serious crime. She certainly didn't want to muddy the waters with unfounded suspicions. "Mr. Bradford and I don't always see eye to eye," she said.

"There's no thought in your mind that he might be connected with Harry Wainwright's murder?"

"None at all." Why was she being so protective of Andrew Bradford? "How about you?" she asked.

"Well, it's true he has no apparent motive," the inspector said slowly. "There's no possible way Harry's death could benefit him. And in my experience," he added with a wry smile, "there's no murder without a motive. It seems to me that the motive is pretty clear in this case. All these people stand to inherit now Harry's no longer standing in their way."

"Sounds too simple," Kate said.

"Murder is usually quite simple," the inspector said.

IT WAS SEVERAL HOURS before Andrew emerged from the library again.

Kate was waiting for him in the vestibule. "How did it go?" she asked.

He sighed wearily, glancing around as if to make sure no one was within earshot. "About as one might expect, Kate. Everyone except Hilary insisted he or she liked Harry Wainwright. None of the family admitted to quarreling with him on Wednesday or seeing anyone else doing so." He raked a hand through his hair, tousling it unmercifully.

"None of them, of course, *resented* Harry. It was entirely up to Frederick to leave his money to anyone he wanted to."

He laughed. "Sikander said his religion teaches that each person is born into a certain station and must stay in it for life. That is his karma."

Kate frowned. "Is that supposed to mean he couldn't have killed for gain because he isn't allowed to gain?"

"Something like that, I imagine."

"What happens now?"

"The coroner's inquest, probably on Monday. A funeral. In the meantime, the investigation will go on."

Kate shivered. "Will there be questions at the inquest?"

He nodded. "And probably precious few answers. The verdict will no doubt be murder by person or persons unknown."

"Who do *you* think killed Harry?" Kate asked.

"I'm afraid to even hazard a guess."

Kate put her hand on his arm. The inspector had come out of the library, followed by Constable Taylor, and was looking around carefully, his gaze lingering on the umbrella stand. Something teased at Kate's memory—the umbrella stand lying on its side when she'd arrived, Lottie saying she'd knocked it over. But what else?

"An interesting collection that," the inspector said. "I noticed it when I came in last night."

"The colonel's father collected them," Andrew offered.

"Did he now? That would be Robert, the one who was a hero in the Boer War?" The inspector inclined his head toward the constable. "Might be as well to take that in, Taylor," he said, gesturing at the umbrella stand. "I'll let the colonel know we're borrowing it. See if you can find him will you, Mr. Bradford?"

As Andrew headed along the hall toward Frederick's study, Kate asked, "Do you know what kind of blunt instrument Harry was hit with?"

Her casual voice didn't fool Inspector Erskine. He shot a glance at the umbrella stand, then looked at her, his grizzled eyebrows meeting over the bridge of his nose. "I believe your politicians in America would say no comment," he said.

"Keeping it under your hat, are you?" she asked.

"You're a verra smart lassie," he said.

Chapter Six

As the grave-side service ended, Kate was surprised to see Detective Inspector Erskine hovering nearby. She hadn't noticed him among the small group of mourners. Because of the persistent rain almost everyone was shielded by an umbrella.

"What do you suppose Erskine's doing here?" she asked Bennett, who was standing next to her.

Bennett shrugged. Kate bit back a sigh of frustration. During the past few days she'd been trying to get her relatives to talk to see if they'd tell her anything they hadn't told the inspector. But following what Mrs. Hogarth had insisted on calling the "crowner's" inquest, which had taken place in the courthouse at Hambury, the county seat, everyone had acted as if they were afraid they'd incriminate themselves if they even opened their mouths. The coroner's verdict had been as Andrew had predicted—murder by some person or persons unknown.

"Who do *you* think killed Harry?" she asked Bennett, figuring the direct approach was worth a try.

"Maybe his sister did it," he said, looking across the grave to where Hilary, Frederick and Andrew were talking to Mrs. Sanderham, a frazzled-looking woman in tweeds and sensible shoes, who had kept watching the others with hard, cold eyes.

"Why?" Kate asked. "The inspector says there's no such thing as murder without a motive."

"*I* think Hilary bumped him off," Robbie said.

His voice, coming from behind Kate, made her jump. She hadn't even known he was listening. Bennett's face turned purple. She thought for a minute he was going to hit his son, but he managed to restrain himself.

"That's a slanderous thing to say about a fine woman," he snapped. Then he turned on Kate. "Will you for God's sake stop asking questions? You're just stirring up trouble."

"The old man's hormones are giving him hell," Robbie said cheerfully as Bennett strode away toward the parking area.

So Robbie knew about his father's interest in Hilary. She looked at him, then averted her eyes as he bestowed another of his suggestive smiles on her. She had no wish to get into a discussion with Robbie on the subject of hormones.

"Where's Joss?" she asked, looking around.

"She went to her father's car." Elaine volunteered. "She was upset, poor kid. Said it reminded her of her mother's funeral."

"She have any more visions?" Robbie asked, chuckling and tossing back his long blond hair. "This is one weird bunch of people, if you ask me. What with Jossie seeing bodies in the woods and Sikander twisting himself into a yoga pretzel every chance he gets, a murderer on the loose fits right in."

"Wouldn't surprise me if it wasn't Sikander who killed Harry," Elaine said. "That guy gives me the creeps."

"Nah," Robbie said. "Too much of a wimp. You're my favorite candidate. Hell hath no fury like a woman scorned."

Elaine's face flushed as painfully as it had that night at dinner. "I was not flirting with Harry," she said through her teeth. "I was asking him for a loan." Immediately she bit her lip and looked pleadingly at Kate. "Please don't tell my dad," she begged. "He'd kill me." With a hostile glance at her brother, she turned away and hurried to catch up with Lottie and Emory, who had driven her and Robbie over in Hilary's Austin.

"Harry laughed at her," Robbie confided sotto voce before he, too, followed the others.

So much for the loving relationship between twins, Kate thought.

The inspector fell into step beside her as she headed toward the gates. Kate walked briskly, anxious to comfort Jocelyn. The inspector kept up.

"Just as well the family's staying at Farrington Hall for a wee while," he remarked in a voice that was far from casual.

"No progress?" Kate asked.

The inspector had returned to the house on the weekend, politely inviting people into the library for more questions.

"Verra little," he said. "How about you, Miss Kate? You seemed to be in the midst of some heated discussion just now."

"That was just the Cobys being silly," she said. "I don't think they like each other very much." She hesitated. "Do police officers always attend the funerals of murder victims?" she asked, before he could question her further.

"I do," he said, giving her his shy smile. "I live in hopes the murderer will be there looking suitably guilty."

Nobody had looked particularly guilty to Kate. Nor had anyone seemed griefstricken. Frederick had looked grim. So had Andrew. The rest of the family had appeared chilled and anxious, which was probably how she had looked herself.

"Do you think the murderer *was* here?" Kate asked as they reached the parking area.

"Oh, yes," Erskine replied, then he dipped his umbrella in lieu of farewell and hurried over to his own car.

Leaving Kate even more chilled.

THE RAIN HAD STOPPED during the night and the sun shone in an intensely blue sky, but the tall bushes in the rhododendron walk were still heavy with moisture. As Kate raised her camera, Jocelyn reached for one of the magnificent mauve blooms. Rainwater sprayed her face and she shook her head laughing.

"That's perfect," Kate muttered.

"I should think you got enough pictures of me the other day," Jocelyn said, looking self-conscious. "I'm not at all photogenic."

"Let me be the judge of that," Kate said. "The other pictures were mostly group shots, anyway."

In an effort to alleviate the general depression after the inquest, Kate had talked everyone into letting her take their photographs. Her efforts had successfully distracted the family, but she wasn't expecting much in the way of results. Lottie was the only one who had managed a smile.

"Daddy wants to pack me off to stay with Grandma and Granddad Bradford in Kent," Jocelyn blurted out.

"He's worried about your safety," Kate said, fitting a different filter onto her camera.

"He's worried the murderer might get nervous about my fuzzy things and decide to shut me up," Jocelyn said with a lugubrious expression. "He wouldn't dare, it seems to me. It would look too obvious. But if Daddy sent me away, the killer might follow me." She shuddered. "I'm safer here with Daddy than anywhere else, Kate. I've got you to protect me, too."

Kate smiled affectionately at her and started shooting pictures again. "All the same, Joss—" she began.

"Daddy's awfully handsome, don't you think?" Jocelyn interrupted. "When he came for me at school my friends all went gaga over him." She sighed. "I'm just getting to know him, Kate. And the inspector won't let any of the rest of you leave until he finds out who killed Harry. Why should I be treated differently? I told Daddy I'd run away if he insisted." She smiled faintly. "He wasn't too pleased."

"That's hardly a surprise."

"He said, 'We'll have to have a little chat about discipline one of these days,'" Jocelyn said in a fair imitation of her father at his most British.

"Now, perhaps?" Andrew himself said, abruptly appearing behind Jocelyn in Kate's viewfinder.

Kate's heart jerked. From the *surprise* of seeing him, of course, not just the *fact* of seeing him.

Laughing, Jocelyn flung her arms around her father, her face alight with love. "Eavesdropper," she accused.

Andrew hugged her back. "Rotten child," he said fondly.

Kate snapped off several shots before they realized what she was up to. Then they broke away from each other, looking slightly embarrassed at being caught in a demonstration of affection.

"Why don't we go sit in the gazebo?" Andrew suggested, smiling at Kate. "I need to talk to this rebellious creature."

"And I want to talk to you," Kate said. "I hoped to have a chance on the weekend, but Joss said you were working."

He nodded. "A rather sticky estate settlement. I'm sorry I wasn't available."

For a change they sounded friendly, Jocelyn thought, feeling pleased.

"I'm not leaving Farrington Hall, Daddy," she warned as they started walking toward the gazebo.

"Jocelyn Bradford—" Andrew began in a threatening tone.

But then Kate interrupted, putting her hand on his arm. "Maybe we should go somewhere else," she suggested.

Puzzled, Jocelyn looked across at the Victorian gazebo and saw two people sitting on one of the benches. Hilary Wainwright and Bennett Coby, talking very earnestly. Jocelyn supposed Kate didn't want to intrude on their conversation. "Let's go to the maze, then," she said.

"I remember Grandpa Will talking about this maze," Kate said as they changed direction. "I've never been in one before." At the entrance, she hesitated, looking nervous. "Are we sure we know how to do this?" she asked.

"It's fairly simple," Jocelyn assured her. "You start off going to the right, then there are a couple of sharp left—" Quite suddenly she felt as though she'd walked right into an ice cave. There were goose bumps on her arms and a chill running down her spine. Pulling down the shirtsleeves she'd rolled up earlier, she frowned and came to a complete stop. "I don't remember the temperature changing," she muttered. She couldn't breathe. Where had all the air gone?

All at once she realized what was happening. The high hedges were blurring in front of her eyes in a familiar way. Images were starting to form, wavery and unfocused images imposed on the hedges, like ghost pictures in the background of a television screen when channels got crossed. Shaking her head, she took a step backward, bumping into her father. Muttering an apology, she tried to pull herself together, but she could not force herself to walk on.

Kate had turned around and was looking at her oddly. Her father's hand had come up to her shoulder.

"Are you feeling all right, Fishface?" he asked.

"I don't think I do remember the way after all," Jocelyn said, her voice sounding too high even to her own ears.

Andrew frowned at her. "What's the problem?"

Jocelyn had no real answer to give. To her relief, the cold sensation was passing. She must have been mistaken, thinking she was in for another fuzzy thing. She'd just taken a chill, coming into the shadowy maze. But she still didn't want to go on. "Perhaps we could come back tomorrow," she said.

"Something *is* wrong," Kate said, looking concerned.

Jocelyn shook her head and squared her shoulders. She didn't want Kate thinking she was altogether weird. She wanted Kate to like her. And she certainly didn't want her father getting any more ideas about sending her away. "It's all right," she said. "I remember now. It's this way."

She led them along the next path, ignoring the new wave of anxiety that assailed her. If there was something in the maze, then she had to face up to it, she told herself. Daddy had said Bradfords weren't allowed to be cowards.

A moment later, she stopped again. So did Kate and Andrew. The sound of voices had come so suddenly it had been a shock. The high thick hedges acted as a buffer so the voices were muffled, but there was no mistaking Lottie's twang. The next few words were louder as Lottie raised her voice. "I'm not paying you to sit around on your arse looking like you're fifteen ounces to the pound. People are going to wonder if you don't join in the conversation. Why can't you act normally?''

"How can I? It isn't normal, any of it."

Emory's voice, very clear. Lottie's had sounded slurred, Jocelyn realized.

"We shouldn't be listening," Kate whispered.

"No," Andrew agreed.

Neither of them made any move to go.

The voices murmured on for a while, then Emory said very clearly, "You should tell the inspector."

"Not bloody likely," Lottie said.

Then she added something in a much lower voice that Jocelyn couldn't catch. Emory responded, just as quietly, then there was a silence that seemed to last a long time. All at once footsteps vibrated on the packed dirt path and Jocelyn realized either Emory or Lottie or both were coming out of the maze. Exchanging a swift glance, they all ducked into a side path. A minute later, the footsteps went past their hiding place and faded away.

"What do you suppose that was all about?" Andrew asked.

"Emory didn't stammer," Jocelyn pointed out.

Kate shrugged. "Sometimes stammerers speak more clearly when they get angry or upset."

"Shall we go on to the middle?" Andrew asked.

It was completely silent in the maze now except for the sound of a bee buzzing nearby. Still leading the way, Jocelyn felt another wave of coldness, like a blast from the Arctic. "Not far now," she said, more to hear her own voice than to reassure the others.

And then they rounded the last corner. Lottie was lying on her back on the marble bench at the open center of the maze, wearing a pink polyester pantsuit. Her eyes were open as if she were gazing up at the blue sky, but behind the gold-rimmed spectacles they had a blank, unfocused look to them.

She was dead. Jocelyn was quite sure she was dead. Emory, she thought. He must have killed her. Blackness was forming behind her eyelids, moving, tearing to show her a picture of Lottie with blood on the back of her head, just like Harry. Behind her she heard the sudden swift intake of her father's breath, and Kate's hand came to grip her shoulder as though to stop her from going forward. A heartbeat, and Jocelyn grasped the significance of the green wine bottle that rested on Lottie's round body. Both of Lottie's hands were clasped around it. She let her breath out in a whoosh of relief. "She's tiddly," she exclaimed.

"G'day," Lottie said abruptly, sliding her eyes sideways to acknowledge their presence.

"Are you okay?" Kate asked.

"Abso-bloody-lutely," Lottie said. "Am I drunk? Pie-eyed." Sitting up, she took a swig from the bottle and grimaced. "Dregs," she complained, setting the bottle carefully on the ground.

It was from her own winery, Andrew realized. "Perhaps we should be getting back to the house," he suggested. "It's almost teatime."

"Want to sober me up, do you, mate?" Lottie asked. "Why? I've a beaut of a glow going." She bestowed a rather ferocious grin on Jocelyn. "Seen any more pictures in your head, pet?"

Jocelyn shook her head.

"Tha's a relief. Makes me nervous having someone around who sees all." She wagged her head and almost toppled over. "The trouble all goes back to the secret, you know," she said to Kate. "Expect you heard about the Wainwright secret?"

"I don't think so," Kate said, sitting down next to her. "Why don't you tell me about it?"

Lottie put her head on one side. "Le'see, your grand-dad was the eldest brother—William, right? He didn't tell you?"

"Tell me what?"

Lottie screwed up one eye in a truly gruesome grimace that Andrew supposed was meant to be a wink.

"I'm no fool. Abso-bloody-lutely not."

That said, she seemed to collapse forward, as if all the air had gone out of her. Andrew and Kate grabbed for her and managed to stop her from slumping to the ground.

"What on earth has she been drinking?" Jocelyn asked.

Andrew toed over the bottle so she and Kate could see the label.

"Well, that explains a lot," Kate said. "Emory gave me a bottle of that stuff. I opened it up and took a sip—it tasted like a lumberyard. I poured it down the toilet." She took a better grip around Lottie's shoulders.

"I need to go to the loo," Lottie whined.

Andrew laughed. "We'd best get her indoors."

Kate nodded. Hoisting her camera bag to her shoulder, she took a firm grip under one of Lottie's arms, while Andrew got hold of the other. Then she said, "Hold on a minute," and leaned over to pick up something from the ground at the side of the bench. "I thought I saw something glint," she said, holding up a pair of glasses that were identical to Lottie's. "They must be Emory's," she added, and stuck them in the side pocket of her camera bag. "Ready," she told Andrew.

"Heave ho," he said, and they lifted together, Kate staggering under the woman's weight. Then they eased her through the narrow paths in a sort of crablike procession, with Jocelyn leading the way, carrying the empty wine bottle.

"I hope nobody sees us," Kate muttered as they emerged from the maze.

"Not our reputations at stake," Andrew said, but when Kate glared at him he suggested they take the back staircase, which was hidden away beyond a door inside the rear hall.

The staircase was enclosed and very narrow, almost impossible to navigate without ricocheting against the walls, but at least they managed to avoid detection. They left Lottie lying on her bed, minus her glasses and shoes and covered with a blanket.

"I sincerely hope if she really does need to go to the loo, she'll be able to get there under her own steam," Andrew said, after closing Lottie's door.

Kate smiled at him. They were both slightly out of breath. "I'm afraid Lottie likes her own wine too much," she said. "Maybe that's why the winery isn't doing so well?"

"One of the reasons, perhaps," Andrew said lightly, not wanting to go into the other reasons, which only he knew about.

"What was all that about a Wainwright secret, do you suppose?" Jocelyn asked as they reached the main staircase.

Kate and Andrew paused and looked at each other. "I haven't the faintest idea," Andrew said. "Kate?"

"First I've heard of it," Kate said. "It has to be connected with the brothers leaving home, don't you think?"

Jocelyn nodded thoughtfully. Kate had filled her in on the family history the previous weekend, realizing she'd missed most of it when she'd bolted from the dining room.

"Lottie asked if Grandpa had told me about it," Kate pointed out to Andrew. "And she said everything goes *back* to the Wainwright secret. Perhaps there was some specific incident that triggered Robert's anger. D'you think we should talk to the others about it?" She sighed, shaking her head. "A waste of time, probably. I've been questioning them all for days, watching to see if their body language gave anything away. And what did I get? Zilch."

"Body language!" Afterward Andrew was astonished at the strength of the fury that filled him. But at the time all he could think was that she had put herself at risk. "Good Lord, Kate, you can't go around quizzing everyone. What if you rubbed the wrong person the wrong way?"

"I'm sure Kate was very discreet, Daddy," Jocelyn said staunchly. "Don't be beastly."

"Look, Andrew, surely we can discuss this calmly," Kate said. "There are several things I'm concerned with."

Andrew glanced at his watch. "Sorry, Kate, I've used up my spare time," he said rather stiffly. "I've several telephone calls to make—the estate problem I told you about. Perhaps we can talk tomorrow. Though I do think these matters are best left to the police."

"But nobody's telling Erskine anything!"

"Nevertheless."

Why couldn't they be friends? Jocelyn wondered. The three of them could have a smashing time together. She sighed. The problem was, Daddy spent most of his time shut up in his room, working on papers sent down from London or talking on the telephone to his office. He did try to spend time with Jocelyn in the evenings, but he didn't seem to have time for Kate. Yet she had a hunch he liked her, and her hunches were always right. Perhaps if she put her thinking cap on, she could think of a way to get them together. It was certainly worth a try.

KATE CONTINUED DOWNSTAIRS, fuming silently about Andrew's snotty attitude and feeling at loose ends. Jocelyn had wandered off behind her father, looking preoccupied. At the foot of the stairs, she hesitated, pulling the spectacles she'd found out of the camera bag. There was a small marble-topped table near the front door that held a stack of mail. She'd leave the glasses there until Emory turned up to claim them.

Setting them down on top of the pile, she adjusted the strap of her camera bag on her shoulder, frowning down at the glasses. Something didn't look right, but it was a moment before she realized what it was. Glasses usually distorted print when they were laid on top of it. These didn't.

Picking them up, she put them on. She could see through them perfectly well. Plain glass? How very odd. Clutching them, she decided it might be a good idea to return them to Emory herself.

Emory was sitting on the sofa in the library, reading a newspaper. Apparently he had no difficulty reading the fairly small print. "Did you lose your glasses?" Kate asked.

He looked blankly at her, then touched his nose, as though expecting to find them there. "Looks as if I d-did," he said.

"I found them in the maze," she told him.

He took them from her and put them on. His fingers were trembling, she noted. And he'd turned pink behind the ears.

"Thanks, K-Kate," he said. Then he snapped the newspaper and brought it infinitesimally closer. "Much b-better," he said.

Definitely dotty, she thought, echoing Jocelyn's earlier comment. Could she ask him why Lottie was paying him? she wondered. Probably not a wise thing to do. Besides which, he was hardly likely to tell her. "Andrew and I put

Lottie to bed," she told him, sitting down opposite him. "She's drunk."

"Is that s-so?" he said, keeping his face hidden behind the paper.

"She told me about the Wainwright secret," she added.

He lowered the paper, his round face a total blank. "What's th-that?" he asked.

"You've never heard of it?"

He shook his head.

"Lottie hinted it might be connected to Harry's murder," she said, stretching the truth slightly.

He immediately looked terrified. "Lottie over d-d-dramatizes everything," he said. "She d-doesn't know anything at all about Harry's murder. She t-told you that before. So d-did I. Why d-d-do you keep on asking questions?"

With that, he began reading again with great concentration, and it was obvious he wasn't going to tell her any more. But he knew more, she felt sure. He'd protested a little too much.

CLOSING THE DOOR that led from the back entryway, Lottie climbed the first dimly lit and narrow flight of stairs to the shadowy landing. She stood still for a minute, catching her breath, leaning on the cane she'd just recovered from under one of the maze's privet hedges. It was bloody quiet, she thought. Too early for the sensible people to be out and about. Why the hell had the silly bugger wanted to meet her at six o'bloody clock in the morning?

So no one would see them, of course. The first suggestion had been the river, as if she were crazy enough to meet there. "My arthritis is acting up," she'd said. "I can't walk that far." Then she'd suggested this back staircase. It was apparently little used. She hadn't even known it was there until Andrew and Kate had hauled her up it the previous day.

And her excuse had been accepted, confirming her low opinion of certain people's intelligence. If anybody tried anything here she'd scream like a stuck pig. The inner walls of this fancy mausoleum might be inches thick, but she had a voice like a kookaburra when she wanted to use it.

She leaned more heavily on the cane. The excuse about arthritis hadn't been a total lie. Her hip was giving her serious grief. Not as much as her head, though. Lord what a hangover she'd had this morning. Served her right, of course, but that didn't make the nauseating pain any easier to bear.

It was after six now. Maybe she'd asked for too much. Maybe "her friend" had decided the cane wasn't worth it, or that she wouldn't carry out her threat. She *would* tell, though, if she didn't get her money. Too right, she would.

A door opened above and she saw a figure on the upper landing, wearing slacks and a blue sweater. The person hesitated briefly, then continued down the uncarpeted stairs, not looking a bit pleased to see her. She saw the stuffed envelope that had to be the cash she'd demanded. It was going to be all right then. Relief shuddered through her.

"This is what you want, cobber?" she said, grinning, holding the cane out, then pulling it back sharply. "Regular panic merchant, aren't you? Thought Harry's killer might be."

Her friend's face tightened to a grim mask.

"Don't do yer block," she said hastily. Handing over the cane, she snatched the envelope from the outstretched hand. "Glad to give it the flick, to tell you the truth."

The person lifted the cane, looking at the knob on top closely as if to make sure it was the right one. There was no change of expression in the eyes staring at her, nothing to give her any premonition of sudden movement.

The cane came whistling at her, straight for her head, taking her completely by surprise. She ducked and the blow caught her on the shoulder, spinning her around, the pain of it knocking the wind out of her so that she couldn't have yelled even if she hadn't been caught off guard. Another vicious blow landed on the back of her head. As pain rocketed through her skull, sending showers of glaring light tumbling in kaleidoscopic designs in front of her eyes, her attacker reached out and pushed her into space.

She was falling, turning over and over, bumping on every step, blackness reaching out to envelop her. Then there was silence.

Chapter Seven

"Frederick and I thought we might take you all to Windsor today," Hilary announced at breakfast, waving the teapot around. "Inspector Erskine says it's all right. He has no reason to confine any of us to the house at the moment."

The "at the moment" chilled Jocelyn to the bone, but nobody else seemed bothered by it.

"We can take a good look round," Hilary went on. "Have lunch out. What do you think?"

Most of the family seemed thrilled by the idea of getting away from the house, except for Kate. "Do you mind if I don't join you?" she asked, without giving any excuses.

"I think I'll stay here, too," Jocelyn said quickly.

None of them seemed to mind, though the colonel did dart a rather alarmed glance at her. He'd been nervous around her ever since her premonition about Harry's death.

"I've too much work to do," Andrew said.

Jocelyn immediately decided today would be a good time for her father and Kate to get together.

Right after breakfast, she took Kate aside and got her to agree that a picnic lunch by the river might be nice, as long as they went in the other direction from where... Kate hadn't needed to complete the sentence. Jocelyn had no desire to return to the spot where they had found Harry's body.

A couple of hours later, she approached her father. "The whole idea of me coming down here was so we could get better acquainted," she pointed out. "We can't get acquainted with you shut up in your room working."

Andrew glanced up from the papers spread all over the desk in the corner of his bedroom, looking as shamefaced as she had intended him to look. "A picnic you say? Why not."

Next she tracked down Mrs. Hogarth, whom she found whirring around with a vacuum in one of the bedrooms.

"Them girls wouldn't know clean if it looked 'em in the face," the housekeeper complained, switching off the machine. "I'm forever on at them—doesn't help my indigestion one bit."

Jocelyn was afraid she wouldn't take kindly to the idea of preparing a picnic lunch, but she seemed quite willing to go down to the sparkling black-and-white kitchen to help Jocelyn put something together.

"There's a bit of 'am left from last night's dinner," she said. "'And me out some salad cream from the fridge, there's a dear. Three people, you said?"

"Daddy and Kate and me," Jocelyn said, crouching to pet Gray Boy, who was winding around her ankles, purring like mad.

Mrs. Hogarth shot her a look, but didn't say anything. After wrapping the sandwiches in grease-proof paper, she brought out a marvelously equipped picnic hamper from a cupboard and was filling a vacuum bottle with hot tea, when Kate came into the kitchen. Gray Boy immediately went over to rub himself against her legs. He obviously liked Kate a lot, too.

"All ready," Mrs. Hogarth said with a smile for Kate.

"I was going to help," Kate exclaimed.

"Bless your 'eart, dearie, it's no trouble," the house-keeper said.

Kate picked up the cat and started petting him. "Have you worked here long?" she asked Mrs. Hogarth.

"Came here as a girl of fourteen," the housekeeper said. "Mr. Robert was in charge then. The family had a butler named Thomas and I married him when I was eighteen. Died ten years ago of a stroke."

"You must have known all the Wainwright brothers, then," Kate said, feeling suddenly excited.

"Not personally, ducks. They'd all gone before I started 'ere."

She turned around and started sprinkling scouring powder into a sink that looked perfectly clean to Kate.

"Did your husband ever tell you what they were like?"

Mrs. Hogarth didn't answer.

Kate waited. Jocelyn shot her a knowing glance, obviously guessing what she was after.

"A wild lot by all accounts," Mrs. Hogarth said finally. "Always after the girls. Lords of the manor, Thomas said, like back in feudal times. Heavy drinkers the lot."

"That doesn't seem to have changed except for Frederick," Kate murmured. "George spent a lot of time in Australian pubs and Sikander said Alexander drank, too. My grandfather had to have his martinis at the end of the day, though he never got drunk. I don't know about Charles, but his daughter, Jennifer, was evidently an alcoholic."

"Sins of the fathers," Mrs. Hogarth muttered.

Kate studied Mrs. Hogarth's back for a minute, then decided to risk the question. "Did you ever hear of the Wainwright secret?"

The housekeeper shook her head firmly.

"Do you know why the brothers left home?"

"Mr. Robert got tired of their nonsense. Packed them off. No secret to that." She shrugged. "Better get off on that picnic if you're going," she said abruptly.

Defeated, Kate pulled the cat off her shoulder, where he'd draped himself, and helped Jocelyn hoist the picnic basket. "She suffers from indigestion," Jocelyn murmured.

Kate grinned, then together they started out the door.

"Have a good time, all of you," Mrs. Hogarth called after them.

Kate looked at Jocelyn. "All of us?"

"Daddy's coming, too," the girl explained. "You said you wanted to talk to him, so this should be a good chance. You don't mind him coming, do you?"

Kate regarded her face suspiciously for a moment, but she looked remarkably innocent. "No, of course I don't mind," she said, and had to admit to herself that was an understatement. She was really feeling absurdly pleased.

ANDREW WAS WAITING on the terrace. He looked very surprised when he saw Kate, but courteously refrained from saying anything. Nor did he comment when Jocelyn complained about the weight of the picnic basket. He simply took over her side of the hamper, with a smile for Kate that caused all kinds of havoc in her nervous system. She really did like his smile, she decided. It always started slow, filling his eyes with light before spreading to his well-shaped mouth.

She breathed deeply of the pollution-free air as they walked briskly down the driveway, feeling a surge of well-being that was like a tonic to her soul. It had been cold earlier, but the temperature had climbed and now the air was warm.

Andrew was dressed casually again in white twill pants and a blue shirt with rolled-up sleeves that were tight over his biceps. There was more color in his face today. And he was walking along in a vigorous way.

"Are you feeling better?" she asked him.

"Much. It feels splendid to be out getting some exercise. I was afraid my muscles were going to atrophy."

She managed not to look at any of the said muscles. "It's a lovely day for a picnic," she commented inanely.

He smiled again, which set another wave of activity surging through her bloodstream. When he worked at it, this man was far too attractive for her peace of mind.

"Do you have the impression my daughter manipulated this meeting?" he asked with a glance over his shoulder to where Jocelyn was trailing behind them. "Did she tell you I was coming?"

"Not until a few minutes ago."

He nodded. "Just as I thought. Sly little boots. She didn't happen to mention to me that you were included in the invitation, either—she just accused me of parental neglect."

"Do you mind that I'm here?" Kate asked.

He gave her that slow smile again, which caused her breath to become trapped in her throat.

"Not in the least."

"Why are you being so nice to me?" she asked suspiciously.

A spark of laughter showed up in the back of his gray eyes. "I've decided to stop fighting my attraction to you."

"Oh." She couldn't think of a thing to say.

Andrew laughed. "Don't look so worried, Kate. We'll have it out later. Have you forgiven me for spying?"

She was sure she must look sheepish. "I guess so. Once I had time to think it over, I could see it was practical of

Uncle Frederick to check everybody out if he was considering including them in his will." She glanced at him sharply. "That doesn't mean I came here expecting to get something."

"In school we used to say pax when we made up after a quarrel," Andrew said. "It's Latin for peace."

She smiled at him. "I'm a pacifist myself."

There was a moment's silence, then he said. "Have you seen Lottie this morning?"

Lottie hadn't appeared at tea or dinner or breakfast. "I don't think she went to Windsor," Kate said. "But I haven't seen her around. I imagine she's sleeping it off."

They had reached the end of the driveway and turned onto a little country lane flanked by tall hedges foaming with creamy blossom. Trees arched over their heads, filtering the sunshine into bars of light and shade. Kate wished she'd brought her camera with her. She glanced over her shoulder to confirm that Jocelyn was still some distance behind them. She was picking buttercups from the lane's grassy verge, taking her time.

"I want to talk to you about Lottie," Kate said. "Why on earth would she be paying her own brother? And what for?"

"Look here, Kate," Andrew said. "I avoided letting you pin me down yesterday because I knew you'd question me about Lottie and Emory and I wasn't ready to talk about them. One of the phone calls I made was an effort to clear things up, but I couldn't reach the person I needed. Is it any use asking you to drop the subject for now?"

"No," Kate said.

Andrew shot her a glance that was half amused, half exasperated, then he seemed to make up his mind to something. "The man you know as Emory is not Lottie's brother," he said.

Kate was so astonished she almost dropped her side of the basket, but recovered in time to save it. "But they look..."

"Almost identical. But they aren't related. Though I didn't reveal it the other night, I've known for some time that Emory Wainwright died several years ago. Did you notice that Lottie looked relieved under all her bluster when I gave my report? She must have thought I'd overlooked Emory's death."

"The man who's supposed to be Emory wears plain glasses," Kate said. Briefly she explained how she'd discovered that. "He dyes his hair, too. If you look at him closely, you'll see he has dark roots." She pondered a moment, then added, "Obviously he's trying to look more like Lottie so everyone will accept him as her twin. But why the deception?"

Andrew laughed shortly. "Frederick summoned Emory and Lottie. Lottie saw a chance to get two shares in Uncle Frederick's will."

Kate whistled under her breath. "So she hired someone to impersonate Emory." She paused, then asked, "Who is he?"

"Damned if I know."

Kate frowned. "Lottie probably didn't think anyone here knew Emory was dead." Suddenly horrified, she exclaimed, "You don't suppose Harry found out?"

"I don't know that, either."

Kate was thinking fast. "Jocelyn overheard Lottie having an argument with Harry on Wednesday. She told me so while we were at the river, waiting for the police to come."

It was his turn to glance over his shoulder. Jocelyn was making a chain out of the golden-hued flowers she'd gathered. "We'll have a talk, Fishface and I," Andrew said grimly. "She had no business keeping that from the inspector. Why didn't *you* tell Erskine?"

"I thought it was up to Joss," she said lamely, and couldn't resist adding, "I guess I thought if I told him all that I'd have to tell him about your quarrel with Harry, too."

There was a question in her voice as she ended the sentence and she half expected Andrew to get all stiff and defensive again.

But instead he said, "If the three of us put our heads together perhaps we can come up with something that would be useful to the police."

She nodded, feeling relieved. "Let's go for it."

"That was pretty clever of you, working all that out with the hair and the glasses," Andrew said.

Kate laughed. "I'm a smart lassie, the inspector says."

"Yes, well, I'm not surprised. He's obviously smitten."

"That's ridiculous," Kate said, noting that Andrew's voice had gone back to being dry and stuffy again.

"Is it?"

It wasn't, of course. She'd received the same impression. "I'm not interested in the inspector in the least," she said firmly.

"The odd thing is that I knew that," Andrew said with a self-deprecating smile. "But I still experienced . . . pangs. Which made me realize just how attracted I am to you."

They had turned onto the footpath that ran alongside the river. By unspoken consent, they stopped walking. Their eyes met and awareness leaped between them. It had been there all along of course, but suppressed. Now it was out in the open.

Not knowing exactly how to respond, she said the first thing that came into her head. "Emory wasn't murdered, was he?"

Andrew smiled wryly, obviously aware that she was evading the issue at hand. "Word was he died of a stroke."

"Well, that's a relief."

"I don't suppose Emory thought so."

How could she not laugh? Right from the first Andrew's wit had delighted her, even when it was directed at her. She'd always liked men who had a sense of humor. Pity she hadn't remembered that when she'd met Paul Milton.

"You have a lovely laugh, Kate," he said quietly.

She was suddenly afraid to look at him.

ANDREW WAITED until they'd demolished Mrs. Hogarth's sandwiches, then he poured tea all around and looked sternly at his daughter. "Right, Fishface, time for the third degree."

They were sitting under an ancient oak tree, having avoided a nearby clump of beeches that looked like the one where they had laid Harry's body. Kate shuddered as Harry's face flashed into her mind—slack and lifeless, pale eyes staring emptily.

They were at least a couple of miles downriver from that spot, she reminded herself. The water was deeper here and moved lazily with the gentle slope of the land, splashing musically around some large flat rocks that had apparently been placed there to serve as stepping stones. It was peaceful and warm even in the shade. They had spread the blue-and-white tablecloth as a blanket to sit on.

Jocelyn groaned. "What did I do now?" she asked.

"Kate told me you overheard Lottie quarreling with Harry on Wednesday. You should have told the inspector."

He sounded stern, but Jocelyn didn't appear intimidated. "You said I shouldn't repeat hearsay," she said bluntly.

So that was how Andrew had stopped her telling of his argument with Harry. Score one for Joss, Kate thought.

"You could have told *me*," Andrew pointed out.

"I tried to on Thursday morning and you said you didn't want to listen to a load of gossip."

Andrew laughed. "All right, Fishface, I give in. I apologize. Now, what was Lottie going on about?"

Jocelyn gave him a smile that held a definite aura of triumph. "Well . . ." Her brow puckered, then she said, "On Wednesday morning when we arrived, you were busy talking to the colonel, and I got bored. So I walked across the meadow to the river." She shuddered, and fiddled with the buttercup chain she'd hung around her neck. "When I came back I thought I'd look in the library for some helpful books."

She glanced at Kate. "I have to do homework because I got out of school early. But I didn't go in the library, after all, because Lottie and Harry were there. I heard Lottie asking Harry for a loan. She said she needed money for the winery and Frederick wouldn't give her any more."

"What was Harry's response?"

"He laughed at her. Said she was a bit premature—he didn't have the loot yet and when he did get it nobody else was going to get a smell of it. Lottie was really angry. Her chest puffed up just like a pigeon's. I decided it wasn't a good time to interrupt, so I sort of tiptoed away."

"They didn't say anything about Emory?"

"Not while I was there."

Andrew sighed.

"You must think I'm an awful snoop, Daddy."

He grinned, then reached out to tug her long braid lightly. "In this case, your snooping may prove useful, Fishface. Just don't make a habit of it."

Kate was becoming more and more puzzled by Andrew's attitude toward his daughter. He might have neglected her in her early years, but he sure seemed fond of her now. The nickname he'd given her was hardly flattering, but it was always said with a great tenderness. His face softened when he looked at her. But at the same time there was an expression in his gray eyes that was hard to pin down. It was almost…uncertain. And occasionally full of something very like pain.

Jocelyn was smiling at him, her gaze adoring. There was no mistaking how she felt about him.

"Lottie paid someone to pose as Emory—Lottie asked Harry for a loan," Kate murmured. "This plot is getting thicker."

They sipped their tea in silence, then Andrew murmured, "Seems several people had it in for Harry. Elaine—"

"Surely she wouldn't murder Harry simply because he rejected her."

"Who knows? Then there's Sikander. Harry insulted him."

"Elaine voted for Sikander," Kate said. "Bennett thought Mrs. Sanderham might have done it. Robbie accused Elaine. Evidently she asked Harry for a loan, also."

Andrew frowned.

"Then there's you," Kate added.

He laughed and tapped Jocelyn on the knee. "Better tell Kate about my tiff with Harry, Fishface," he said. "She's very curious about it."

"So am I," Jocelyn said. Then she frowned. "You said you didn't want me to tell anybody, that it wasn't important but people might misunderstand."

"We can trust Kate," Andrew said. "Which reminds me, Fishface. I meant to tell you that if you have any more fuzzy things and I'm not available, you can tell Kate about them.''

Astonished and gratified, Kate stared at him, awed by the trust he was placing in her. He returned her gaze levelly for a second, then he smiled and her pulse went into double time. No doubt about it. This was one very sexy male.

Jocelyn was obviously delighted that things were going so smoothly between her father and Kate. Turning to face Kate, she grinned mischievously at her. ''I didn't hear much, just Harry saying if he wasn't a gentleman he'd tell Daddy exactly what the situation was all those years ago. Then Daddy said if Harry was a gentleman there wouldn't be a situation. And he should stay away from me.''

''I'm sure glad that's all cleared up,'' Kate said dryly.

Andrew shrugged, then sprawled flat on his back beside her, clasping his hands behind his head. ''It was just a silly argument,'' he said. ''What can you offer?''

Looking at him stretched out like that, his muscular body so close to her, his flat stomach within touching distance, she couldn't remember a thing. She had a sudden vision of herself sprawling right along with him, hip to hip, breast to chest. ''The thing was,'' she said hastily, ''according to what you told me, when the inspector questioned everybody, almost all of them lied.''

Twin lines formed above the bridge of his nose. She found herself wanting to smooth them with her fingertips. ''Everybody told Erskine they had nothing against Harry, right?'' she said hastily. ''But we know from Joss that probably wasn't true for Lottie, and we can be pretty sure Sikander disliked him. Elaine, too. I know Hilary didn't like him—she told me so. Hilary also told me she was afraid, but I don't know what of. I tried to find out from her after the funeral and she said I must have been mistaken—she hadn't said that at all. But I wasn't mistaken.''

She hesitated. "Hilary said even Frederick didn't care for Harry all that much. Then there's Bennett. At the funeral, Robbie teased him about Hilary and he got all hot under the collar. He looked really *murderous.*"

She pondered for a minute. "Sikander pulled his nose when he said he hadn't noticed anything out of the ordinary on Wednesday evening. People do that when they're lying."

"Some sort of Pinocchio complex?" Andrew asked with deceptive mildness, watching her face with sly amusement. "They think their noses are going to grow."

Kate decided to ignore the remark. "Lottie shook her head at Emory when he started to say something about Harry," she went on. "She definitely wanted him to shut up."

Andrew nodded. "We need to have words with Madam Lottie. I intended waiting until I could find out the pseudo Emory's true identity, but I think we'd better get right to it."

The sound of that "we" brought Kate a warm feeling. "Frederick and Robbie seem to be the only people with alibis," she said. "Frederick heard Robbie playing the piano, which places both of them. But I'm not sure I believe in Bennett's lonely walk. And Elaine looked shifty when she said she was doing her nails." She laughed, looking at Andrew. "Elaine rather likes you, doesn't she?"

"No more than Robbie likes you."

Kate became aware that Jocelyn was watching them both very closely. "What do Frederick and Hilary think?" she asked hastily. "I haven't had the heart to question them."

"They are totally bewildered. Frederick feels responsible because he brought everyone together. Not much doubt he thinks one of the family did it to eliminate the competition."

"So where are we?" Kate asked.

"Back at the beginning," Jocelyn said. "We still don't know who killed Harry."

"I just *have* to talk to everyone again, ask them about the Wainwright secret," Kate said with a sigh.

"We'll talk to them together," Andrew said immediately. "I won't have you risk your neck asking the wrong sort of questions."

She should have bridled at the implied criticism of that remark, but she was savoring the sound of the word "together."

"You *are* bossy, Daddy," Jocelyn said.

"Women like dominant men," he said.

"Do they, now?" Kate said, her feminist hackles rising automatically.

"If you two are going to fight, I'm going for a walk," Jocelyn said, bouncing lightly to her feet.

"Not out of sight, Fishface," Andrew said.

The implied warning of danger made Kate shiver, but the girl merely nodded and headed downriver, where the path stretched a long way in clear view.

"*Are* we going to fight?" Andrew asked.

Kate shook her head. "It's too nice a day."

"It is, indeed."

Kate was tracing the fleur-de-lis pattern on the tablecloth with one finger, not looking at Andrew, but she could feel him looking at her. A kind of lethargy had come over her suddenly, an after-lunch somnolent feeling. No, not somnolent. Every cell in her body was awake.

"I do believe Fishface is being discreet," Andrew said.

Kate swallowed. Her throat had suddenly become dry. Perhaps she should pour herself some more tea. No. She didn't want to move. Andrew was sitting very close to her, his head turned toward her. Tension arced between them, almost palpable, definitely sexual.

Jocelyn was still strolling away from them, bending to examine things in the water from time to time, not looking back. Kate could hear insects humming in the grass. In the sky, exuberant white clouds played hide-and-seek with the sun.

"Andrew," Kate murmured.

"Yes."

What had she meant to say? Nothing. Just his name.

His fingers touched her hair, then slid up under it to clasp the back of her neck. She felt the shock of his touch travel all the way down her spine.

It all seemed unreal—the leaves of the oak tree rustling in the slight breeze, the river splashing merrily, the cheery sound of birdsong—all this, even though a man had died in that river a week ago.

They were alive, she and Andrew.

She turned her head, giving in to the gentle pressure of his fingers. The clear air seemed to shimmer between them. There was a pause the length of a heartbeat while she looked into those wonderfully clear gray eyes, then his mouth touched hers.

"I've wanted to do this," he said against her lips.

It was a long, discovering kiss, at first merely a slow brushing of his mouth on hers. Then his lips hardened and his free arm slipped around her and held her close, his mouth moving impatiently, passionately.

Kate responded with unthinking ardor, making incoherent little sounds in her throat, her breath mingling with his. When at last he drew away she was so shaken all she could do was stare at him.

Another heartbeat and he murmured, "I think Jocelyn's about to come back."

Kate turned her head. Jocelyn was standing quite still, looking at the river, as far along the path as she could go without getting out of sight. Was her stillness intended to warn them that she was about to turn around?

"She's a lovely girl," Kate said warmly. "Such an interesting mixture of shyness and boldness and tact." She hesitated. "It's obvious she's going to be a tall woman, but apart from that, she doesn't resemble you at all. Does she look like her mother?"

Andrew didn't answer right away and when Kate glanced at him she surprised a look of anguish on his face. "What's wrong?" she exclaimed. "Did I say something I shouldn't have?"

His face had cleared immediately. Now he smiled. "Bit of a twinge from the old lungs," he said.

Would a mere twinge cause an expression of anguish? Was it the mention of Jocelyn's mother that had caused his reaction? What exactly was the story there?

Feeling slightly awkward, she turned away to watch Jocelyn again. She wanted so much to ask Andrew why he'd seen so little of Jocelyn over the years, but she didn't want him telling her it was none of her business and spoiling the good feeling that had begun to grow between them.

"LET'S NOT go back yet," Jocelyn begged after they'd packed up the picnic things. "Let's go for a walk. We could leave the hamper under the tree and fetch it on the way back."

"Your father should probably rest for a while," Kate said.

"I've been resting," Andrew said firmly.

"Then could we go to Allercott?" Kate asked. "I have a couple of rolls of film..." Rummaging in her purse, she pulled out the containers of film she'd used up on her first day in England. She made a sound of exasperation. "I knew I should have brought along my camera bag—the pictures I took of the family and Jocelyn are still in there."

"Next time," Andrew said, his smile promising more lovely days like this. "On to Allercott," he said cheerfully, setting foot on the first stepping stone.

The old village was beautiful, featuring imposing Tudor and Georgian houses set cheek by jowl with tiny cottages. There was also a church that dated back to the seventeenth century, a pub with a swinging sign that featured a posturing cavalier, a small supermarket and some interesting-looking shops, which included a chemist's, where Kate dropped off her films to be processed.

Just as Kate was beginning to feel thirsty again, they came upon a pretty inn whose garden, literally crammed with flowers of all descriptions, was also a tea garden.

"Did you know this place was here?" she asked as she shared the pot of fragrant tea among the three of them.

Andrew shook his head. "It's not, usually," he said, looking directly into her eyes.

It was the most romantic, whimsical thing anyone had ever said to her.

Her appreciative smile warmed the cold places that had long existed in Andrew's heart. He really liked her face, he decided. There was such radiance in it when she smiled. Her brown eyes were full of soft light. He was glad she hadn't burned out on smiling altogether. He thought he would remember her smile long after she'd returned to America, and was startled by the flash of sadness the thought brought with it.

And then he glanced at his daughter. There was an expression on her face he'd never seen there before. A blank, lost expression that made his heart contract. Surely she wasn't upset by his attention to Kate. She'd maneuvered them together, after all—

"What is it, Fishface?" he asked.

She didn't answer and he was shocked to see that all the color had drained from her face.

"She's ill," Kate said, putting her arm around Jocelyn's shoulders.

Jocelyn shook her head slowly, still with that blank expression in her eyes. "Not ill," she murmured. Then her eyes cleared and she looked in a frightened way at Andrew. "I think we ought to go back now," she said in a shaky voice.

"Why?" Kate demanded, leaning forward.

"I don't know why," Jocelyn said, looking as if at any minute she was going to burst into tears. "I only know something's wrong, dreadfully wrong."

The sun chose that moment to disappear behind a cloud Andrew could have sworn wasn't in sight a moment ago. The colors in the garden seemed suddenly subdued and there was a definite chill in the air. Whatever it was that affected his daughter from time to time—intuition or ESP—something was obviously terrifying her now. "Let's go," he said.

Chapter Eight

Standing at the window of his room, fists clenched on the sill, Sikander stared down at the courtyard unseeingly.

Those damnable socks. What was he to do with them? Why had he even picked them up that day? Deliberately he flattened his hands. He *had* picked them up. The fact could not be changed, so he must have the wisdom to accept it. He had hung the socks in his bathroom to dry, then put them away with his own socks in his bureau drawer. But their presence had weighed on him ever since; they had niggled at his mind all day, spoiling his enjoyment of the trip to Windsor.

What enjoyment? It had been a disappointment when Kate and Jocelyn had decided not to accompany them. The others were friendly enough to his face, but he sensed wariness in them, no doubt because of Andrew Bradford's report. It was not fair. He had made a mistake in the past, yes; he had no one to blame but himself. But he had paid for his misconduct.

Was he making another mistake now, keeping those socks hidden away?

Pulling abruptly back from the window, he pushed his spectacles firmly into place, straightened his bow tie and tugged at his sleeveless pullover. It was unbearable to stand there idle while his thoughts scurried like mice. He needed the calm, the purification of yoga. He would go down to the courtyard straightaway, while the others were changing for dinner and would not be likely to disturb him.

Opening the door that led to the back staircase, he fumbled for the light switch. Even when he found it, the stairway wasn't well lit. The stairs were narrow. Possibly they had been intended for use by the servants in the old days when servants were not supposed to be seen by guests in the house. His own room had formerly served as servant's quarters, Aunt Hilary had told him. Sikander was glad he was not a servant. He wanted—how he wanted—to be his own master.

What was he to do about those socks?

Turning the corner on the lower landing, he stopped dead, looking down, his breath catching in his throat. It appeared very much as if someone was lying at the bottom of the stairs. But why would anyone do that? Unless they were ill?

Gripping the handrail, he slowly, reluctantly, descended the final flight. The person at the bottom was Lottie Wainwright, sprawled against the door that led to the back hall. She was obviously unconscious, her sturdily shod feet sticking out from under a long mackintosh. Was she drunk again? Emory had said at dinner yesterday that she had gone to bed early with a headache and did not wish to be disturbed in the morning. But Robbie had told Sikander he'd seen Andrew and Kate helping Lottie into the house in the afternoon. She was swacked, he'd said with a grin.

Squatting, Sikander touched the woman's arm in a gingerly way. Her eyes were closed, her face devoid of color. "Lottie," he whispered, then added more loudly, "Lottie, wake up!"

He felt suddenly afraid. Terrified. So terrified, the short hairs on the back of his neck stood on end. His chest felt hollow and his heart ricocheted against his ribs. "Lottie," he said again.

And then he saw that there was a small stain on the collar of Lottie's mackintosh, a stain that looked reddish brown in the dim light. More of the reddish brown color had spread across the slate floor beneath her head and had seeped into the edges of her short blond hair.

Suddenly understanding, Sikander jerked upright. A scream was lodged somewhere in his throat, but he could not seem to release it. He must tell someone. Now. At once. But he could not open the door without moving Lottie's body. Backing away, he stumbled against the stairs and almost fell, recovered, then turned and raced up to the first landing, where he pulled open the door and simultaneously found his voice. "Help!" he shouted. "Here at once, I tell you. Help!"

THE MOMENT THEY TURNED from the lane into the driveway to Farrington Hall, they saw the police cars. The significance of their presence hit Andrew like a blow to his solar plexus.

"Too many cars," he muttered, quickening his step.

"What do you mean?" Jocelyn asked, turning pale again.

He shook his head, not wanting to say in front of her that there were too many police cars for follow-up activities. Something new had evidently occurred.

People were milling around in the vestibule. Hilary was pacing back and forth, throwing her arms about. "It was such a lovely day in Windsor," she said to Andrew, taking hold of his arm with a grip that felt like steel.

Obviously bewildered, Kate looked helplessly at Andrew.

"Hush," Bennett said, taking hold of Hilary's other arm. "It's all right, dear. You couldn't know. None of us knew."

"Such a lovely day," Hilary sobbed. "Who would imagine we'd come home to this."

"We just arrived a little while ago ourselves," Bennett added, which was hardly any more enlightening.

"Why are the police here?" Kate asked.

Jocelyn's face was as white as her shirt collar. Tugging her father aside, she whispered urgently to him, "Something's happened to Lottie. I knew I shouldn't have ignored that chilly feeling going into the maze yesterday." She looked up at Andrew, her eyes wide with fear. "There was a fuzzy thing trying to come and I pushed it away. It was trying to come back when we were having tea at the inn."

Andrew put an arm tightly around her and looked at Sikander. "What's going on here?" he demanded.

Sikander's mouth looked pinched, his dark eyes, magnified behind his spectacles, were owllike with fear. "Mrs. Hogarth had no occasion to go down the back stairs, you see, so it was not till we came back that Lottie was found."

"What *happened* to Lottie?" Andrew shouted.

Jocelyn's body jerked as though electricity had gone through it.

Sikander pushed his glasses back into position and regarded him nervously. "I found her lying at the bottom of the back stairs with blood coming out of her head."

"She fell downstairs?" Kate asked.

He shook his head. "Uncle Frederick telephoned for an ambulance. When it came the attendants said the police station must be rung up because she had not fallen accidentally."

"Dear God!" Kate exclaimed.

"Is she dead?" Andrew asked.

Sikander shook his head. "Not dead, no. But it is thought she might not recover. She was taken to hospital in the ambulance. Emory accompanied her."

His hands were tightly clasped to his chest and suppressed emotion was making his slight frame tremble like an aspen in a storm. His eyes blinked convulsively. He was in shock, Andrew realized. Which was hardly surprising.

Andrew wished he could sit down. Since his illness it had happened like this, a sudden loss of energy, a feeling that his knees were going to give out. Kate's hand slipped under his free arm and he glanced at her gratefully, though he wasn't sure if she meant to support him or if she was looking for the warmth of human contact. To make contact himself, he covered her hand with his own and gripped it tightly.

Detective Inspector Erskine appeared in the vestibule a few minutes later, accompanied by Frederick, and suggested they all wait in the drawing room. Mrs. Hogarth, green around the gills, put a cloth on the round table and served strong hot tea, which she insisted would make them all feel better.

The tea did seem to help and Bennett kept urging everyone to drink more. By the time the inspector returned, Sikander and Hilary were beginning to recover. At least Hilary had stopped pacing and Sikander had stopped wringing his hands. Jocelyn's face was still ghastly, however. Kate had her arm about the girl, holding her closely. Frederick was obviously considerably shaken, too. For the past fifteen minutes, he'd stood by the window, looking out, his shoulders stooped, his gray head bowed as though in prayer. Robbie was sitting on the piano bench, Elaine by his side. They both looked feverish.

Kate was trembling, Andrew discovered when he took hold of her free hand. "We should have told the inspector about Lottie yesterday," she muttered.

"We weren't to know this was going to happen," Andrew murmured, knowing it was a small crumb of comfort. "Let me tell Erskine, all right? I'll fill him in on the facts about Emory at the same time."

She nodded agreement, just as Erskine tapped on a glass for attention. "Miss Lottie was struck on the head before she fell or was pushed down the stairs," he said sternly. "Apparently she was assaulted fairly early, before the family left for Windsor. I will talk to each of you in turn."

He turned to Frederick, who was now standing beside him. Andrew had never seen Frederick stoop like that— he'd always had such a military posture. He looked as if he had aged ten years or more. "The library has been prepared for us again?"

Frederick nodded.

Andrew was allowed to be present as each person was called in for questioning. The pink-cheeked constable took notes.

"Bad business this," Erskine observed to Andrew when it was his turn to be questioned.

Andrew nodded. "Any clues?" he asked.

"One or two," the inspector said ambiguously. "It's like building a wall, one brick at a time. Do you have any bricks to offer yourself?"

Andrew didn't hesitate this time. "Emory Wainwright died several years ago," he said. "The man calling himself Lottie's twin brother is an impostor."

The inspector looked at him with narrowed eyes. "Why did you no tell me this afore?"

"I have no proof. I'm awaiting documentation from Australia."

"But you are sure of your facts?"

"I was told by my Australian colleague that there was no room for doubt. And I have some slight confirmation myself." Briefly he described the incident in the maze. "Lottie was evidently paying the man to pose as Emory. I would imagine she thought that if Frederick was going to leave her any money she might well claim two shares. I also heard the pseudo Emory say she should tell the inspector something. Do you have any idea what that might have been about?"

"I do not."

The inspector assessed Andrew's face shrewdly for a minute. "You might find this so-called Emory Wainwright for me," he suggested.

"I understand he went along in the ambulance."

"Och!" The inspector was instantly furious. "I gave instructions nobody was to leave this house. What if he was the one who attacked her?" Getting up, he strode from the room. He was gone several minutes, then came back brushing his hands together. "He'll be brought back at once," he announced. "Now," he said, sitting down, "I understand you possess written reports on the various members of this family."

"Those are confidential papers," Andrew protested. "I'll have to get Frederick's permission to show them to you."

"I suggest you do that."

The inspector's hazel eyes looked as opaque as pebbles newly washed in a brook, Andrew noted. "I'll see what I can do," he promised.

It took him a while to find Frederick. He was sitting on a leather sofa in his study with his arm around his wife. Hilary was sipping a brandy, calm now, but still very pale. When Andrew told him what the inspector wanted Frederick pursed up his mouth. His weathered face, usually so ruddy, was gray.

"I suppose we'll have to give him the reports," Frederick said with a sigh. "He could subpoena them later if we don't."

Coming downstairs a few minutes later, Andrew met Kate coming up. She looked even paler than Hilary.

"Jocelyn's lying down in her room," she said. "She wanted to be alone for a while. I'm just going to check on her."

"Thank you for taking care of her," Andrew said, then hesitated. "I didn't tell Erskine she'd had another episode."

"Good. We have to protect her as best we can."

"Are you all right?" he asked.

"I'm not sure I'll ever be all right again. I can't believe someone would do this—someone we know."

"I'm having a similar reaction," Andrew said. "I'm afraid I have to give the inspector my reports," he added, indicating his briefcase. "Somebody talked."

There was a look of strain around her dark eyes. "I think we should tell the police every single thing we know."

"As long as it's something we know for sure," he answered.

A flash of suspicion showed in her face. "You're asking me not to talk about your quarrel with Harry?"

"Actually, I was thinking of Lottie rambling on about some sort of Wainwright secret. I'd rather look into that myself." He paused. "However, my quarrel with Harry had nothing to do with Harry's death. Or with Lottie's accident," he added emphatically. He touched her cheek. "We have to trust each other, Kate."

She leaned her face into the palm of his hand. "I know," she murmured. "I just keep remembering that while we were at the river, Lottie was lying down there at the foot of the back stairs, bleeding. While we were . . .''

"Kissing," he finished for her. "We didn't know, Kate." Taking her in his arms, he kissed her very gently, and felt warmth and comfort fill him. He wished he could stand there forever on that staircase, kissing Kate. He didn't want ever again to think about violence and fraud and mysterious happenings. "We'll get through this, Kate," he murmured, observing that her eyes seemed darker than ever against the pallor of her face.

"Will Lottie?" she asked.

It was all she could do to drag herself up the rest of the stairs. Why did she feel so exhausted? she wondered as she paused on the landing. Shock still affecting her, probably. She wished she could take a nap and wake up to find that the past couple of hours had been a terrible nightmare, nothing more. But she couldn't. She had to check on Jocelyn and she had yet to have her time with the inspector.

Where was everybody? The house felt unnaturally still, as if it were empty. Almost as eerily still as the first time she'd come into it. Such a big house. Its high ceilings and wide passageways seemed to absorb all sound.

On the heels of this thought, she heard a door open along the hall. Still leaning on the banister, she saw Elaine emerge, close the door quietly and tiptoe away in the opposite direction, entering another room at the far end. So puzzled was she by Elaine's furtive behavior, it was a moment before she realized the room Elaine had come out of was her own.

What the hell was Elaine up to?

Entering her bedroom, Kate could see no sign of disturbance. In the massive wardrobe, her clothes hung as she'd left them; her suitcases were still stacked on top of it. Closing the mirrored door, she went methodically through the chest of drawers and dressing table. Nothing had been disturbed.

Puzzled, she gazed around the room again, her glance falling on her camera bag. But when she squatted and opened it, everything seemed okay.

She had closed the zipper and was getting to her feet, when she remembered the containers of film that should have been in the gadget bag. Opening it again, she searched the bag thoroughly. The containers were not there.

But she was willing to swear Elaine had not carried anything out of the room.

Feeling foolish, she got down on her knees by the bed and looked under it. Something glinted, far back against the wall. Taking a pencil from the nightstand and lying flat, she reached for it and pulled it out. A plastic container. Empty. Lying flat again she fished some more and brought out the second container. Also empty.

There was one place she still hadn't searched. Standing up, she maneuvered the nightstand to one side. And there was all her film, stuck down behind it, unwound and exposed.

There was a sour taste in her mouth, a coldness inside her. Why had Elaine exposed her film? What possible reason could she have had?

THE MAN WHO CALLED himself Emory Wainwright came into the library escorted by a police sergeant Andrew hadn't seen before. He was obviously in shock, his pudgy body trembling. The eyes behind the gold-rimmed spectacles looked faded and watery.

"She died," he said, slumping onto a chair. "Lottie d-died. Before we got to the hospital."

"I'm sorry," the inspector said softly. Andrew reached over to clasp Emory on the shoulder. The shoulder felt loose, as though the man's frame were in the process of dissolving.

"I lovcd that old g-girl," Emory muttered.

The inspector looked at him with obviously sincere sympathy. "I'm sure you did, sir." There was a short silence, then the inspector glanced at Andrew and took a deep breath. "I dislike bothering you at a time like this, sir, but I must ask you where you keep your passport."

"Top d-d-dressing table drawer, under my sh-shirts," Emory said in a numb way, apparently not recognizing the significance of the request.

The inspector nodded at the sergeant, who left the room.

"When did you last see Lottie?" Erskine asked.

"Last n-night about half past seven," Emory replied, still looking dazed. "She was in her room lying d-down. She felt c-crook—unwell."

"She'd been drinking heavily, I understand."

Emory nodded. "I asked her if she w-wanted to go to d-dinner, but she said n-no. She said not to wake her in the morning. That's why I d-didn't ask her this morning if she wanted to go to Windsor. If only I'd g-gone looking for her..."

"Have you any idea—" Erskine broke off as the sergeant returned and handed a passport to the inspector.

Emory's eyes followed the movement, widening as he belatedly recognized the implication.

The inspector glanced at the document, then handed it to Andrew. "At least you didn't come into the country using Emory Wainwright's identity," he commented.

Emory's face showed resignation now. The belligerence had gone out of his rotund body like air escaping from a balloon.

"Lottie thought it would be too dangerous," he said without a trace of a stammer.

Andrew examined the passport carefully. The photograph had evidently been taken after the man had dyed his hair, but the name on the document was Roger Stoane.

"Good Lord!" Andrew exclaimed. "You're the husband!"

The Australian lowered his head for a moment, then pulled off his gold-rimmed spectacles and sighed. "Thank God I don't have to keep wearing these bloody things."

Andrew handed the passport back to the inspector, who tapped it lightly against the palm of his other hand, looking thoughtful. "I'll just keep this a wee while," he said, fixing the Australian with a baleful stare. "Would you care to explain yourself?" he asked with obvious sarcasm.

The man spread his palms in a helpless gesture. "Lottie said it wouldn't be like nicking because we used to be married. We were married for five years, but she got impatient with me—I'm a bit slow sometimes—and decided we should get divorced. But she kept me on at the winery for old times' sake."

The inspector shot a few rapid-fire questions at him and the answers confirmed Andrew's opinion that Lottie had planned to pass Roger off as Emory in case there was any chance of inheriting from Frederick.

"Once Emory died, the winery started going down the gurgler—the drain," the man added. "Lottie wrote and asked Frederick for money. He sent her some, but it's gone now."

Andrew exclaimed under his breath, but the inspector seemed unsurprised. "Colonel Wainwright told me as much during our first interview," he said to Andrew.

"Lottie asked Harry for a loan, too," Roger volunteered. "He just laughed. Said all he had were prospects."

Andrew was relieved he wouldn't have to confess that Jocelyn had overheard that particular conversation. Nevertheless it was an opening he should probably take advantage of. There was something he still hadn't told the inspector in regard to Frederick's will. But client confidentiality prevailed. It was Frederick's place to enlighten the inspector. Perhaps he already had.

Andrew looked at Roger, who was visibly perspiring. "I take it the real Emory stammered."

Roger Stoane nodded. "Lottie wasn't sure if anyone in the family knew that, so she didn't want to take chances. Bloody awful thing to keep up."

"You were overheard arguing with Lottie in the maze yesterday," the inspector broke in. "What was it you thought she should tell me?"

"That I wasn't Emory," Roger said promptly.

Too promptly? Andrew wondered.

Erskine kept his gaze fixed on the man's face, waiting.

"I thought Lottie should tell you about the cane," Roger said, slumping in apparent resignation.

Erskine blinked. "What cane would that be?" he asked. He didn't do anything obvious such as lean forward, but the angle of his head, the sudden glint in his eyes, gave Andrew the impression he wanted to. Body language, he thought. Kate had a point, after all.

"Harry was carrying a cane when he went off home on Wednesday. I started to tell you, but Lottie stopped me and changed it to a coat. The cane was back in the umbrella stand the next day, Thursday. Lottie knew that because her arthritis was bothering her, so she used it when we all went looking for the body Bradford's little girl said she'd seen. When we heard about Harry getting killed, Lottie realized there was no blamed way Harry could have brought it back, so..."

"So the murderer must have," Erskine finished for him. "Did Lottie have any idea who that might have been?"

"She wouldn't say."

The inspector fixed Stoane with a direct gaze again, but this time he didn't offer anything more. "Where is that walking stick now?" Erskine asked.

"I don't know. Lottie hid it under one of those high hedges in the maze. She wanted to think about it awhile." He frowned. "She got it out when we came home from the inquest and used it the rest of the day to see if anyone showed any interest. But nobody did. I haven't seen it since."

"Somebody was interested in that cane, after all," Andrew murmured, feeling chilled to the bone.

Erskine nodded, then dispatched the sergeant to search Lottie's room. "We looked everywhere for that damned walking stick," he muttered, sounding disgusted.

"You knew Harry had a cane with him?" Andrew asked.

The inspector didn't answer. "What did the walking stick look like?" he asked Roger.

Roger made a vague movement with his right hand. "Wooden, with cracks in it, as if it had dried out a bit. Sort of knob on the end. I'm up the creek, aren't I?" His voice shook.

The inspector regarded him coldly. "Conspiracy to commit fraud comes to mind. Depends on whether the colonel wants to press charges. Depends on whether you were involved in the assault on Lottie Wainwright."

"I wasn't involved at all. Dinkie die," Roger insisted, sitting bolt upright, color draining from his face. "I loved Lottie, Inspector, in spite of the divorce. When I got up this morning, around half past seven, I went straight down to breakfast. Afterward I went into the library to read the newspapers while I waited for the others. I didn't see Lottie again until we came home and Sikander..." His voice trailed away and he swallowed visibly.

"Was anyone else in the library?" Erskine asked.

Roger shook his head. "Not until just before we left."

Sighing, the inspector cautioned him not to mention the walking stick to anyone, then asked Constable Taylor to bring Frederick Wainwright to the library.

When Frederick arrived, he asked immediately if the inspector had heard anything from the hospital.

"I'm afraid so, sir," the inspector said.

"She's dead," Roger said. "Lottie's dead."

Frederick swung around and walked over to the spiral staircase, where he stood gripping the metal rail, his back turned.

Exchanging a glance with Erskine, Andrew stood up and went over to him, touching his shoulder. "Steady on, old chap," he murmured.

Frederick nodded. With an obvious effort he straightened his shoulders. Returning to the desk, he offered condolences to the man he still thought of as Lottie's brother.

Quickly the inspector enlightened him, acquainting him with Roger's true identity and the plan Lottie had cooked up. "Do you wish to press charges?" he asked.

For a moment Frederick seemed too confused to respond. Andrew wasn't surprised. This shock on top of the other was more than enough to confuse any man.

At last Frederick took a deep breath and sighed. "I don't see much point in dragging this through the courts," he said.

The color was returning to his face, Andrew was glad to see.

Roger had wilted with obvious relief.

"However," Frederick added, tugging at his mustache, "I can't say I think very highly of your character, Mr. Stoane. You didn't have to agree to defraud me."

"Wasn't much use saying no to Lottie," Roger said.

A gleam of agreement showed briefly in Frederick's eyes, then he glanced at the inspector. "You don't think this man is responsible for the assault on Lottie?" he asked.

Andrew wouldn't have thought Roger's face could blanch any whiter, but it did.

Erskine shook his head and Roger wilted again. "If at all possible, I'd appreciate your letting Mr. Stoane stay on for a while," the inspector said.

"If you deem it necessary," Frederick said immediately. "You can count on me for full cooperation, Inspector."

The inspector smiled at him gratefully.

"A good man, the colonel," he said as soon as the two men had left the room.

"The best," Andrew agreed. "You don't think it's possible Lottie hid the walking stick because *she* killed Harry with it?" he asked.

Erskine sighed. "A Mrs. Freemantle remembers Lottie buying postcards at half past five that particular Wednesday. Not the kind of woman you'd forget easily. The old gardener remembers Lottie and Emory—Roger—driving in about half past six. It's possible they could have parked the car somewhere, hiked to the river, struck Harry down, dragged him into the river and hiked back, but it seems unlikely. If that were the case we'd have two killers. Lottie and whoever brained her. Roger wasn't likely to do both— without Lottie he has no claim to anything." Erskine paused, sighing. "As for the rest of the family—nobody was ever with anybody when anything happened, so the field's still wide open."

"Kate and Jocelyn and I were together," Andrew pointed out.

"Not this morning you weren't," Erskine said crossly. "I don't know which is the more frustrating—when everybody's got a damned alibi or nobody's got one, which is the case here." He took a deep breath. "Where the hell's Sergeant Cooper?"

As though on cue, the sergeant entered the room. "Nothing in Lottie Wainwright's bedroom, sir," he said.

Andrew could have sworn he heard the inspector grind his teeth.

"Go look under the hedges in that damn maze," Erskine said.

"All of them, sir?" the sergeant asked.

The inspector glared at him, and he about-turned smartly and left the room.

"I take it the missing cane could be the murder weapon?" Andrew said.

Erskine leaned back in his chair, looking more relaxed now. "The postmortem turned up splinters of wood embedded in the tissue of Harry Wainwright's head wound. Stinkwood. Does that mean anything to you?"

Andrew shook his head.

"I'm told one of the places stinkwood trees are found is in South Africa. Settlers used it to make furniture. Robert Wainwright fought in the Boer War—the South African War."

"And Robert collected walking sticks."

"Precisely."

The inspector seemed to be considering something. Andrew waited him out and after a few minutes he leaned forward.

"This stinkwood business is between you and me, Mr. Bradford. We don't want the killer knowing how much we know, you understand."

Andrew nodded.

"To recapitulate," Erskine went on, "Roger Stoane and Lottie saw Harry with a walking stick on Wednesday evening. No walking stick was found near the body. According to Roger, the walking stick showed up in the umbrella stand the next day.''

''Carefully washed, I should imagine.''

''Aye, no doubt. But usually such things are not as clean as the person thinks. But we don't have the walking stick, so we don't know. Lottie hid the walking stick as soon as she realized it might be the murder weapon. Why? Why not bring it to my attention. Who was she protecting?''

''She'd asked Harry for a loan, remember. The winery is on its last legs. So she might have planned on some blackmail. The question is did she know *who* to blackmail.''

''Evidently she did,'' Erskine said dryly. ''The police surgeon told me there were fragments of wood in her head wound, also. I'm willing to wager they'll turn out to be stinkwood.''

Andrew pursed up his mouth in a soundless whistle. ''If you could find that cane . . .''

''I've an idea the walking stick may have disappeared forever this time.'' He leaned back, steepling his fingers. ''When Lottie was found, she was wearing a mackintosh over her nightie and there was mud on her shoes. But it was a warm sunny day today. It was cold early this morn, however. And probably dew on the ground. So it seems possible she might have gone out to the maze straight from her bed.''

''To recover the walking stick.''

''And why would she do that, unless she intended giving it to someone?''

''The someone who killed Harry.''

''Possibly.''

Andrew sighed. ''You're still working on the assumption that one of the potential heirs killed Harry?''

''Till something better comes along.'' The inspector stood up and held out his hand to Andrew. ''I need hardly warn you again to keep mum about all this," he said as they shook hands.

Andrew nodded and turned away, only to see Kate coming into the room. She was frowning, carrying something wrapped in a silk scarf, which she set on the desk in front of the inspector and Andrew. "I checked on Jocelyn," she told Andrew. "She's still asleep. I made sure her door was locked when I left." She glanced at the inspector. "How is Lottie?"

"She died on the way to the hospital," Andrew said softly.

Kate shuddered convulsively and sat down on the chair Andrew had vacated. "Dear God," she murmured. "It seems so much worse, when you know—" She broke off and reached a hand toward him.

He took hold of it and clasped it tightly. Her face was the color of putty, her lovely brown eyes moist.

"How could the murderer leave Lottie bleeding to death while he or she went calmly sight-seeing in Windsor?"

"Not calmly, I shouldn't think," Andrew said.

Kate swallowed again. She was holding on to his hand as if it were a lifeline. Not that he minded that at all. Her hand felt very natural in his, as if it belonged there.

"It's so awful," she murmured. "I really had my doubts about Lottie. I was about ready to decide she and Emory had killed Harry, but now..." She looked sharply at the inspector. "Do you think we're in danger, any of us?"

"Not unless you have it in mind to blackmail anyone."

"You think that's what Lottie was doing?"

"Yon's a smart lassie," Erskine said to Andrew. "Now, what was it you wanted to show me?" he asked Kate.

Making an obvious effort to pull herself together, Kate reached forward and unfolded the scarf, revealing two cylindrical plastic containers and what at first glance looked like long curling strips of brown-and-black plastic.

"Two rolls of thirty-five millimeter film were removed from my camera bag," she said. "I found this mess behind my nightstand. The plastic containers were under my bed."

Erskine's shrewd gaze was on her face. "You've an idea who's responsible?"

Kate nodded. "Elaine Coby. I saw her coming out of my room a little while ago." She glanced at Andrew. "It was right after we talked on the stairs."

"But you didna actually see the girl take the film out?" Erskine asked.

Kate shook her head. "Seems a bit coincidental that she'd be sneaking around my room for any other reason."

"Aye." The inspector sighed. "Unfortunately she can deny any knowledge quite easily."

"I didn't handle either the film or the containers," Kate pointed out. "I picked the film up in the scarf thinking you might be able to turn up some fingerprints."

The inspector smiled wryly. "That's not always as easy as the television would make you think, lassie. But we'll check, you may be sure. In the meantime, it might be as well to have a wee word with Miss Coby. What was on these rolls of film?"

Kate frowned. "One was mostly pictures of Jocelyn, some by herself, some with Andrew. The other roll was of the family. I took everybody's picture after we came back from the inquest on Monday afternoon."

"Tell me about those pictures," the inspector suggested.

She thought for a minute. "There were a few group shots. A couple of Uncle Frederick and Aunt Hilary together. One or two of Bennett holding the cat. Robbie and

Elaine on the terrace steps. Lottie and Emory in the court-yard.''

The inspector blinked. "Exactly how did you pose Lot-tie and Emory?"

Curiosity showed in the slight narrowing of her eyes, but she answered right away. "Emory on the bench, Lottie standing beside him."

"Can you remember anything else?"

"Well, Lottie was leaning on her—" Her eyes widened and she sat forward abruptly. "The cane," she said.

"What?" Erskine asked in a deceptively calm voice.

"When you first showed interest in the umbrella stand, I knew there was something I should remember, but I didn't know what. When I arrived here the umbrella stand had been knocked over. Lottie said she'd tipped it over in her hurry to go out when they all went to look for the body." She paused. "You know, before anybody knew there really was a body. Lottie apologized to Hilary for not pick-ing the stand up. She had an arthritic hip and couldn't bend. But she didn't put the cane back that she'd bor-rowed. And she didn't use it again until Monday after-noon. She had it when I took her photo. It had a knob on the end of it rather than a handle." Her eyes widened again.

With excitement, Andrew thought. He was getting pretty good at this body-language business.

"That's it, isn't it?" she exclaimed. "The cane's the murder weapon. Lottie had it. Does that mean…" Her face fell. "She'd hardly hit *herself* on the head, would she? Emory then… he said she should tell you something. Was it something to do with the cane?"

The inspector nodded, his gaze fixed on her face. An-drew didn't blame him for that; the changing expressions as her thoughts raced were wonderful to see.

"I saw Emory with the sergeant a while back," she was saying now. She glanced at Andrew. "Did you—I mean, is it okay to..."

"The man who called himself Emory Wainwright is Roger Stoane, Lottie's one-time husband," the inspector said.

Kate shot a glance at Andrew. "Did you know that?"

He shook his head. "The inspector checked his passport."

"So you think the killer is Emory—Roger?"

Erskine spread his hands, palms up. "There's no motive for him to kill Harry or Lottie. Better for him if Lottie were alive to claim any possible inheritance."

"So you're no further forward? Except you have the murder weapon."

"We don't have it," the inspector said heavily. "We've no idea where the damn thing is. You don't happen to know where Lottie went after you took her photograph?"

Kate shook her head. "I went to watch Sikander practicing yoga. I didn't see Lottie again that day until teatime."

"And the next day was Harry's funeral," Andrew said, "and the day after that Lottie was drunk in the maze. Yesterday."

Andrew glanced at Kate and saw that she was pale again. "What is it?" he demanded.

"The murderer," she said faintly. "The murderer would have had a good reason to expose my film. Because of Lottie on there with the cane. Elaine..."

"Let's no be jumping to conclusions," Erskine warned. He glanced up as the sergeant came into the room. "Anything?"

The man shook his head. "Not so far. I've some men checking around the grounds."

The inspector sighed. Then he looked at the fireplace. "Are there ashes in there?" he asked.

The sergeant walked over to take a look. "Clean as a whistle."

"Check the other fireplaces in the rest of the house."

"There was a fire in the dining room this morning," Andrew volunteered.

"Get Mrs. Hogarth in here," the inspector called after the sergeant.

"I thought you were going to talk to Elaine," Kate said.

"All in good time, lassie," the inspector said.

The housekeeper arrived a minute later. Her hands were covered in flour, and she was wiping them on her apron. There were twin spots of color on her round cheeks. "That officer wouldn't give me time to wash me 'ands," she complained.

"Who asked you to light the fire in the dining room this morning?" the inspector said calmly.

"Nobody *asked* me. One of my jobs. It was chilly early. Warm later, like midsummer, but cold still at seven, which was when I lit it, just before breakfast."

The inspector sighed. "I don't suppose you saw anybody burning anything in it, did you?"

"I didn't stand guard over it."

"Did you clean out the ashes yet?"

"I can't do everything, can I?"

"Thank you, Mrs. Hogarth," Erskine said. "Dyspeptic old hen," he mutttered darkly after she'd left.

"She suffers from indigestion," Kate murmured soothingly.

He raised his grizzled eyebrows. "That's a poor reputation for a cook to have."

At that moment, the sergeant returned and was dispatched to collect the dining-room fireplace ashes for analysis. He went off with a long-suffering expression on his weathered, countryman's face.

"Ask Miss Elaine Coby to come down here first, will you?" Erskine called after him.

"YOU WANTED to see me, Inspector?" Elaine Coby asked from the doorway a few minutes later.

Kate's heart thudded against her ribs.

The inspector gestured at a chair.

"I heard Lottie died, is that true?" Elaine asked in a faint voice as she came forward.

"It is, I'm afraid," the inspector said. Then he looked at her very sternly. "Miss Kate has a question for you," he said, then paused, watching her face closely.

Kate watched her, too, waiting for her reaction to the spirals of film on the desk. But Elaine just glanced at them, frowned briefly, then sat down and looked inquiringly at Kate.

"I saw you coming out of my room," Kate said.

Once again an all-encompassing blush raced from below Elaine's blouse collar, up over her bony throat and thin face to her wildly teased hair. A second later the color receded completely, leaving her skin pasty, her eyes dull.

The inspector had watched this phenomenon with narrowed eyes. Now he leaned forward on the desk and said, "Don't ever lie, lassie. It'll do you no good with a blush like that."

Elaine bent her head, her fingers agitatedly pleating the fabric of her flowered skirt. After a long moment, she mumbled, "I'm sorry. Really, I am."

"Why did you destroy my film?" Kate demanded.

Elaine's head came up. She looked totally mystified. "What film?" she asked.

"That film," Kate said, nodding at the desk. "It was taken from my camera bag, exposed and stuck behind my nightstand."

"Not by me," Elaine said firmly. No telltale blush gave the lie to her words.

"You're asking us to believe you just wandered into my room by mistake and waltzed out again without touching anything? Today of all days."

Elaine hesitated, her lower lip trembling. "I was upset. I didn't know what to do with myself. I just went in to look at your clothes."

Kate had to strain to hear her voice. She was almost whispering.

"I do that sometimes," she admitted. "You've got such pretty clothes. You're always so, so..." She gestured vaguely as words failed her.

Kate fixed her gaze on Elaine's face. "There were family pictures on one of those rolls. The ones I took after the inquest. You're quite sure you didn't get into my camera bag?"

"I didn't go near it," Elaine said defiantly, her voice returning to her. Then her expression altered, becoming a rueful grimace. "If I'd known *that* roll of film was around, I might have done away with it, but I didn't."

"Why would you even want to?" Kate demanded.

The girl's eyes looked hunted, going from the inspector to Kate to Andrew and back again. "I just hate anyone taking pictures of me, that's all," she blurted out. She glared at Kate. "You didn't even ask me. You just started taking pictures of me and Robbie."

"But I don't understand..." Kate began.

"No, you wouldn't, would you?" Elaine said bitterly. "You with your perfect body and your perfect clothes and your perfect face. Your straight nose that I would die for."

She looked pleadingly at the inspector. "I'm going to get a nose job, just as soon as I have the money. It costs such an awful lot of money and Daddy had to pay Mother's bills, so there hasn't been enough. He doesn't want me to do it, anyway. He says what's inside is more important." She swung around to Kate again. "I know what you're thinking. Even if I had the money I couldn't just order the nose I want. But I could get mine improved, couldn't I?"

"If a nose job would make you feel good about yourself then you ought to have a nose job," Kate said softly, all traces of anger swallowed up in a burst of sympathy.

Elaine didn't seem to hear. "I *hate* having my picture taken," she declared. "Is that such a crime?"

Kate touched her arm. "It's okay, Elaine. I understand."

"I'm sorry I went in your room, Kate," she said more reasonably. "But I absolutely didn't move anything."

"You believe her?" Erskine asked after Elaine had left the room.

Kate nodded, sighing. "As you said, Inspector, it's impossible for anyone who blushes like that to tell a lie." She shook her head. "Which means we still don't know who exposed my film. Though we can certainly guess why." She shuddered. "The thought that the murderer was in my room . . ." She took a deep breath, striving for control.

"Are you finished with us?" Andrew asked.

"Aye." Erskine looked from Andrew to Kate. "If you've told me everything you have to tell."

"I have," Andrew said promptly.

"Me, too," Kate said, trying not to feel guilty. She and Andrew were still holding a few things back. "Do you have any idea who killed Harry and Lottie?" she asked the inspector as she stood up.

"Och, yes," he said.

Kate started with surprise.

"I've muckle ideas. But no proof, lassie. Not one iota of proof."

Chapter Nine

There were sounds coming from the attics above her bedroom. Putting down her book, Jocelyn sat up straighter in her bed and listened, staring up at the ceiling. It sounded as if somebody was dragging something across the floor up there.

She was being silly. Her imagination was running away with her. Not surprising, considering what had happened to Lottie the previous week.

There it was again—a scuffling sound. Sighing, she swung her legs off the bed. If she didn't investigate, she'd lie awake listening all night. She'd better ask her father to go with her. He wouldn't be in bed yet. It was only ten o'clock. But then, approaching his door, she heard his bathwater running. Well, she'd tried. Padding on along the hall, she turned the corner and went up the stairs to the attics. Now that she was up and moving around she felt a lot braver.

The attic door was open and she almost had heart failure listening to the weird sounds while she fumbled around for the light switch. But then her fingers found the switch and a dim bulb came on, showing the shadowy silhouettes of boxes and weird bundles, pieces of furniture and rolled-up carpets. Dust motes hung in the air, moving gently.

The shuffling sound began again. Jocelyn hesitated, her heart bumping erratically against her ribs. Then she took a couple of steps forward and saw Gray Boy wrestling with a hank of knitting wool that he'd pulled out of a box. Letting her pent-up breath go in one explosive whoosh, she scooped up the cat and dashed out of the attic, pulling the door closed behind her, not caring that she'd left the light on in there.

Taking the cat into her bedroom, she plunked him on the bed and climbed up herself. A few minutes later she was once more deeply engrossed in *The Forsyte Saga*. Gray Boy began giving himself a bath.

It wasn't a sound that grabbed her attention this time. It was a sensation. Something about the attic. She could *feel* it above her head, like a cavern, with shadows reaching out from the corners. Gritting her teeth, she tried again to read.

Gray Boy had stuck his rear leg up behind his head, but instead of washing it, he paused, his ears cocked, his eyes fixed on the ceiling. At the same time a picture was forming between Jocelyn's eyes and her book. A picture of the attic and someone lying in a pool of blood.

No! Not again. Not ever again.

Terrified, Jocelyn jumped out of bed, sending Gray Boy flying. She had to find something to do. If she kept busy she could sometimes avoid an onslaught. Reading was too hypnotic. Talking might work… "Come here, Gray Boy," she called softly.

The cat had shot under the bed, obviously put out by Jocelyn's sudden movement. Now he emerged slowly, stretching his front paws, then his hind paws, rolling over so that she could rub his tummy.

Picking him up, hugging him while she walked to and fro in her bedroom, trying to stay warm, trying to stop shivering, Jocelyn said, "Did I ever tell you about my grandpa?

Mummy's father. He made biscuits, which Kate would call 'cookies.' Isn't that a funny word? *Cookies*. Where do you suppose Americans got that from? Little things you cook?''

The cat butted her chin with his head. The picture hadn't faded yet; it was still hovering in the air around her, bringing with it the awful smell of danger and death. A metallic smell. She could see the silhouettes of boxes and old furniture. The floor was so dusty she could taste the grit in her teeth. And there, right there on the dusty floor... Whose body was it? *No! Don't think about it. Don't let it happen.*

"Grandpa was awfully rich," she confided to the cat. "It's nice to be very rich, I suppose, but I think perhaps having a lot of money isolates one.'' Gray Boy patted her cheek with one paw, as if he knew she needed distraction.

"The money all comes to me when I'm twenty-one," she went on. "Daddy says by then I ought to be sensible enough to handle it. I expect he's right. I certainly don't intend to be isolated, though.'' The cat was purring noisily and she went on talking to him, trying desperately to hold back the picture that kept threatening to come through.

KATE LAY on top of her bed, wrapped in a blue silk kimono, mentally reviewing all the people at Farrington Hall, trying to decide which of them was most likely to be the killer. When she looked at the happenings of the past couple of weeks clinically, as if they were a puzzle to be solved, she could close her mind to the horror of it all for a while.

She didn't want to believe one of her relatives was a killer—that was the trouble. And her thoughts kept returning to Andrew. His fight with Harry had still not been explained to her satisfaction. And he'd seemed to avoid her since their picnic. Not that there had been much opportunity to get together, what with the inquest and Lottie's funeral and Inspector Erskine and his cohorts hovering around.

It was impossible for her to think about Andrew objectively. Whatever feelings she had for him were intensely subjective. If Andrew Bradford turned out to be a killer, she would shut herself up in a cave somewhere and live out her life in chastity—because it would be obvious she had no judgment at all where men were concerned.

There was a glimmer of an idea that was trying to come through. Something to do with different ways of looking at things. As she was trying to track down the nebulous thought, somebody knocked at her bedroom door and she shot off the bed like a rocket. God, her nerves were in pieces.

"Who is it?" she whispered through the closed door.

"It's me—Joss," a recognizable voice whispered back.

Letting out the breath she'd been holding, Kate opened her door to find Jocelyn standing there barefooted, in a pink nightgown, clutching the cat, her light blue eyes luminous.

"Come on in," Kate said, then noticed the girl was shivering. Taking the cat from her, she pulled back the covers on her bed and gestured Jocelyn in. Tucking her in warmly, she sat down beside her, rubbing Gray Boy's right ear in the way that made him purr like distant thunder.

"I heard noises in the attics above my room," Jocelyn explained. "Finally, I took a look and found Gray Boy playing with some knitting wool. I brought him into bed with me, and he kept staring at the ceiling with his ears pricked up and his eyes round as saucers, as if he could hear something, too."

"That was very brave of you to go up there alone, but a bit foolhardy," Kate scolded.

Jocclyn nodded. "I went to get Daddy, but he was in the bath, so I came down here."

She was very pale, Kate noted. "Did you have another fuzzy thing, Joss?" she asked.

The girl bit her lower lip, hesitated and finally blurted out, "A little bit of one, but it didn't come to anything. It was more an idea that someone—or some*thing* was in the attics. I managed to fight it off."

She looked at Kate in a pleading way that tugged at Kate's heart. "I don't *want* to see any more fuzzy things," she said. "They frighten me, Kate. They really do."

Kate stroked a few strands of hair away from the girl's forehead. "Tomorrow morning, we'll go root around the attics and make sure nothing's there. That'll make you feel better."

"I do love you, Kate," Jocelyn said.

Tears pricked behind Kate's eyelids. Leaning over, she kissed the girl gently on the cheek.

Jocelyn flung her arms around her neck and hugged her. Then, as Kate drew away, she asked, "May I please stay here the rest of the night?"

"Sure you can," Kate said warmly.

Jocelyn burrowed into Kate's downy pillows, her eyes drifting shut. She seemed about to drop off, but then she roused herself. "Daddy said he'd come in later to make sure I was all right. Could you tell him where I am? He'll have a fit if he finds my room empty."

"Sure," Kate said.

Jocelyn's eyes opened again. "You do like Daddy now, don't you?" She frowned. "I read somewhere that some specialists working with an encephalograph have decided that if your brain waves match those of a prospective partner the attraction is immediate. Do you suppose there's anything in it?"

Kate laughed. Jocelyn was evidently still working on her campaign to get Andrew and Kate together. "It's as good an explanation as any, I guess." She wasn't about to tell Jocelyn that her brain waves worked overtime where Andrew was concerned.

"It wasn't Daddy's fault he didn't travel with Mummy," Jocelyn said. "Mummy usually had a friend with her, you see."

"A friend?"

The girl sighed deeply. "A man. She was so beautiful, Kate. Men liked her a lot. And she just couldn't seem to settle for one man. There was always a new one."

Kate mentally apologized to Andrew for blaming him for neglecting his wife. He could hardly have gone traveling with her if she was always accompanied by another man. All the same, he shouldn't have left Jocelyn in a situation like that.

"You mustn't think Mummy neglected me," Jocelyn continued. "She always loved me, which is why I managed to come through it all without getting too messed up."

But not without getting too grown-up too soon, Kate thought.

Jocelyn yawned hugely and closed her eyes again. "You will tell Daddy where I am, won't you?"

"I'll tell him," Kate promised. And maybe give him a piece of her mind at the same time, she thought.

Jocelyn was already asleep.

ANDREW CAME TO HIS DOOR clad only in light blue pajama bottoms. His blond hair was damp. Jocelyn had been right about him taking a bath. It had to have been a bath—Farrington Hall didn't run to showers.

"Come in," he said at once, adding, "I'm on the telephone. My father." Striding across the room, he picked up the telephone receiver and spoke into it. "All right, Dad, did you remember anything?"

Kate felt awkward about interrupting him, but there wasn't much she could do about it. Closing the door, she tried to look as if she wasn't listening, letting her gaze wander around the room, noting that it was as luxuriously furnished as her own.

"Nineteen thirty-three," Andrew said.

Kate shot a glance at him. He held her gaze, his own eyes serious. "All we know is that Lottie said there was some kind of secret connected with the Wainwrights," he said after another minute. "I was hoping you could shed some light."

He listened again, frowning. His naked muscular torso was something to see, Kate thought, feeling abruptly warm.

"Of course I'll avoid offending Frederick," he said. After he hung up the receiver, he raised both palms in a helpless gesture. "My father's convinced one of Frederick's relations finished Harry off simply to get him out of the running. Lottie, he thinks, must have seen or heard something that made her a threat. He doesn't remember any Wainwright secret, I'm afraid." He sighed. "The thing is, in 1933 my father was only eleven years old. My grandfather represented the Wainwrights then and *he* died several years ago."

He made a vain attempt to smooth his tousled hair with his fingers, looking at her questioningly, obviously wondering belatedly what she was doing there.

Kate explained about Jocelyn's change of sleeping accommodations. "It's no problem," she assured him. "I've got an enormous bed." God, she thought, that almost sounded like an invitation.

A glint of devilment had appeared in his gray eyes. "I'll remember that," he said. "Thank you for looking after her."

Silence fell between them. The memory of the kisses they'd shared loomed large in Kate's mind. And judging by the softened expression on his face, he was remembering, too.

"Kate," he said softly, walking toward her.

His fingers reached out to touch her face, his thumb lightly tracing her cheekbone, moving down to the corner of her mouth. His gray eyes shone with tenderness.

Suddenly, inexplicably, Kate's own eyes filled with tears. "Oh, Andrew, it's all so awful. First Harry, then Lottie. Something terribly evil and dangerous is on the loose in this house. I feel it all around me, all the time, no matter how I try to shut it out. I've tried to be objective about it, keeping my mind occupied with questions and possible answers, as if it were all some mystery novel and not real life. But it is real—all of it."

He took her in his arms, cradling her head with one hand, pulling it into his shoulder, shushing her gently. "It's all right," he murmured.

"No, it's not," she muttered, her body shuddering.

"For now it is," he answered. "At this moment. Here. You and me together."

Her breasts were pressing against Andrew's smooth bare chest, with only the silk of her kimono separating their bodies.

When he kissed her gently, delicately, his mouth was warm and comforting on hers. Kate reached up to touch his still-damp hair. It clung to her fingers, feeling alive, so alive. Abruptly she pulled away.

He looked at her inquiringly.

"I didn't come here for this," she said.

"It's a wonderful idea all the same, don't you think?" He tipped her chin with his free hand so that he could look directly into her eyes. "I've wanted to be with you like this ever since our picnic, but I was afraid."

When she looked at him questioningly, he laughed shortly. "I'm quite terrified of the strong feelings I have for you, Kate." He studied her face, a gentle smile curving his mouth. "I do believe you're frightened, too."

"Petrified," she admitted.

He laughed and pulled her in close. "I've never been a promiscuous sort of chap," he said solemnly. "I've always felt that love should precede lust. I could love you, Kate." He grinned. "Which doesn't mean I don't lust after you also."

She stared at him mutely.

"This is your cue to say you could love me, too."

She tried to pull away, but he held on to her. "We haven't known each other long enough to talk about love," she protested.

"That occurred to me, also," he said with a wry smile. "I'm not usually swept off my feet quite so quickly. That's why I was so terrified." His fingers lightly outlined the rim of her ear. "I think we may be like soldiers who've gone through combat together—they often form a strong bond. We've shared some very intense experiences. Perhaps they've speeded up our metabolism, our chemistry."

"Our brain waves," Kate murmured, but refused to explain. "I'm very sexually attracted to you, Andrew," she admitted. "But I don't have a good track record when it comes to recognizing love."

"You thought you were in love with Paul Milton, did you?"

"I *was* in love with him." She hesitated, then added lamely, "I think."

They both laughed, then Andrew cupped her face with both hands, holding her gaze, his eyes reflecting the light of his bedside lamp. He was looking at her as though she were the most desirable woman he had ever seen and there was no way she could withstand the tidal wave of emotion that was rushing through her. Love, yes, she could love this man.

"It doesn't seem right to feel like this," she murmured. "Lottie's funeral this morning—Harry's death."

"Intense feelings need a way to escape," he said softly. "Is this really such a bad way to let them go?"

She made no protest when he gently removed her kimono and eased her down beside him on the bed, his lips finding hers again, shaping her mouth to his, drawing the essence of her out of her body and into his. A long sweet breathless time later, he began kissing her throat, her breasts. Without any hesitation at all, her body responded to the gentle demands of his lips and hands.

She could feel his heart beating as he held her close, his lower body urging hers to rhythmic unhurried movement. Her fingers lingered over the masculine texture of his skin. He had a wonderful body, smooth and muscular.

"Rowing," he murmured, evidently reading her mind.

She laughed, deep in her throat. "Competitively?"

"Of course." His hands moved over her. "You?"

"Nautilus equipment."

He laughed also, sounding short of breath. When had he removed his pajama bottoms? She hadn't noticed. It didn't matter. She could only marvel at the firmness of him, the wonderfully clean smell of him. Her whole body felt languorous, as though warmed by a tropical sun.

A moment later all thought was shattered as he entered her and the languor was replaced by urgency. Their movements brought to life a fierce longing in her body, sending ripple after ripple of heat along her thighs. Her mouth demanded kisses that were driving and intrusive; her hands urged him closer as pressure built in her body and, inevitably, exploded. A second later, his own release sent a wave of sweetness surging through her, and then she fell gently through warm heavy air into a place of calm peace. For a long time they held each other, murmuring occasionally, kissing softly.

Kate wanted to prolong this lovely time of afterward, wanted not to think about anything but the two of them and the joyous experience they had just shared. But eventually the practical side of her nature reasserted itself and she knew that the brief time of forgetfulness had come to an end.

"We have to talk," she said as they sat side by side on Andrew's bed, wrapped in their respective robes. "I didn't come here just to tell you that Jocelyn was in my room. I thought you should know she's had some kind of experience again. A feeling that something was wrong in the attics."

Andrew raked a hand through his hair. "Oh, God, not another one."

"I've promised her I'll explore the attics with her in the morning. Just to be sure..."

"I'll go with you," he said at once. "I don't want either of you poking into things on your own. It's not safe."

It would be safer with a big strong man to take care of them, supposedly. Well, Kate admitted to herself with a nervous laugh, it probably would. "Joss is scared, Andrew," she said. "So am I."

"Me, too," he admitted. "There's an atmosphere in this house that—" He broke off. "Perhaps some of Jocelyn's fuzzy things are rubbing off on me."

"Maybe she inherited her ability from you," Kate said, watching his face.

Sure enough, he flinched.

"I think it's time you told me about your relationship with Jocelyn," she said gently. "Sometimes you look at her so...questioningly."

He nodded. Then, lowering his head, he took her hand between both of his and began outlining her fingers with one of his own. "Has Fishface told you much about her mother?"

"A little. She wanted to assure me you hadn't neglected her deliberately. She told me that her mother had... friends." She touched his face lightly with her free hand. "I have to tell you, Andrew, I don't think you should have left Joss in a situation like that. As far as I can tell she's been shuttling around the world with her mother and whoever Mother happened to be dallying with at the moment. You might have done something about that."

He sighed. "I wanted to, Kate, believe me." He put his arms around her. "I don't normally talk about my wife, because it sounds as though I'm...whining, complaining. It's very important to me that you think well of me, however."

She looked at him. "Tell me about her."

He sighed. "I married Olivia when I was twenty-two, still in university. She was enchanting, sweet, childlike, innocent, yet passionate." He sighed. "Unfortunately I was too enamored to realize that her passionate nature would not long be content with one man. Her father had been very strict with her, had barely let her out of his sight. As my wife, she felt she would be free of her father and could do as she wished. When she discovered she was pregnant, I was afraid she'd hate the very idea—but to my surprise and relief she seemed delighted. That's why she'd wanted to be married, she told me. She wanted to be a respectable lady with a baby. A few weeks later she left me and went to live with a woman friend in Majorca. She said she wanted to be by herself while the baby grew inside her. She was adamant. Short of tossing her over my shoulder and carrying her home, there wasn't much I could do."

"But that's—" She broke off. "I'm sorry, go on."

He gave her a strained smile. "When Jocelyn was born, I went to Majorca determined to bring her and Olivia home with me." He looked down at his hands, which were clenched on his knees, the knuckles white with pressure. "Olivia refused to leave. When I threatened to take my daughter, she said I couldn't have her because she wasn't my daughter."

Kate frowned. "I don't . . ."

"I didn't believe her at first, but then she told me she'd taken a lover within a month of our marriage. She had tired of him quickly, she said, and he wasn't at all interested in claiming the baby, but if I went to court to try to get custody of Jocelyn, she would tell everyone who the real father was. If I left Jocelyn with her, she would allow me to see her when I wanted to. And she would let the child believe I was her father. I could take it or leave it."

The anguish she had seen on his face before had returned.

"I flew back to England. But I couldn't get Jocelyn's little fish face out of my mind. I loved her the moment I saw her, you see. So I accepted Olivia's terms. I knew the child was safe with her—there was no doubt ever that Olivia loved her. Whenever I could I visited her."

His face was bleak. Kate wanted to touch him, but didn't want to stop him talking. She was almost sure he had never told this story to anyone before.

After a minute or two, he continued. "When Olivia knew she was dying, she sent for me." He swallowed visibly.

Kate did touch him then, taking his hand and gripping it tightly. And after a moment, he went on again. "On her deathbed, Olivia told me Jocelyn was mine, after all. She hadn't wanted me ever to know because she was afraid I'd take Jocelyn away from her."

Remembering again the anguish that had shown on his face from time to time, Kate said, "You didn't believe her?"

He sighed explosively. "Olivia always told whatever story was most useful to her. Dying, she wanted Jocelyn to be cared for. So in order to make sure I'd care for her, she swore she was my daughter." He laughed shortly, a bitter sound. "She didn't need to—I'd have taken care of her, anyway. It's just that—I wish I knew for sure. It would make me so happy to know for sure that she's mine."

"Surely there are blood tests...."

"I looked into that. A blood test would show if she wasn't my daughter, but wouldn't prove she was. There is one small possibility... but I'm not sure I want to explore it. If she's *not* mine, I don't want to know it. I'd rather just hope...."

He looked at Kate directly and she could have cried out at the hopelessness on his face. "Olivia never told you the name of the man she originally said was Jocelyn's father?"

"Oh, yes. I knew all along. It was Harry Wainwright."

Numb with shock, Kate could only stare at him.

Andrew smiled tiredly. "Olivia met Harry in a London nightclub. I checked and he was in London at that time, all right. Staying in the same hotel as Olivia. And every time I came down here and Harry showed up, he'd make some comment about Jocelyn, hinting around that she was his daughter, making me furious. This trip was the first time I'd brought Jocelyn with me. I had some stupid idea about seeing them together, making up my mind if there was any resemblance.''

"And was there?"

"Not really. But as you pointed out, she doesn't look like me, either."

She could see that he had tortured himself over Jocelyn's parentage. And she could see how angry it must have made him when Harry had made comments about Jocelyn and asked the girl to give him a kiss.

So now she knew why Andrew had fought with Harry. And why he'd been so frantic about Jocelyn overhearing some of that quarrel. Just how angry had Harry made Andrew? she wondered. "You lied to me, Andrew," she said evenly. "You told me your argument with Harry was just a silly little quarrel."

He drew in a long breath, then let it out. "He needled me about Jocelyn being his daughter. I told him if I heard any more of his damned nonsense I'd punch him on the nose."

He sighed. "He said that if he wasn't a gentleman he'd tell me exactly what the situation was, and I said if he was a gentleman there would never have been a situation. And I told him to stay away from my daughter. That's the part that Jocelyn overheard. Luckily the only part."

He was holding both her hands now, his gray eyes solemn.

"I didn't kill Harry Wainwright, Kate," he said. "It's very important to me that you believe me."

She met his gaze with a direct one of her own. "I believe you," she said softly, trying not to listen to the part of her mind that was reminding her she'd also believed Paul Milton was visiting his invalid mother in Arizona.

He let out his breath on a long sigh, then took her into his arms and held her without speaking for a long time. And between them a feeling arose that was beyond sexual attraction, beyond emotion—a feeling that was beyond any Kate could remember experiencing. Gazing at the glowing lamp next to Andrew's bed, she narrowed her eyes against the glare, and the light through the amber globe seemed to splinter into a hundred fragments. Gold, she thought. The color of love was gold and Andrew was covered in it. She loved the man—no doubt about it.

Chapter Ten

Kate knelt in front of a large and ancient wooden cabinet, wondering if it would be unethical to open it. Hilary had authorized them to look through the attics after Jocelyn had explained she'd found the cat hunting in there, which might indicate the presence of mice. But that permission surely didn't include carte blanche to go through personal belongings. So far they hadn't seen anything that even remotely fitted into Jocelyn's vision.

"I didn't expect quite as much clutter," Andrew said ruefully, smiling at her, his slate gray eyes full of memories of their night together.

God, she felt wonderful this morning, Kate thought as she smiled back at him. She felt all pumped up, as if she'd been working out with weights. Her skin and eyes and hair must be glowing, revealing to anyone who cared to look at her that she had spent the night making love.

Today Andrew was wearing a black polo shirt that hugged all his lovely muscles, and blue jeans that clung lovingly to his trim hips. The pallor that had hovered around his eyes and mouth was no longer in evidence. He looked completely well—vigorous and virile. As he held her gaze, she glimpsed how lonely her life would be when she returned to Seattle, having known and loved Andrew

Bradford. She suppressed the thought. Time enough to think about that when it happened.

"Look at this super hat," Jocelyn said, and they both jumped as if they'd been caught doing something improper.

Jocelyn had been rooting around in the adjoining room and now stood framed in the arched entrance, wearing a large white picture hat that had artificial rosebuds around the crown. The hat looked ludicrous with Jocelyn's cowboy shirt, but it cast shadows under her cheekbones and made her eyes luminous.

Looking at her solemn heart-shaped face, Kate caught her breath. The promise of beauty was unmistakable. Andrew was staring at her, too. Taking her gently by the arm, he led her to an ornate mirror that hung on the wall above a pair of Windsor chairs.

Jocelyn stared at her reflection for a full minute without speaking, then she said huskily, "I'm not all that bad, am I?"

"Another year or two and you're going to drive men to distraction," Andrew said.

"Like Mummy," Jocelyn said complacently.

Andrew winced. So did Kate. Andrew's description of Olivia was still fresh in her mind. So were his doubts about Jocelyn's parentage. When Kate had crept back to her bedroom at five this morning, Jocelyn had been sleeping soundly. Kate hadn't been able to resist studying her face in the cool light of dawn, looking for traces of her father's features . . . or Harry's. Jocelyn had awakened and caught her staring and Kate had made some lame remark about checking to see if Jocelyn was asleep. There could be no more of that.

"Are you getting anything?" Andrew asked the girl.

"Vibes, you mean?" Jocelyn asked, looking serious again. "I'm not a radio, Daddy."

"What was it like then, last night, the feeling you had?"

"Just knowing that something awful was connected with this attic," Jocelyn said after a moment's thought. "Or will be." She shuddered. "I don't have it now. And I don't want it to come back." Obviously closing her mind to the memory, she began preening again in front of the mirror.

Kate smiled affectionately at her, glad of the resilience of childhood that had helped the girl recover from her fears of the previous night. And then she realized that Andrew had turned away and was rooting through some stuff on an old bureau nearby. "You've found something?" she asked.

He nodded without turning around, lifting down a pile of manila folders from the top of the bureau. They were labeled "medical records," Kate noted idly. Beneath them was a large book with edges that glinted gold in the attic light. "Looks like a photograph album," Andrew said, sitting down in one of the Windsor chairs to examine his find.

Jocelyn had gone back to the next room and Kate knelt down beside Andrew's chair, squinting at the book. "I hate to sound like a complaining American," she said, "but one thing I've noticed about this house is a total lack of adequate lighting. Do English people *like* shadows?"

Andrew smiled absently. He was studying the flyleaf where "Wainwright" was written in faded ink. The first few pages were disappointing—full of old photographs of grim-faced people in static poses. The only person Kate recognized was her great-grandfather Robert Wainwright, in a shot taken around the time the dining-room portrait had been painted.

Then Andrew turned to a baby picture that was identified. William Wainwright—1907. Kate's grandfather, looking like a child's doll in a lace-trimmed christening gown twice as long as himself, propped against cushions, eyes wide and innocent.

The next two babies wore the same gown for their introduction to the camera. George 1908, Charles 1910. Andrew turned another page. And revealed two more babies sitting side by side, wearing knitted rompers and fuzzy white hats. They were so completely identical it was obvious they were twins. The same hand had written underneath—Alexander and Gillian, born January 21, 1913.

Gillian?

Kate sat very still, staring over Andrew's arm at the photograph.

"I've never heard of a Gillian Wainwright," Andrew muttered.

Certainly nobody had ever mentioned Gillian to Kate. And as Andrew leafed through the album, turning up Frederick's baby picture, then going on, she saw that Gillian Wainwright had not died as a baby. She was included in group photographs with her brothers and parents— Robert and Elizabeth. In most of these Robert was beside or behind her, smiling at her instead of the camera, his hand touching her shoulder. There was only one photograph of her alone—wearing a lovely white gown, her blond hair parted in the middle and waving over her ears. The picture was labeled—"Gillian on her twentieth birthday, January 31, 1933." It was the last photo in the book, though there were many pages left to go.

Nineteen thirty-three. The year four of her brothers had been sent away by their father.

"Judging by the body language, Robert idolized her," Kate murmured. She waited for Andrew to make some scathing comment, but he was evidently too stunned to think of one.

"Could this be the Wainwright secret Lottie had referred to?" Kate asked softly.

Andrew sighed audibly. "Damned if I know what to think. I suppose I'll have to ring up my father again, ask him if he knows anything about Gillian. Why wouldn't Frederick ever..."

He put a hand to his blond head, worrying his hair unmercifully. This time Kate gave in to the impulse that had affected her so often before—she reached out and combed his hair into place with her fingers. He had wonderful hair, crisp and clean. She loved the feel of it against her fingers.

Andrew's eyes darkened. "You're playing with fire, young woman," he murmured.

Immediately she subsided, clasping her hands in her lap, smiling demurely at him. But then as her gaze fell on the book in his lap, she straightened up again. "There must be a way to find out what happened to Gillian." She considered for a minute, then said, "I planned on talking to everyone about the Wainwright secret, remember? What with Lottie's death and the investigation and funeral and all I didn't get around to it. I could ask them about Gillian at the same time, using the excuse that I have to take all their photographs again because the last bunch got lost. I want to redo the pictures, anyway."

Andrew's jaw had acquired a belligerent angle. "I don't want you taking any risks, Kate."

About to bristle with irritation, Kate stopped herself. Having someone care about your safety wasn't all that bad, she decided. "You could come with me," she suggested.

He stood up, placing the album where he'd found it. Then he put out a hand to help Kate to her feet. With a quick glance at the next room, from which the rustling sounds of Jocelyn's explorations could be heard, he took her in his arms and kissed her gently. "Promise you'll be discreet?" he asked.

She wasn't at all sure discretion was the way to go. Somebody needed to fling back the curtains of the past and stir up all the dust that had settled on this family.

"Kate?" he murmured. "Two people have died. One of them the day after she mentioned the Wainwright secret."

"I'll be discreet," she said, crossing her fingers behind his back.

KATE READIED HER CAMERA as she moved cautiously forward into the drawing room. Robbie was playing the piano with great drama, his head now tilted back, now hunched forward, now rolling sideways, his long blond hair flying. He spent most of his time playing and Kate had become accustomed to hearing piano music at all hours of the day.

Kate couldn't see that his playing lacked passion, as the reviewers had reportedly said. But, then, she was no expert.

She snapped a picture as Robbie reached the finale with much spectacular hand movement. He wasn't startled by the flash, she noted. He must have been aware she was there—she'd suspected all that drama might be for her benefit.

"Shostakovich?" she queried.

He nodded, then tapped the piano bench. "Take a seat."

His eyes had acquired a familiar smoldering expression. Kate sighed. No way was she going to get too close to this young man, even with Andrew standing in the doorway. "I've been sitting around too much," she said, and busied herself refocusing the camera. "Did your grandfather Charles play?" she asked as she looked through the viewfinder again.

"Never," Robbie said, smirking for the camera, flipping his hair away from his shoulders with the back of one hand.

"What about your mother?"

"Mother didn't do anything but drink and gamble. How about going into Allercott for lunch? It's a nice walk."

"We have other things to do," Andrew said with a falsely apologetic note in his voice.

Startled, Robbie turned on the bench and shot him a look that should have dropped him on the spot.

"Nice of you to ask, though," Andrew added, quite unperturbed.

"I'm not eating lunch," Kate said hastily as Robbie's nostrils flared. "I need to lose a few pounds."

It was entirely the wrong thing to say. It gave him an excuse to appraise her from head to toe and back again. "You look fine to me."

Kate gritted her teeth into what she hoped was a smile. "How did you get along with your grandfather?" she asked.

He shrugged. "He was okay. Not too friendly. Why do you want to know all this stuff?"

"Kate's interested in the Wainwright family," Andrew offered, still hanging back in the doorway. "She thinks it's romantic the way the four brothers all went away and only Frederick stayed home. I guess there was only Frederick?"

Andrew's patronizing "us-boys-understand-these-silly-women tone" had made Kate bristle, but when she saw what he was driving at she kept her temper.

Robbie shrugged again. Subtlety wasn't working.

"Imagine having four brothers," Kate said brightly. "Not a single girl in the bunch."

"Sounds good to me," Robbie said. "Where's Jocelyn today?" he asked Andrew. "She's usually hot on Kate's heels."

"She's showing Hilary a hat she found," Andrew said.

"She have any more of those weird trances or whatever you call them?"

Andrew shook his head, clamping his lips together. Robbie was treading on thin ice.

Perhaps he realized it. At any rate, he changed the subject hastily. "What do you think the chances are of Frederick leaving me any money?" he asked. "You're his solicitor. You must know. And now that Harry's dead, it seems to me..."

"That's privileged information," Andrew said tersely.

Kate didn't blame him for letting his anger show. Considering that two people had been killed, possibly with a motive of financial gain, Robbie's question had been tactless, to say the least.

"Do you need money, Robbie?" she asked, suppressing her own distaste in the hope of getting information.

"Doesn't everyone?"

He turned back to the piano and started playing softly, this time a piece Kate didn't recognize.

"I have a friend who's an architect," he said dreamily, still playing. "He'd love to design a house for me, not a house like this monstrosity, a contemporary house, with wonderful acoustics—a house made for music." He sighed. "It would take a heap of money."

There was such a yearning in his voice that Kate found herself sympathizing with him in spite of herself. "What would you do with such a house?" she asked softly.

"Play the piano all day and make love to beautiful women all night," he said promptly, with a sidelong glance at her that was almost a leer.

Whenever she was around Robbie Coby, she found herself wanting to slap him. Exchanging a glance with Andrew, she stalked to the doorway. Andrew followed her out.

"Don't ever leave me alone with that young man," Kate said as soon as they were out of earshot.

"Not on your life," Andrew said grimly.

SIKANDER WAS STANDING on his head on the front terrace. Jocelyn had brought out a cushion and was trying to emulate him, with much flailing of her legs. Kate took several shots of Sikander, which evidently disturbed his concentration. Lowering himself gracefully, he shot her a dark glance, then assumed the lotus position, his open hands resting palm upward on his knees, thumbs and index fingers lightly touching.

"Contentment in all things must be cultivated," he said to Jocelyn, who was now trying to get her feet tucked in like his.

He didn't look all that contented himself, Kate thought. Since Lottie's death he had seemed jumpy, easily irritated. The grim line of his mouth didn't seem to promise much success in the relaxation he was trying to achieve.

"Did your grandfather Alexander practice yoga?" Kate asked, getting down beside him to try out the position herself.

He glanced at her without moving his head. "My grandfather did not adopt the ways of India," he said. "He was forever an Englishman, and so, out of place."

"Did he ever talk to you about what it was like growing up in a large family? As an only child I can't imagine having that many siblings around." She paused. "There were five of them, weren't there? William, Charles, Alexander, George, Frederick. Yes, that's right. Five."

Andrew's eyebrows had climbed almost to his hairline. Kate made a face at him.

Sikander had closed his eyes. He was certainly good-looking, Kate thought. Not really attractive, though. Why was that? Something cold about him. Cold enough to kill?

What was he so nervous about? she wondered. His breathing was rapid and he kept swallowing convulsively, his bow tie riding up and down over his rather prominent Adam's apple. "Grandfather did not share any such experiences with me," he said after a short silence. "He was quite distant usually."

Jocelyn was looking at her curiously. Her clever mind had apparently deduced that Kate was on the track of something.

"There is a story about a holy man of India," Sikander continued. "He thought he would be more holy if he consumed a page of the Christian Bible every day. All went well until he ate a page that was illustrated. Then he died. It transpired that the materials used in the color printing were toxic."

Kate and Andrew exchanged a startled glance. What was the point of the story? Kate wondered, suddenly feeling chilled.

One more try, she decided. "It's odd that there were no twins in our grandfathers' generation, isn't it?"

"Such happenings frequently skip a generation, I believe," Sikander said.

Jocelyn was definitely interested now. Her eyes were narrowed almost to slits and she was looking directly at Kate. Kate shook her head at her. Obviously she wasn't going to get anywhere with Sikander. Surely if he had known anything about Gillian he would have mentioned it by now.

"I must concentrate now," Sikander said fretfully. "It is not possible to relieve stress without peacefulness."

"Are you under stress, Sikander?" Kate asked.

A muscle twitched in Sikander's cheek, but he didn't answer.

"Was that story supposed to be a threat?" Kate muttered to Andrew as they reentered the house, Jocelyn right behind them, obviously still bursting with curiosity. "If I keep turning pages I'm going to die?"

"Perhaps he thinks he has to entertain us and that's his weird way of doing it," Jocelyn said from behind them.

Andrew nodded, but didn't look convinced.

THEY FOUND ELAINE in the kitchen, hands deep in an odd-looking mixture she said was Muesli, the healthiest breakfast in the world. Behind her Mrs. Hogarth rolled her eyes at the ceiling.

Kate had stashed her camera alongside one of the vestibule statues before approaching Elaine. The young woman had stayed away from her since her passionate outburst about photographs and it seemed politic to avoid that subject entirely.

"We're off for a walk in the grounds," Andrew said, as they'd agreed. "Would you like to come along?"

To Kate's surprise Elaine accepted eagerly. She shouldn't have been surprised, of course, she thought as they emerged onto the terrace. Elaine had slipped her hand into Andrew's arm in a very proprietary way and was gazing rapturously up into his face. Andrew, poor dear, looked highly uncomfortable and kept casting pleading glances over his shoulder, but there wasn't any tactful way Kate or Jocelyn could rescue him.

Kate felt slightly uneasy as they wandered through the topiary garden. She didn't care for that particular form of garden ornamentation. In her opinion, a tree should be left alone to grow naturally. But her discomfort seemed to go beyond that. It had something to do with the rows of windows looking down at them from the looming mansion. At this hour of the day the sun was shining on the glass, making it impossible to know if anyone was standing there, watching them.

Probably Gray Boy was sitting on a windowsill, she scolded herself. She was imagining a threatening situation where none existed. Yet still she kept looking over her shoulder.

"My grandfather Charles was very strict," Elaine said, apparently in answer to a question from Andrew.

Kate decided she'd better pay attention.

"I didn't like him," Elaine continued artlessly. "I'm sure he was the reason Mother started drinking. He was a perfectionist, eh, never satisfied with anything she did. Mother spent her life trying to please him."

"Maybe he had a tough time as a child," Kate said soothingly. "Four brothers. Perhaps he didn't get enough attention from his parents."

Elaine shrugged.

"He was the third child, after all," Kate continued. "Maybe he resented his older siblings. Maybe he was taking that resentment out on his daughter."

Andrew looked sideways at her, obviously wondering where she was heading. She wished she knew. "I always wanted brothers and sisters," she said. "Especially a sister. Maybe Charles would have been kinder to Jennifer if he'd had a sister." She gave Andrew a triumphant glance.

However, her cleverness was wasted. Elaine just shrugged again, looking bewildered. But then she brightened. "I know all about resenting a brother," she said. "When Robbie and I were growing up, all anybody worried about was his piano playing. Nobody cared about what I might want to do.''

"What *do* you want to do?" Jocelyn asked.

"I want a beauty business of my own," Elaine said immediately, flashing the girl a grateful glance. "I've got it all planned." Her blue eyes shone with eagerness and she looked very pretty. "I'd play taped reggae, eh? With subliminal messages about relaxation. All my clients would feel and look wonderful when they left."

They had reached the driveway and started following it around to the right, walking slowly. Turning her head toward the house, Kate glanced up at its facade. And saw movement at one of the windows. Someone *was* watching. Dropping back a pace behind the others, she counted windows. Robbie's room? The front door was open to let in today's warm spring air, but she couldn't hear the piano. Why would Robbie be watching them?

"It would be a full-service beauty parlor," Elaine said, gesticulating. "We'd give facials and body wraps and massage and manicures, pedicures, and I would supervise every part of it personally. I couldn't do it without a lot of capital, of course." She glanced eagerly at Andrew. "That's why—"

She broke off, but Kate was sure she could fill in the blanks. Elaine, too, was hoping to inherit. Had she been trying to get Harry to finance her plans when she'd asked him for a loan? Had it occurred to her that if Harry was dead she might inherit from Frederick herself? Somehow Kate couldn't make herself believe in Elaine as a killer. For one thing, she didn't look strong enough for the particular crimes that had been committed.

"Could you cut *my* hair?" Jocelyn asked abruptly.

Elaine stopped walking, her face coming alive with pleasure. Lifting Jocelyn's chin, she studied her face in a very professional way. "Your hair should be chin length," she said decisively. "Curving in toward your face to give it a frame, make it look more oval. Parted on the side would be more interesting than the way you have it. And we could cut you some bangs to soften your forehead."

"Bangs? Oh—you mean a fringe. Could you make it go up and across like Kate's?" Jocelyn asked.

Elaine glanced at Kate and nodded. "Would you like me to do it now?"

"Could you?" Jocelyn's voice had risen with excitement.

Elaine smiled, looking pretty again. She needed to smile more, Kate thought. A smile could work wonders on any face, even one plastered with too much makeup.

"Do I have any say in the matter?" Andrew asked mildly.

Jocelyn rolled her eyes. "Oh, Daddy, I suppose you want me to go on looking like a little girl forever?"

"You look fine to me, Fishface," Andrew said. "But I suppose you have to start making these decisions for yourself."

Jocelyn hugged him, then whirled around to Elaine. "Come along before he changes his mind," she cried happily.

"I think someone was watching us," Kate said to Andrew as Elaine and Jocelyn hurried past the rhododendron walk. Jocelyn was lifting her braid and making scissoring movements in the air. Kate shuddered, wondering how Joss would look when she next appeared. "I'd swear someone was looking out one of the second-floor windows. Robbie's unless my count is off."

"Robbie likes watching you," Andrew pointed out.

Kate shook her head. "This seemed more…menacing."

"I think we have to be careful not to overdramatize every situation," Andrew said.

"Thanks a lot," Kate said hotly, then let out a breath. "I'm sorry. You're right, of course. After two murders, it's very easy to see a threat in perfectly innocent happenings." She sighed. "We don't seem to be getting very far, do we?"

"A police detective I know told me the only way to build a case was with one brick of evidence at a time. Let's look at what we've learned. Robbie and Elaine both want money. Badly."

"Enough to kill for it?"

Andrew shrugged. "Who knows. What about Sikander?"

"He doesn't take kindly to being laughed at. Do you suppose Lottie laughed at him? She could be a very irritating woman."

"Harry insulted Sikander," Andrew murmured. "How far do you suppose he'd go to avenge an insult?"

"Well, he did spend time in jail. Is it such a very long step from embezzling money to killing for money? And he does seem to be under some kind of strain, don't you think?"

Andrew seemed about to say something more, but stopped abruptly. They had reached the courtyard, and Frederick Wainwright was sitting at one of the tables, talking to a couple of men in working clothes. Frederick was quite a contrast to the men, dressed in a beautifully cut tweed hacking jacket and impeccably creased brown trousers.

When the men left, Kate went off to get a pot of tea from the kitchen and Andrew sat down with Frederick. He thought the older man looked overwhelmingly exhausted, sitting there with the sunlight on his face. Even his mustache looked droopy, uncared for. His formerly hearty manner was noticeably absent, as was the vigor that had always marked his features. Remembering what he'd told them about his doctor's warnings, Andrew asked, "Are you feeling all right, old chap?"

Frederick mustered a smile. "I feel so responsible," he said heavily. "It was I who brought all my relations to Farrington Hall and exposed them to the horrors of murder."

"It's hardly your fault Harry and Lottie were killed," Kate protested, setting a loaded tray down on the table.

Frederick wasn't comforted. "Harry warned me not to tell everyone I'd named him my heir. He was afraid it would put him in danger. And it did."

"You agree with the inspector, then? You think one of us killed him in order to inherit?" Kate asked as she poured tea.

"I haven't been able to think of another reason," he said. He attempted a smile. "I certainly don't suspect you, my dear, if that's what you're afraid of. You weren't even in the country, after all."

Had Erskine told him one of his father's canes had been used as the murder weapon? Andrew wondered. He certainly couldn't ask him. "Keep mum," the inspector had ordered.

"Where's that nice little girl of yours, Andrew?" Frederick asked.

Andrew laughed. "Elaine's cutting her hair, Lord help us."

"She hasn't had any more of those worrying episodes, I trust?"

"None at all," Andrew said. The manner in which a question was asked certainly made a difference, he thought. He'd taken immediate offense at Robbie's curiosity, but Frederick's concern was obvious. However, there was no point worrying Frederick about Jocelyn. He had enough on his mind. "I'm quite sure that was an isolated incident," he said firmly.

Frederick looked relieved. "I've worried about her," he admitted. "Must be a burden, an unusual ability like that."

"Why do you suppose anyone would kill Lottie?" Kate asked her uncle after a moment's silence.

Frederick shuddered slightly and took a moment to reply. "The inspector thinks she must have guessed who the murderer was and he—or she—had no choice but to—" He broke off and reached for the teapot to fill their cups again. His hands were shaking.

"Lottie was a strange person," Frederick said slowly. "Witness this absurd notion of passing off her ex-husband as Emory."

Picking up his cup, he took a sip of tea, and Andrew noticed that his fingers were still unsteady. He looked so mournful, so unwell, it would be positively cruel to bring up anything that might further distress him. Catching Kate's eye, he tried to communicate this with a tightening of his lips, and Kate nodded, understanding immediately. Gillian would have to wait for another time. For the life of him he couldn't see how Gillian's existence had anything to do with the murders, anyway.

"I do feel speculation is fruitless," Frederick said. He tugged lightly at his mustache for a moment, then looked at Kate fondly. "I'm aware, my dear, that you're very interested in finding the guilty person, as we all are," he said. "But it seems perhaps your interest is more persistent. I'm concerned that you might ask the wrong person the wrong question and put yourself at risk. Far better to leave these matters to the police, who know what they're doing, don't you think? Inspector Erskine seems a competent chap. I'm sure he's capable of finding our murderer for us."

"Hear, hear," Andrew said. "I've been telling her much the same thing myself."

Kate made a face at him, then smiled at Frederick, evidently touched by his obvious concern for her. "You're probably both right," she said in a demure voice that didn't fool Andrew for a second.

An instant later, she changed the subject to the weather, and the flowers blooming in containers around the courtyard. Andrew was glad to see that Frederick's face had lost some of its gray cast when they left him fifteen minutes later.

"Uncle Frederick reminds me of my grandfather Will," Kate said as she and Andrew walked around the side of the house. "Grandfather was never a demonstrative person, but occasionally he dropped his guard enough to show that he did care for me. I always wondered why he felt it necessary to cover up the fact."

"Frederick is obviously very fond of you," Andrew said.

"He looks terrible," she said worriedly.

Andrew nodded. "That's why I didn't want you harassing him about Gillian."

Her brown eyes flashed. "I do not harass people."

They were approaching the rhododendron walk and he abruptly pulled her over to it, taking her into his arms as soon as he judged he and Kate were out of sight.

"You've a tendency to get much too lordly, Andrew Bradford," she muttered when he finally stopped kissing her.

He grinned, looking down into her face. "My mother says I'm occasionally as arrogant as my father used to be before she remodeled him."

She laughed and he kissed her lightly. As usual, she smelled wonderful. A hint of some delicate scent clung to her skin. Running his thumb and forefinger over her lips, he formed her mouth into a smile. "I'm sorry, Kate," he murmured. "I didn't mean to be lordly." He rested his cheek against her hair, which also smelled marvelous. He could spend a lifetime inhaling Kate's fragrance, he thought. "May I come and visit you later?" he asked.

Her face moved gently against his, but then she sighed. "What if Joss comes down again?"

"My room then."

"Where would she go first?"

He frowned. "We'll have to work something out. I seem to want you most dreadfully."

Moving his head, he kissed her again, his mouth playful on hers, now touching, now withdrawing, his lips firm, then pliant. She joined in the teasing game, her lips following his lead, opening to his, her tongue darting to find the tender corner of his mouth. There was a tightness, a warm contraction in her lower body, and heat flamed through her veins. When he released her, she held on to him for a moment, unable to stand upright by herself. Her heart was pounding.

"Either we stop, or I throw you over my shoulder and make a dash for the main staircase," Andrew said huskily.

"Just try it," Kate warned, eyes flashing again. Then she laughed and drew away from him. "We still have people to talk to," she reminded him with obvious reluctance.

"So we have." He smiled at her. "I'm sorry, Kate. I get distracted when you're nearby."

"You don't have to apologize for that," she assured him.

The short interlude in the rhododendron walk had lightened her mood considerably, she thought as they walked on. If only she and Andrew had met under different circumstances. But then they might not have been drawn together quite so quickly. If they had not been soldiers in combat . . .

The thought reminded her of the seriousness of their quest, and she shivered, causing Andrew to look at her questioningly. "Goose walked over my..." She broke off, shuddering again.

They had reached the steps to the terrace. Glancing up, Kate saw it again—that slight shadowy movement in that same second-story window. A cloud going over the sun, she told herself. But the sky was totally clear today, the sun shining brightly. Which made it all the more difficult to explain away the chill that was penetrating clear through to her bones.

Chapter Eleven

Hilary Wainwright sat unusually still on the library sofa, her slender hands clasped loosely in her lap, her head inclined downward at an angle that suggested weariness.

Hesitating in the doorway, as yet unseen, Bennett Coby let his eyes fill with her. "Hilary," he said quietly. "Thank you for meeting me, my dear. I wasn't sure you would."

Her head lifted, and for just a moment her face lit with an inner glow that gave him hope. Then her expression changed, assuming its usual hunted expression, and she began nervously picking at the buttoned cuffs of her blouse sleeves.

"I was able to come because Frederick is taking a nap." She frowned. "He never used to take naps. I'm worried about his health, Bennett—he really seems . . ."

Bennett strode across the library and knelt in front of her, taking her hands between both of his. He had not come here to discuss Frederick's health. "I see you alone so rarely," he complained.

She looked worriedly toward the library doorway. "It's not a good idea, Bennett," she said. "Please do get up and take a seat. If someone were to come in . . ."

He disregarded her plea, dropping a soft kiss on her hands. "I've waited ten years to be with you again. But even if it were thirty, it wouldn't alter the fact that I love you."

Her gray-green eyes looked like mist over the sea. "You shouldn't have come back," she said nervously.

"I was invited. How could I have stayed away?"

For a long moment he held her gaze and saw love in her eyes, then he laid his head in her lap and put his arms around her.

"Oh, my dear," she murmured. Then she glanced in an alarmed manner toward the library door. "Someone's coming," she whispered. But it was already too late.

KATE BLINKED, then blinked again. Oh, Lord, Bennett and Hilary, caught in flagrante delicto, or at the very least in an unmistakably intimate position.

As she and Andrew hesitated in the doorway, Bennett got awkwardly to his feet, his rather weak chin assuming a defiant angle. "So now you know," he said.

"Yes, indeed," Andrew murmured.

Bennett sat down next to Hilary. "I fell in love with Hilary when I visited ten years ago," he confessed with great dignity, seeming relieved to talk about it. "I was at the end of my tether with Jennifer's drinking. Hilary was kind, compassionate. And she was lonely herself. Frederick was always wound up in some political brouhaha. It just happened."

Was he saying they'd had an affair? Kate wondered, exchanging an embarrassed glance with Andrew.

"We knew nothing could come of it, of course," Bennett said, gazing at Hilary.

Kate's heart contracted at the anguish on his face. How cruel love could be.

"Hilary is loyal to Frederick, as I was to Jennifer," Bennett continued steadily. "Now I'm alone, but Hilary—" He looked at Andrew. "I'm an honorable man. I won't deliberately break up Hilary's marriage."

"I always thought you and Frederick were perfectly happy," Andrew said to Hilary, sitting down abruptly in a nearby chair. It was obvious that Bennett's declaration had caused him far more surprise than it had Kate.

"We were in the beginning," Hilary said falteringly. "Frederick was an important man—thirty-two, handsome, clever. I was flattered when he showed an interest in me. I was barely out of grammar school. And my parents kept reminding me I wasn't a beauty, I should grasp whatever opportunity I could."

"*I* think you are the most beautiful woman in the world," Bennett said softly.

Her gaze met his and held there, creating a stillness in the room that spoke volumes. There was pain in her eyes, too, Kate saw, and yearning. But almost immediately she became agitated again, her hands fluttering around as though at any moment she would take flight like a startled doe into the forest of her conventional upbringing.

"Perhaps we should tell Andrew all of it," she whispered.

Bennett shook his head. "I don't think—"

Hilary raised her hands as though in supplication, then turned to Andrew. "Harry knew," she said flatly. "He's been blackmailing me steadily for ten years."

A wave of dislike for the dead man went through Kate, leaving a sour taste in her mouth. Walking over to the fireplace, she stood with her back to it and looked down at Hilary and Bennett. "You don't have to worry about us telling the inspector," she said carefully. "But you must realize, if Harry was blackmailing you, it looks bad. I think perhaps it might be better if you told the inspector yourselves."

The two older people moved together as if seeking refuge. Bennett took hold of Hilary's hand and Hilary looked at him in a frightened way that aroused all Kate's compassion.

"I can't do that," Hilary said, sounding unexpectedly firm. "If Frederick found out...he'd be devastated. It was ten years ago, Kate. Ten years. This time, well, we haven't..." She shook her head, looking agitatedly at Kate and Andrew. "In spite of the way it appears, I'm very fond of Frederick. We've been together a long time. I'm his *wife*, Kate. He's already worried...these dreadful murders."

"He's afraid the scandal will affect his chances for the knighthood," Bennett said flatly.

Hilary looked at him reproachfully. "He hasn't given the effect on the title a single thought."

Bennett appeared rather cynical about that, but didn't comment further.

After a moment, Hilary went on. "Frederick's health is an added consideration at the moment." She looked pleadingly at Bennett, pulling her hand free and fussing with her hair. "You do understand, don't you? I can't let Frederick suffer because you and I were foolish. It was to protect him that I paid Harry."

"I understand," Bennett said softly.

"I'm not sure I do," Andrew said. "Why would Harry come to you for money? Frederick was always generous with him."

Hilary smiled sadly. "Harry was always looking for funds, in case any of his established sources dried up. He never demanded too much," she added. "'Just a few quid to tide me over,' he'd say."

"But it *was* blackmail."

"Oh, yes. Harry had seen us coming out of the Hambury Inn, you see. It was very stupid of us, but we were both unhappy, both swept away. I couldn't let Harry tell Frederick, he'd have made it sound cheap and awful.''

They both looked so miserable, Kate felt it would be a kindness to change the subject, but she had no idea how to go about it in the discreet manner Andrew had ordained.

But while she was still searching for words, Andrew took the lead, asking Bennett if his father-in-law hadn't missed having his brothers around after he'd gone to live in Canada.

Understandably puzzled, Bennett hesitated for a minute, then shook his head. "No love lost there.''

"What about Gillian?'' Andrew asked.

Kate stared at him. Was this what he called being discreet?

Hilary looked from Andrew to Kate with a very alarmed expression on her delicate features. "We don't talk about Gillian,'' she said. There was a note of hysteria in her voice.

"Why not?'' Kate asked, making her voice soft. Hilary seemed ready to fly apart into a million pieces.

"It upsets Frederick,'' Hilary said, as if that should take care of the whole subject.

"I'm amazed you even know about Gillian,'' Bennett said. "I always got the impression she'd been swept under the mat.'' He shrugged. "Yes, as a matter of fact, Charles did miss her. She died shortly after he left England, I understand. But he mentioned her often. Evidently Jennifer resembled her.''

"What did Gililian die of?'' Kate asked in what she hoped was a calm voice. Her heart was pounding with excitement, though she had no idea what use this information might be.

Bennett looked thoughtful. "I never heard. Charles was secretive about her death. His mother died soon after, you know. Charles seemed to think she died of a broken heart.''

"You believe that's scientifically possible?" Andrew asked.

"Oh, yes," Bennett said, gazing at Hilary with his heart in his eyes.

"Aunt Hilary," Kate said. "Do you know anything about Gillian's death?"

The older woman shook her head abruptly, pressing her lips together. "I was a baby when she died. Frederick was barely seventeen."

Kate stood up. "I'm sorry we had to put you through this," she said. "We certainly won't repeat anything you've told us."

Andrew stood up without saying anything and followed her out of the room. "Kate," he said softly as they walked across the vestibule. "I'm not too sure . . ."

She shook her head. "Bennett's too nice a guy, Andrew. I can't imagine him becoming enraged enough to strike anyone."

"That isn't what I meant," Andrew said. "I was talking about the blackmail—" He broke off abruptly.

Kate saw what he had seen. Roger Stoane aka Emory Wainwright was just coming out of the kitchen. He greeted them genially, but warily. He'd been making himself scarce since his unmasking, taking most of his meals in his room, barely venturing out in public at all.

"Did you ever hear of a Gillian Wainwright?" Kate asked him.

Andrew made a startled exclamation. "Good Lord, Kate—what happened to that discretion we talked about?"

"I'm tired of pussyfooting," she informed him. "Besides, you weren't too discreet in there," she added, gesturing toward the library. "You came right out with it and it worked."

She looked back at Roger, who seemed fairly bewildered by all this. "Gillian Wainwright was Lottie's father's sister," she told him. "Did Lottie ever talk about her to you?"

Roger shook his head. "Nobody ever mentioned a sheila called Gillian to me." He pressed his lips together. "I don't want to talk about any of the bloody Wainwrights. You and young Jocelyn are the only ones who even bother to talk to me since word got out. All I want is to shove off for Australia and get on with my life. I shouldn't have come. I shouldn't have let Lottie talk me into it."

He blinked apologetically. "I'm sorry, Kate. None of this is your fault. I shouldn't be taking it out on you. It's just that I'm worried and upset, you see. Lottie wasn't a bad old girl, just frantic about the winery coming a cropper. People didn't work as well for her as they did for Emory because she was a woman, and she didn't really know how to do the job—she'd only handled the bookkeeping part of it when Emory was alive. Now I've got to work out what I'm going to do when I get back to Australia. I don't mean to grizzle, but I'm out of a job, aren't I? Too young to loaf about. But who's going to hire a man who's going on fifty?" Shaking his head, he walked toward the front door without waiting for a response from either of them.

"What now?" Kate asked, looking dazedly after him. "I feel as though my head's stuffed with more questions than ever."

"I suppose Jocelyn's still with Elaine," Andrew muttered. "I would think she's safe with her, wouldn't you?"

Kate nodded.

"I've an idea," he said, frowning. "It might or might not . . ." Nodding as if with sudden decision, he took her elbow and started walking her toward the front door. "Let's get my car, shall we? I think we should go into Hambury."

As THE ROVER SPED along country roads, Andrew said, "After we've seen to the errand I have in mind, we'll go in to see Inspector Erskine and bring him up to date."

"We can't do that," Kate said at once. "I promised Hilary and Bennett we wouldn't tell anyone...."

He made his voice deliberately cold. "If Gillian *is* the key to the mystery, don't you think the murderer will decide we are getting too close for comfort? And should be eliminated. He's killed twice, Kate. What does he have to lose?"

She turned away, her chin lifted in the proud way he usually admired, but which now seemed unbearably stubborn.

"Kate," he said, making an effort to soften his voice. "We have to turn *everything* over to the inspector. It's dangerous to go on poking around by ourselves. Be reasonable."

"In other words, I shouldn't get my knickers in a twist." Her voice was cold enough to freeze blood.

"Right," he said, knowing his agreement would infuriate her, but feeling the risk was worth it if it stopped her from exposing herself to danger.

There was an awkward silence, broken only by the sound of the engine. Then Kate said flatly, "I won't betray Hilary's secret."

"It's hardly a betrayal," he protested. "Two murders have been committed. Blackmail is a very credible motive."

"I don't believe either Bennett or Hilary is a murderer. Hilary's a sweetheart. And Bennett's a nice quiet guy."

"Newspapers are full of stories about quiet people who do terrible things in the name of love," Andrew said grimly.

She was still staring straight ahead. "I shouldn't have invited you to come with me while I questioned everyone," she said finally. "I'll know better from now on." She

darted a glance at him. "If we're going to be so scrupu-
lously honest maybe I ought to tell the inspector about your
motive, too."

She was just hitting back, he told himself, even as he felt
as if she'd stabbed him to the heart.

"That wasn't fair," she said abruptly. "I'm sorry. Of
course I'm not going to tell the inspector any such thing."

Later he thought that perhaps it was at this moment he
knew for certain that he loved Kate Wainwright. Even furious with him as she was, she could still be fair-minded.

He took his left hand off the steering wheel and put it
over her hands, which were clasped tensely in her lap.
"Please don't be angry with me," he pleaded.

"I'm afraid it's too late." Her hands were unyielding
beneath his. After a moment, he took his hand away, at a
loss to know how to make up with her. Give her time, he
thought.

"So what is your idea?" she asked after a strained silence.

"It occurred to me if there were some scandal attached
to the Wainwright brothers' departure it might have been
published in *The Hambury Echo*. That's where we're going now."

Her anger gave way immediately to excitement, which lit
twin lamps in her wonderful brown eyes. "We might even
find an obituary for Gillian."

"Possibly." He was relieved that they were apparently on
good terms again, but still determined to talk to the inspector. For the moment however, he wasn't about to
damage their accord by trying to force her to agree with
him.

A MIDDLE-AGED WOMAN with wavy gray hair and a
charming manner informed them that of course *The Ham-*

bury Echo kept their old newspapers. On microfilm, as far back as the newspaper had been printed. Yes, she said, after Andrew explained he was a solicitor and needed historical background for a case, there was a viewer they could use. And yes, they could do it straightaway. After showing them how to use the machine she left them to it.

They started with January 1933, as that was the date of Gillian's last photograph. It was slow going. *The Hambury Echo* apparently reported every detail of everything that took place in the county. There were stories about Christmas celebrations, garden fetes, Sunday school picnics, pictures of the mayor opening an amazing number of events.

There was very little in the way of local crime. Some thievery, vandalism, a few fights in the local pubs. But all deaths were apparently due to natural causes or accident.

Until Andrew caught sight of an item about one Dennis Riley, a farm worker from Allercott, who—on Saturday, October 14, 1933—was found beaten to death in a ditch at the side of the Allercott-Market Ridgeway Road.

Kate started scrolling again, but Andrew put out a hand to stop her and read the piece to the end. There was something about it... "Carry on," he said, and watched carefully in the ensuing pages for a follow-up story.

But there was no more mention of the incident in the pages that followed. Kate scrolled onward, but Andrew was no longer paying attention, he was searching his memory, trying to decide what had rung a bell.

"What did you see?" Kate asked.

About to tell her, he stopped himself cold. All he had to do was give her a hint and she'd be questioning everyone in the family again, blithely ignoring any possibility of danger.

"Let's keep reading," he said.

Her eyes narrowed, but she made no protest, simply turning back to the machine.

In February 1934, they found Gillian Wainwright's obituary. Robert's only daughter had died that month of a sudden illness at the age of twenty-one. Survivors, other than her parents, were not listed. No other information, other than time and place of interment, was given.

"No mention of foul play," Andrew muttered. "Probably a wild-goose chase, this whole matter of Gillian and supposed secrets."

"Shall we look for Elizabeth's obit?" Kate asked, fingers poised to scroll again. "Bennett said she died the same year."

"I'm not sure that would enlighten us, but we might as well look at it." Andrew pulled his chair closer to Kate's. It was amazing, he thought, how one wanted to be at different distances from different people. Some people one wanted to keep at arm's length. Others even farther. Some could be allowed within touching distance. Jocelyn could come as close as she wanted to. And Kate . . . there seemed to be a special rule for Kate. He couldn't seem to get quite close enough to her at any time. How absorbed he was becoming in her. He could not—and did not want to—imagine being without her. He realized suddenly that since making love to her he hadn't experienced any more of the sudden bouts of weakness that had been the aftermath of his illness. Obviously she was very good for him, he decided, looking lovingly at her.

"Are you reading this, Andrew?" she asked with a sharp sideways glance.

"Sorry, I got distracted by your nose," he murmured, still gazing at her.

She stared at him for a moment, then laughed. "It's absolutely impossible to stay angry with you. Why my nose?"

"It's so straight. Narrow. Aristocratic. No wonder Elaine wants it."

Her laughter echoed in the little room. Andrew seized the moment to kiss the tender area at the base of her left ear.

"We're here to work," she reminded him. Her voice was definitely breathy. The kiss had affected her, no doubt about that. And she was no longer angry with him. Satisfied for the moment, Andrew fixed his attention on the screen.

Elizabeth Wainwright's obituary was no more revealing than Gillian's. She had simply died a few weeks after her daughter.

"Maybe Elizabeth did die of a broken heart," Kate said when they were back in the Rover. "That would hardly be surprising. After all, she had six children and she lost five of them, one way or another, within a few months."

In spite of Kate's renewed objections, Andrew insisted on stopping off at the police station on the way home. But to Andrew's disappointment and Kate's relief, Inspector Erskine was out.

"I think I'll pop up to London tonight," Andrew said as he turned the car into the driveway leading to Farrington Hall.

"Alone?" Kate asked.

"Alone," he said firmly. Might as well be hung for the whole sheep, he decided. "I'd appreciate it if you'd keep an eye on Fishface for me. And not ask anyone any more questions." He looked at her pleadingly, softening his voice. "Please, Kate, promise me you'll behave."

"You're holding out on me," she accused. "You saw something in that newspaper. What was it?"

"Nothing of the sort," he said, but he could see from the mutinous set of her mouth and chin that she was not convinced and she wasn't going to make him any promises.

JOCELYN WAS WAITING impatiently for them, sitting on the top step of the terrace with Elaine Coby. Her hair had acquired a glossy sheen and swung like a bell when she moved her head. A small section of strands, lifted at the front, feathered across her forehead in the same way as Kate's. The rest of her hair framed her heart-shaped face and shining eyes in a way that made her look absolutely beautiful and awakened memories of her mother in the days when Andrew had first known and loved her.

She stood up as Andrew and Kate got out of the car, her hands going for security into her jeans pockets. She was so obviously nervous about her father's reaction that he hurried through the topiary garden and up the steps to reassure her.

Hands on her shoulders, he gazed delightedly at her. "You look smashing," he declared.

"Gorgeous," Kate added.

"I can't call you Fishface anymore," Andrew said sadly.

She flung her arms around him and hugged him enthusiastically. "Of course you can, Daddy," she protested. "That's your special name for me and you can call me by it as long as I live."

Andrew smiled at Elaine. "You're obviously very good."

She flushed, looking very pretty herself. "I liked doing it," she said simply. "Jocelyn's a nice girl."

As the flush faded, Andrew noticed for the first time that her expression seemed strained. "Is anything wrong?" he asked.

Jocelyn had been turning around for Kate's benefit, so she could admire her hair from the back. Before Elaine could answer, she said, "Oh, Daddy, it's awful, the inspector came back and Mr. Coby's been in with him for hours."

"We haven't been gone for hours," Andrew objected, even while he exchanged a glance with Kate. "I'd better see what's up," he said.

Elaine brightened. "Thank you, Andrew," she said. "I'd feel better if I knew what was going on."

Andrew started toward the front entrance, Kate on his heels. In the doorway he hesitated and turned back. "Did the inspector ask to see Bennett, or did Bennett go in voluntarily?" he asked.

"The inspector asked for him as soon as he got here," Elaine said.

"It doesn't look good, does it?" Kate whispered as they headed toward the library.

Bennett, white-faced, sitting in a straight chair on the opposite side of the desk to the inspector, greeted them with a wan smile. "I didn't have a chance to confess, after all," he told Kate. "The inspector already knew."

Kate frowned. "But I didn't—it wasn't me who..."

"I think Miss Kate is trying to say that she didn't inform me of your conversation," the inspector said dryly. He looked reproachfully at Kate. "I was told about this relationship by Mrs. Sanderham, Harry Wainwright's sister. Apparently Harry told her all about it years ago. However, Miss Kate, as you and Mr. Bradford evidently knew about it, I canna understand why you didna inform me of it."

"We were going to," Andrew said briskly. "We stopped at the police station to see you, less than an hour ago."

"Is that a fact?" the inspector said flatly.

Andrew looked at Bennett. "Did you, that is, have you told the inspector—"

"About the blackmail?" Bennett interrupted. "I've told him everything. I've also told him it's ridiculous to suppose either Hilary or I would kill Harry over a matter of a few pounds a month, which Hilary was perfectly willing to pay.''

The inspector looked skeptical. Then he glanced from Andrew to Kate. "Are you keeping anything else from me?"

Andrew could see an agony of indecision on Kate's face. He spoke quickly, for both of them. "There are one or two things we're sitting on, Inspector, because we don't have any proof. Just some ideas we've had that we want to check up on. As a matter of fact I was going to ask if you've any objection if I make a quick trip to London. I need to look at some papers in my office. If I can find the item I need, I'll pass the information on to you at once, of course."

"Will you, now?" the inspector said heavily.

"Are you through with me?" Bennett asked. "I'd like to make sure Hilary's okay."

The inspector shifted his angry gaze from Andrew's face to Bennett's and sighed audibly. "I suppose there's no point in going over it again," he said. "But I would no advise you to leave this house, Mr. Coby. You might take that as an order rather than a request."

Bennett blanched, then scurried out of the room.

"Is Aunt Hilary unwell?" Kate asked, looking worried.

The inspector sighed. "The lady became somewhat hysterical when I questioned her," he said.

"I should have been here," Andrew said grimly.

"Aye. But you were not. And no one knew where you'd gone. But you've no need to concern yourself. I've no been badgering the lady. I've no wish to badger anybody. All I want is for everyone to tell me the truth."

"We've told you the truth," Kate said.

"With certain omissions, it seems."

There was no possible answer to that. Andrew decided it might be best to appear confident. "There isn't any reason I can't go to London tonight, is there, Inspector?"

"You say you've possible information there?"

"Yes. Something Kate and I were looking into just now might possibly have some bearing on the murders."

"I knew you were holding out on me," Kate muttered, her face darkening.

Andrew avoided her accusing gaze.

"Aye, well, I suppose you can go," the inspector said. "You'll be back when?"

"Tomorrow, no later."

The inspector nodded.

Andrew was quite ready to leave the room while the going was good, but Kate chose that moment to sit down. "Do you think Bennett killed Harry and Lottie?" she asked Erskine.

The Scot's shrewd eyes softened noticeably as he looked at her. No doubt about it, the man was smitten, Andrew thought. Which was too bad for him, he added to himself.

"I don't deal in thoughts, Miss Kate," he said tiredly. "I deal in concrete facts. Blackmail's as good a motive as any, it's true, but in this case the amount was small and it had been going on for ten years. Mr. Coby swears he didn't know about it until he came back to England. Would he really kill Harry Wainwright over something that happened ten years ago? That is," he added thoughtfully, "if both parties are telling the truth and the...incident has not been repeated."

He shook his head. "Why *would* Bennett Coby kill Harry Wainwright? Bennett's a single man now. If Harry had carried out his threat of telling the colonel the two of them were lovers, what would be the worst that could have happened? The colonel might throw his wife out of the house. And then Bennett would be standing there waiting to receive her."

He looked at Andrew, then at Kate, blinking in the odd way he had. "It would have made more sense for Bennett Coby to kill Frederick Wainwright, don't you think?"

Andrew sucked in his breath, but Kate was there before him. "You think it's possible Harry was killed by mistake," she said in a very matter-of-fact tone.

"You don't seem surprised," the inspector said.

"Oh, I am," Kate said. "It's just that a couple of days ago, when I was mulling everything over in my mind, I had the feeling I was looking at it from the wrong angle. And when you implied Harry's death might have been a mistake, I knew that's what my subconscious was trying to tell me. You think the murderer might have intended killing Uncle Frederick."

"It was misty that night," Andrew said quietly.

"Aye. And Harry was struck down from behind. And the two men looked a lot alike."

"Good Lord," Andrew exclaimed. "You're suggesting Bennett meant to kill Frederick so he could have Hilary?"

"I'm no saying anything of the sort," the inspector said shortly. "I'm merely offering a different perspective." He stood up. "I'm off for the day. I put the fear of death in yon Mr. Coby and got nowhere. And I've an idea questioning either of you two again would lead me up the same garden path." He looked at Andrew. "Ring me up when you return, will you?"

"I will," Andrew promised. He was going to have a hell of a time convincing the inspector he'd discovered nothing if that proved to be the case, he thought.

"Have a good trip," Kate said shortly as he headed toward the door.

Tempted to turn back, to apologize, he kept going. If he gave her a single inch, she'd be on at him about what he'd discovered in the newspaper. Better he leave her ignorant but safe, he decided. He'd explain on his return and then she'd forgive him.

He hoped.

Chapter Twelve

The sky was low and densely gray, pregnant with rain. The air seemed unnaturally still. The muggy atmosphere suited Kate's mood admirably. She was furious with Andrew, had awakened several times in the night thinking of things she should have said to him, insults she could have hurled. Taking photographs in the grounds, she kept muttering. Andrew Bradford had treated her like a child—telling her not to ask anyone questions—trying to get her to promise to behave herself, while at the same time he'd refused to share information that had come out of the newspaper.

Following a suddenly frigid blast of cold air around eleven-fifteen, rain began slanting down from billowing clouds. Conversely, Kate's mood lightened. Andrew had been worried about her, she conceded. And according to what he'd told the inspector, his bit of information might not have anything to do with the murders at all.

But who *was* Dennis Riley? she wondered as she ran lightly up the main staircase. She was sure that was the item that had started Andrew off. He'd stopped her from turning to the next page when they'd reached the name Dennis Riley.

In her room, she switched on the light and started toward the bathroom, thinking she'd freshen up before lunch.

Something seemed out of place. A chill quivered down her spine.

There was a piece of paper wedged behind her small jewelry case, held upright so that she could see it was a page torn from a book. Someone had entered her room again. Elaine? Or someone else? Frowning, her heart suddenly beating very rapidly, she gingerly picked up the page by two corners and took it under the hanging light fixture to study it. The paper was thin and of very good quality, slightly yellowed as though with age. The single name Stevenson was printed at the top. Robert Louis Stevenson? she wondered.

The printing was small and fairly dense. But partway down a paragraph had been marked with a small inked x. "I feel very strongly about putting questions," Kate read. "It partakes too much of the style of the day of judgment. You start a question, and it's like starting a stone. You sit quietly on the top of a hill and away the stone goes, starting others."

There was nothing overtly threatening about the passage, but she felt threatened nonetheless. This page had not been put here for her reading entertainment. It had been meant as a warning to stop asking questions.

She flinched as distant lightning forked across the sky, flashing in through her window like a searchlight. Placing the page carefully in her lingerie drawer, she left the room, walking slowly down the hall to the main staircase, trying to contain her anger. She was furious that someone had invaded her privacy for the second time. It seemed obvious to her that this very literary and ambiguous method of warning her had been chosen by the same person who'd exposed her film.

Due to the storm, the vestibule was more shadowy than ever. Kate walked as quietly as she could, willing her Reeboks not to speak on the parquet.

She spent half an hour surveying the library shelves, trying to work out the system employed in organizing them, which proved to be fairly complex. Nor was it simple to find the author she was looking for. She had finally to climb the spiral staircase to the upper gallery. And here she found several books by Stevenson, some of them first editions. All of them had been bound in morocco to preserve them. The paper of at least three seemed similar to the one that had been left in her room. Why hadn't she thought to glance at the page number? It would have greatly simplified her search.

About to go back to her room to check, she hesitated, a pulse hammering in her head at the sound of voices close to the library door. Uncle Frederick. She relaxed. Whom had she expected?

"But it's almost lunchtime, my dear," Frederick said.

"I'm just going to ring up Amy Sanderham," Hilary replied.

"Such an unpleasant woman," Frederick said. "Why bother?"

"There's something I want to discuss with her."

"I'd prefer you had nothing more to do with her," Frederick said firmly.

Hilary's sigh was audible. "Very well, dear," she said. A moment later, both sets of footsteps faded away.

Almost lunchtime. If she went upstairs now she'd probably run into one or other of the relatives and get dragged into the meal herself. Pulling out the next Stevenson on the shelf, she riffled through it, caught sight of a discrepancy in page numbers and ran her finger over the jagged edge of paper left behind when the page had been removed. This was the book. Closing it, she checked the title embossed on the cover. *The Strange Case of Dr. Jekyll and Mr. Hyde.*

She shivered.

Someone had torn that page from this book and put it in her bedroom to frighten her. Who? Everybody used the library from time to time.

With shaking fingers she replaced the book, then descended the spiral stairs. Elaine and Bennett were passing the door when she emerged. When they told her lunch was ready, she murmured something about needing to wash up, and raced up the stairs, reaching her room without running into anyone else.

Sitting down at her dressing table, she planted her elbows on the shining surface and clasped her head in her hands. What on earth was she to do about that page? What she wanted to do was to take it down to the drawing room right now and confront everyone, demanding to know who had torn it out of one of Uncle Frederick's first editions. But that was probably not the most sensible action. Andrew certainly wouldn't think so. How she wished he were here. Straightening, she picked up her hairbrush and began brushing her hair, hoping the action would calm her shattered nerves. She would just have to wait until Andrew returned, she supposed.

She was applying lipstick, when a knock came at her door. She jumped, then walked slowly toward it. "Who is it?" she asked.

"Joss."

Kate flung the door wide, happy to see the girl. She had been studying in her room for most of the morning. Kate had made sure she'd locked herself in, made her promise she wouldn't wander around the house.

She was wearing a Western shirt and blue jeans, as usual, looking wonderfully pretty and up-to-date in her new hairstyle. Gray Boy was draped across her left shoulder. He greeted Kate with a piercing meow.

"Are you feeling better?" Jocelyn asked.

Kate looked at her blankly. Jocelyn giggled. "I came up behind you when you were taking pictures of an oak tree this morning and you were muttering away like a motorboat, all sort of growly and sputtering. I decided discretion was the better part of valor, so I tiptoed away."

To hide her embarrassment, she stroked Gray Boy's head and rubbed his ears in the way he liked best. "I'm sorry, Joss. I got up on the wrong side of my bed, I guess."

"You're mad at Daddy again, aren't you?"

Kate touched her lightly on the nose. "Never you mind who I was mad at. I'm okay now."

"Good." Jocelyn stood up, clutching the cat in both arms. "Then you can come and have lunch with me in my room. I've got it all arranged. I've told Aunt Hilary we won't be down and Mrs. Hogarth is sending one of the maids up with tea and sandwiches."

"I'd love to have lunch with you," Kate said warmly. It had been difficult to get through dinner the previous night without mentioning anything about *The Hambury Echo*. At breakfast this morning the name Dennis Riley had almost slipped off her tongue. Between that and her anger at whoever was trying to frighten her off, it would be as well to avoid the family for a while, at least until Andrew returned.

Jocelyn had draped a small square table with an embroidered cloth and set it with a platter of finger sandwiches and blue-and-white dishes.

Sitting down at the table, Kate smiled, feeling suddenly nostalgic. "Blue Willow," she murmured. "I have a set myself. It belonged to my grandmother. That's amazing we'd own the same dishes."

Jocelyn looked knowing. "An omen, that's what it is." Setting the cat down on her bed, where he immediately curled up and went to sleep, she sat down herself. "I love the blue willow legend. It's all about runaway lovers being changed into birds." She touched her plate. "Here they are, you see, flying above the little bridge. Together forever—" She broke off as a crack of thunder shook the windowpanes and Gray Boy dove under her bed. "Old love stories always end sadly, don't they?" she continued. "I wonder why? There's no reason a love story can't have a happy ending, is there?"

Kate looked at her suspiciously. She was wearing her innocent face again. "I don't think there's a law against happy endings, no."

"You do love Daddy, don't you?"

"We haven't known each other very long, Joss. And you're forgetting I'll be going back to the U.S. soon."

Jocelyn reached for the teapot and began pouring daintily. "You won't be going back, Kate," she said matter-of-factly. "At least not to stay."

"Of course I will," Kate protested, but Jocelyn was shaking her head in a very decided manner. "You're forgetting that I know things," she said as she set the teapot down.

Wishful thinking, Kate thought. Warmth filled her as she realized Jocelyn would hardly be so insistent if she didn't truly want Kate to stay.

"I really love my willow dishes," she said, deliberately changing the subject. "My grandparents were terribly strict and didn't allow me to talk at the dinner table, so I made up stories of my own about the oriental design."

Jocelyn didn't answer. Putting down her half-eaten sandwich, she rose and went to stand by the window. The storm had moved closer, the thunder cracking almost immediately after lightning lit up the sky.

"Maybe you shouldn't stand by the window," Kate said uneasily, rising from her chair.

Once again the girl didn't answer. Kate joined her and stood for a moment looking down at the grounds, where the tops of the trees were tossing back and forth. "It's getting worse, isn't it?" she murmured, then glanced at Jocelyn and realized that no recognition of the storm was showing on her face. Her expression was totally blank, her gaze obviously unseeing, the pupils of her eyes so large that only a rim of pale blue showed around them. "Joss," Kate whispered, but the girl's unnatural stillness did not change.

Because she couldn't think of anything better to do, Kate took hold of the girl's hands. They felt like ice and she clasped them tightly, hoping her own warmth would be absorbed by them.

"So much blood," Jocelyn muttered.

Kate's stomach contracted, her breath catching in her throat.

"Where are you, Joss?" she asked, making her voice gentle.

"Somebody," Jocelyn said. "Blood. Face all bloody."

Kate's pulse hammered in her ears. She didn't know what to do, was almost afraid to move in case she startled the girl and did her harm. "Tell me, Joss," she murmured.

Jocelyn flinched as a sheet of rain drenched the window, backlit by a flash of lightning that cast an eerie light over the flowers in the courtyard far below. But the blankness was still in her eyes.

Should she go for help? Kate wondered. No, she couldn't leave the girl alone in this catatonic state, or whatever it was. And there was no telephone in this room.

"No," Jocelyn wailed in a voice so filled with fear it made the short hairs on the back of Kate's neck bristle as if at an electric shock. The girl's face was working now, her mouth trembling, her eyes wide and staring.

She had to do something. Pulling Jocelyn close, Kate locked her arms around her and held her, shuddering as she felt the coldness of her body. Reaching out carefully, she dragged the comforter from Jocelyn's bed and wrapped it around her, then held her again, rocking her in her arms, trying to communicate caring, safety, warmth, trying to bring the girl back from wherever her mind had wandered to.

And still the wind moaned through cracks in the old stone that surrounded the window and thunder crackled across the sky. She *had* to get help; she couldn't handle this alone. But they had decided, she and Andrew, and the inspector, too, that no one should be told if Jocelyn's episodes returned. There was no way she could summon a doctor without everyone finding out.

Talking helped, Jocelyn had told her. "I'm right here, Joss," she said desperately, rubbing the girl's back through the quilted spread. "I'm not going to let go of you. You don't have to do this alone. Tell me what's happening to you. Tell me what I can do." Keeping her voice calm, she kept talking, not even trying to make sense, just saying things that sounded soothing, comforting. And gradually Jocelyn's body temperature began to return to normal and the warmth of returning blood showed pink in her face.

And then she blinked her eyes and her gaze focused on Kate's face. Almost immediately, her face crumpled and she burst into tears.

Kate continued to hold her, easing her over to the bed so that they could both sit down. Kate's legs felt like overcooked string beans, totally unable to support her.

"I don't know if it was a man or a woman," Jocelyn said when she'd regained her composure. "It was really fuzzy this time, as if everything were happening underwater. It was the same picture that was trying to come before I came down to your room the other night." She raised frightened blue eyes to Kate's face. "Why does this happen to me, Kate. Why?"

Kate pulled her head close to her shoulder and stroked her silky hair. "I don't know, honey. I wish I did. Has anyone else seen you during one of these . . . episodes."

"Mummy did occasionally. They scared her. And I was with Grandma Bradford once. She's a psychotherapist, you know. She's been helping me—she really has. I was doing fine until I came here."

Talking seemed to have helped; she was looking more like her usual self.

Pulling slightly away from Kate, looking embarrassed, she said, "It's so frightening, Kate. I hate to be a coward, but I wish it would just go away."

Kate took her hands and held them. "You said something about blood."

Jocelyn shivered. "There was a lot of it. All over somebody's face, somebody lying on the floor. In the attic."

"The attic!"

"I think so."

"Maybe it was some kind of belated reaction to Lottie's death," Kate suggested. "Sikander said there was blood..."

Jocelyn shook her head. "It wasn't Lottie. It was somebody thinner. Somebody tall, lying on the floor. Wearing trousers, I think. But I don't know if it was a man or a woman. If only I'd been able to see the face . . ."

Bennett? Kate wondered. Or Robbie, Uncle Frederick? They were all tall and slender. So was Andrew.

But Andrew wasn't here.

Jocelyn flinched as lightning and thunder split the clouds apart again.

"I'd better take a look," Kate said, getting up.

"I'll come with you."

About to dissuade the girl, Kate changed her mind. Whatever the reality, it was probably better for her to face it than to go on imagining...

The attics were as eerily dim as before, smelling of dust and musty fabric and unused air. As they entered, a crack of thunder vibrated the roof, making them both jump. Swallowing through a suddenly dry throat, Kate walked the length of the first room, then went on into the next, looking behind boxes and pieces of furniture and stacks of papers. Jocelyn, her white face glimmering in the shadows, watched her from the doorway.

"Nobody here," Kate said when she returned.

Jocelyn let out a long breath and slumped against the doorjamb. "Let's not ever come back in here, all right?"

"Fine with me," Kate said, dusting off her jeans.

Back in Jocelyn's room, they finished their lunch and drained the teapot, Kate keeping a wary eye on Jocelyn, who winced at every lightning flash. There seemed less ferocity in the storm now, as though it were finally passing over.

"I think we should talk to the inspector," Kate said at last.

Jocelyn nodded, still looking shaky. "Should we ring him up?"

Kate shook her head. "Somebody might hear us. We don't want to alarm anybody." Especially the murderer, she thought, but certainly wasn't going to say so. She glanced out of the window. "The rain's letting up, and I don't know about you, but I'd sure like to get out of this house for a while. Why don't we drive to the police station?"

Jocelyn's smile was a little stronger this time around. "Just seeing Inspector Erskine would make me feel better, I think. He's got such a nice craggy face. And he doesn't make fun of my fuzzy things."

"I THINK YOU NEED HELP with your fuzzy things," Kate said carefully as they drove away from Farrington Hall. It had taken them a while to coax Gray Boy out from under Jocelyn's bed and then they had taken him down to stay with Mrs. Hogarth in the kitchen. Now the rain had dwindled to a damp mist, which necessitated the use of windshield wipers, but wasn't hazardous to Kate's driving. "There are experts on ESP and so forth."

Jocelyn nodded. "Grandma Bradford heard about a scholarly type in Edinburgh who has done paranormal research. She's looking into it for me."

"Your grandmother knew about your...problem all along?"

Jocelyn shook her head. "Mummy didn't want me telling anyone. I didn't even tell Daddy. Mummy was afraid I might be taken away from her. But I rang Grandma Bradford up when I knew Mummy was ill. I told her all about it then. Mummy didn't have any symptoms at first, you see, but I *knew* she was very ill and I couldn't persuade her to go to a doctor. So I telephoned Grandma and she talked Mummy into seeing a Harley Street specialist. But he couldn't save her, anyway."

Such a weight of sadness in her voice. Kate took a hand from the steering wheel and touched her knee gently.

Jocelyn managed a smile. "I really am weird, aren't I?"

"No," Kate said firmly. "You are a wonderfully intelligent person with a special gift. It's just a question of learning how to handle that gift."

Jocelyn smiled at her gratefully, then sat back in her seat, obviously feeling much more relaxed.

ONCE AGAIN, the inspector wasn't in, and nobody seemed to know when he would return. Somehow Kate hadn't allowed for that possibility. She had even brought along the Stevenson page, planning on showing it to him. Jocelyn definitely didn't want to talk to anyone else about her fuzzy things, so they walked out of the police station without telling anyone anything. The sun had finally broken through the clouds. The sidewalk was steaming gently.

"What now?" Kate wondered aloud.

"Mrs. Hogarth gave me a shopping list when we left Gray Boy with her," Jocelyn said. "There's a little supermarket around the corner."

Grocery shopping seemed a wonderfully normal thing to do. Kate began to relax as they walked around the store with a small metal cart, picking things up off the shelves. But then someone called out "Miss Wainwright" and Kate almost jumped out of her skin. Obviously she wasn't as relaxed as she'd thought. She turned to see a petite young woman with long riotously curled hair smiling at her. She looked vaguely familiar, but Kate couldn't place her. "You left your film with us to be processed," she said. "It's been ready for some time."

Kate had completely forgotten about the rolls of film she'd dropped off the day of the picnic. "I'll stop by as soon as I've finished here," she said, then started to turn away, only to find a portly middle-aged man blocking her way.

"Did I hear that young lady address you as 'Miss Wainwright'?" the man asked, raising a shapeless tweed hat that had seen better days.

"I'm Kate Wainwright, yes."

He held out his right hand. "Dr. Philip Carlton. I'm your uncle's physician. He told me his relations were coming to visit." He laughed shortly. "Used it as an excuse to postpone his annual physical, actually. I'm glad I had the chance to meet you. You must be the one from America."

Kate nodded, wondering what he'd said that had made some kind of question arise in her mind. "Are you stopping in England long?" the man asked.

"About two weeks to go," Kate said.

"I'm afraid your visit has not been a pleasant one."

There was curiosity showing in his eyes and voice. Well, she wasn't going to satisfy it by talking about the murders. "You must have a poor impression of England," the doctor persisted.

Muttering something noncommittal, Kate started to turn away, then stopped as she realized what had seemed significant. "Uncle Frederick canceled his checkup?" she asked.

The doctor nodded. "Not the first time, either. Objects to being poked at, he says."

"But he said—" She broke off. Frederick had said he'd received bad news about his health from his doctor when he'd gone in for his annual physical. Some other doctor then. No, he'd said Dr. Carlton. She remembered the name because a woman with that name had worked at Sky High Resort.

She became aware that the doctor was waiting for her to finish her sentence. And Jocelyn was staring at her, also. Of course, Jocelyn hadn't been present when Frederick talked about his ill health.

"How *is* my uncle?" Kate asked the man. "I worry about him sometimes. He gets very red in the face. Does he have high blood pressure? Heart trouble?"

"The colonel? Healthy as a horse. He'll probably out-last me," he added, complacently patting his oversize abdomen. "Remind him he's overdue, will you?" he asked.

Kate nodded, her mind churning so rapidly she didn't really notice he'd walked away, until Jocelyn jogged her elbow.

"What's wrong, Kate?" Jocelyn asked, looking alarmed.

Kate shook her head. "Nothing," she said at once. Jocelyn certainly didn't need anything more to worry about. She'd think about all this later, she decided.

"Let's pick up my pictures and go home, okay?" she said as she opened the car door a few minutes later. She even managed a smile. "It ought to be getting close to teatime, don't you think?"

Driving back to the house, she tried to think of any reason Frederick could have for lying about his health, but she couldn't come up with anything at all. Luckily Jocelyn was engrossed in looking at Kate's photographs, admiring the mood shots of Tower Bridge in particular.

Kate was so relieved to see Andrew's Rover drawn up in front of the entrance to Farrington Hall that she was halfway up the steps before she realized the other vehicle was a police car. Sending Jocelyn off to the kitchen with the bag of groceries, she headed for the library.

Inspector Erskine was sitting behind the desk, Andrew opposite. "I've something to tell you," she said to the inspector without pausing for breath.

"All in good time, lassie," the inspector said, indicating Andrew. "We've had a surprising development."

Andrew had stood up when Kate entered the room. Now he set a chair for Kate next to his and sat down with her, taking her hand in his. Agitated as she was, she still felt her usual warm reaction to his touch. She had been angry with him, she remembered. But right now, looking into his concerned gray eyes, she couldn't remember why, could only remember that she loved him. He was still in the business clothes he'd worn to go to London—a dark pin-striped suit, white shirt and what looked like an old school tie. For once his honey blond hair had been combed neatly from its side parting. Every time she saw him she was astonished at how gorgeous he was. Every time she saw him, she wanted to touch him.

"Is Jocelyn all right?" he asked.

"She's fine." No point in worrying him until she had a chance to explain. "What's going on?" she asked.

"I went through the Wainwright papers in my office this morning," he said. "I came across the name Riley."

"I knew that had started you off," she exclaimed.

"The name seemed familiar." He hesitated. "On the way back from London I stopped at *The Hambury Echo* and photocopied that portion of the paper. The inspector has it now."

Inspector Erskine held up a sheet of paper and read from it:

"A worker from a farm near Allercott, one Dennis Riley, was found dead in a ditch yesterday at the side of the Allercott-Market Ridgeway Road. He had been severely beaten, by more than one person, according to the chief constable of the county. The police have no leads at this time. As the altercation had taken place a scant half mile from a local public house where Riley had been drinking and playing darts all evening, it is thought that either robbery was the motive or there had been a drunken quarrel after the pub closed."

Kate frowned. "I'm not sure I understand."

"The name I found in the Wainwright files was *Winnie* Riley," Andrew said.

Kate was still puzzled. "You mean it was a dead end?"

"Not at all," Inspector Erskine said. "According to what Mr. Bradford found out, it seems a Miss Winnie Riley, age fourteen, was employed as a maid by Robert Wainwright in November 1933—soon after Dennis Riley's death."

Kate sat very still. "Mrs. Hogarth came here as a girl of fourteen. She told me so herself."

"And her name is Winifred," Andrew added. He squeezed Kate's hand. "Inspector Erskine sent one of the maids to fetch her, but it seems she's in the middle of making some kind of sauce that is crucial to tonight's dinner and can't be left. We're waiting for her to come now."

"What was it you wanted to say?" the inspector asked.

Kate shook her head. "I think it can wait," she said ambiguously. Telling the inspector and Andrew about Jocelyn's episode, the scary message that had been left in her room or her meeting with Dr. Carlton might just confuse the present issue. But Jocelyn—she'd sent her to take the groceries to Mrs. Hogarth. About to leap from her chair, Kate subsided when someone tapped on the door and opened it and Jocelyn poked her head around the jamb.

"May I come in, Daddy?" the girl asked.

Andrew shook his head. "Afraid not, Fishface. Why don't you wait for me in the drawing room—the others are having tea. Stay with them until I come, all right?"

"Tea? Good. I could eat a horse," Jocelyn said cheerfully. She seemed fully recovered from her earlier experience. "I missed you, Daddy," she added, then glanced at the inspector and looked a question at Kate. Kate shook her head and she nodded conspiratorially and closed the door.

"If Mrs. Hogarth is related to Dennis Riley," Kate said, "what does that mean? Does it make her a suspect as far as Harry and Lottie are concerned? I don't see the connection."

"All in good time, lassie," the inspector said again. And for the moment she had to be content with that.

WINNIE HOGARTH PRIDED herself on her skill with béarnaise sauce. Not everyone could make it successfully. You just couldn't stop stirring, not for a second.

But it was almost impossible to concentrate. A name kept echoing in her mind. *Dennis.* It was Dennis they were wanting to ask her about, she felt sure. She'd known all that past terrible history was going to come out the minute Miss Kate asked her about the Wainwright secret. *Dennis.* Her brother whose broken body had been buried in Saint Mary's churchyard well over forty years ago.

She could see him now, even though she had closed her mind to him all this time. Such a beautiful boy growing into a beautiful man. A bully and a lazy gowk when nobody was watching. Stumbling drunk half the time. She'd have wondered what Miss Gillian saw in him if she hadn't seen them together in her own shabby home—Dennis sober as a judge, laying on the charm with a trowel, smiling at the impressionable girl in a way that would melt the hardest heart, never mind a kind soft one such as Miss Gillian's. Why did wealthy young women never seem to suspect penniless young men might be after more than their bodies?

"Mrs. Hogarth?" The constable was back. And her sauce was ruined. While her mind rummaged in the past the mixture had scorched and stuck to the pan. That's what happened when you stirred up the past. It didn't pay.

Lord, there was such a pain around her heart from thinking about Dennis. Had she loved him, after all, then?

Once maybe, when he was a lad. "I'm coming," she said heavily to the constable. Turning off the gas, she set the pan aside, wondering why her legs were suddenly hurting. They didn't usually, even when she stood the longest time.

She limped into the library, wiping her hands on a dish towel. "A body can't feed this many people when other people keep interrupting with question after question," she said sternly, starting off as she meant to go on.

The inspector gestured at a chair, but she wouldn't sit, even though her indigestion was acting up now, burning at the back of her throat and shooting sharp pains into her chest like darts at a dartboard. She'd feel stronger standing, she decided.

The inspector didn't insist. "You were related to Dennis Riley," he said, making it a statement rather than a question.

"That was all a long time ago," she said.

"But you *were* related?"

"He was my brother." No point in denying it, obviously. "He was a bad lot," she said defensively. "He led me Mum a terrible life for years. And he and me Dad were forever rowing. After they died, I was lucky if Dennis didn't beat me up when he came home drunk, especially if there was no dinner on the table. And how was I supposed to provide dinner with the little bit of money he gave me, I ask you?"

"He was murdered."

"Yes."

"How old were you when Dennis died?" the inspector asked.

The pain seemed to ease slightly. No harm answering this one. "Fourteen," she told him. "We were orphans, both of us. I'd just left school, didn't have a job yet."

"But after Dennis died, Robert Wainwright gave you a job."

She nodded, husbanding her breath, but the inspector seemed to want more. "Me mum taught me to cook and clean before she and my dad took sick," she explained. "Dennis had a job, though—at a farm. He was twenty. But he liked his beer, and women—there wasn't much left from his pay when he got home on a Saturday."

"And then one Saturday he didn't come home," Mr. Andrew said. "He was lying in a ditch at the side of the Allercott-Market Ridgeway Road, beaten and left to die."

"That was verra kind of Mr. Robert to give you a job when your brother died," the inspector said.

"It was." She wasn't going to give an inch more than she had to.

"Who killed your brother?" the inspector asked in a deceptively quiet voice.

Her heart gave a jump and started beating so hard she wondered if the others could hear it. "I don't know," she whispered.

The inspector didn't believe her. She could tell by the way he raised his grizzled eyebrows and cast a glance at Mr. Andrew and Miss Kate. Something was wrong with her breathing suddenly. It was as if she couldn't quite catch her breath. Her eyes were affected, too—the air around her had grown hazy.

"Would you prefer to answer my questions at the police station?" the inspector asked.

She had to strain to hear him. What on earth was wrong with the air in this room? It seemed as if it had water in it. Lord, her legs hurt—she should have sat down when the inspector had told her to. Now she wanted to lie down. *Let the man ask his questions so I can go lie down,* she breathed silently.

"Mrs. Hogarth?"

The pain was there again, rising up into her throat so she couldn't speak, spreading out across her chest and even down into her arm. That bad it was, worse than anything she'd ever felt before. Like a weight pressing against her chest, pushing her down, beating her down.

Somewhere in the room she heard a chair scrape, heard Miss Kate call out, "She's ill, Inspector."

A nice young woman, Miss Kate, she thought vaguely as the room tilted and the floor came up to meet her. Had the lights gone out? No, they were flying around her, popping in front of her eyes like flashbulbs on a camera, making everything look green and purple.

She was lying on the floor. Now what was she doing there? Mrs. Wainwright wasn't going to be happy about that. Someone was lifting her legs up, putting a blanket over her. Mr. Andrew. That was kind of him—to take care of her like this. She wished she could do something for him. "It was because of Miss Gillian," she whispered to the handsome face leaning over her. "Dennis was sweet on Miss Gillian. And Miss Gillian had been seeing him. Rebellious, she was."

"Don't try to talk," Andrew said urgently. "Just rest. The inspector's telephoned for an ambulance."

"That pretty, she was," she persisted, wanting to get the story out now. "Apple of her father's eye. But wild with it. Almost as wild as her brothers. She and Dennis . . ."

"It's all right," Mr. Andrew said. "Don't worry about it now."

"Who is Miss Gillian?" the inspector asked him.

"One of the things we were holding on to, Inspector," Andrew said. "Kate and I discovered photographs of Gillian in the Wainwright family album. She was born in 1913, a twin to Alexander Wainwright. She died in February

1934. I looked for some trace of her in the Wainwright files while I was in London. There were plenty of references to William, Charles, Alexander and George, but no mention of Gillian. My father never heard of her. It's as though she never existed.

"I never told," Mrs. Hogarth muttered. "I promised Mr. Robert I never would, and I didn't. I never told anyone."

"Did the Wainwright brothers kill Dennis because he was seeing their sister?" the inspector asked her.

He wasn't going to leave it be—that much was obvious. She pressed her lips together tightly against another wave of pain. "They followed her when she went to meet Dennis that night," she managed to get out.

"She saw them beat him?"

"That she did, poor thing."

The Wainwright secret, Kate thought. She'd finally found out what it was. The Wainwright brothers were murderers—Charles, George, Alexander, her own grandfather, William. Kneeling on the floor beside the housekeeper, Kate felt sick, but somehow not astonished. There had been a streak of possessiveness in her grandfather that had caused her problems from time to time. Often she'd railed at him that he treated her like a possession. But to beat his sister's lover to death! She felt increasingly nauseated.

The inspector's voice was calm. "Was the colonel with his brothers when they killed Dennis?" he asked.

Kate's head came up and she stared at the inspector. Were his suspicions falling where hers had touched a short time ago?

"I don't know," Mrs. Hogarth said. "I never knew and I never wanted to know. The colonel's been good to me always."

"I take it Robert Wainwright persuaded you not to press charges."

Mrs. Hogarth's color looked somewhat improved now, but she was still breathing in a shallow way and her hand was pressed to her heart. "No witnesses," she gasped. "The police officer who found Dennis knew who done it to him because Dennis lived long enough to tell him, but Mr. Robert . . . he . . ."

"Paid the officer off?"

"Yes."

"And your payment was a job, a home, security," the inspector said, with sympathy in his voice.

"There wasn't anything I could do," the woman said, tears gathering at the corners of her eyes and running down into her hair. "Mr. Robert had already sent the boys away. He was terribly angry."

"Miss Gillian died," Andrew said softly. "What did she die of, Mrs. Hogarth? Do you know?"

Her head moved weakly from side to side. "I promised Mr. Robert," she said, and closed her eyes. It was obvious she wasn't going to tell any more.

"I'M NOT SURE all that helped as far as our current investigation is concerned," the inspector said gloomily. The ambulance men had come and gone, carrying Mrs. Hogarth away with them. Fortunately the men had managed to stabilize her condition before they left.

The ambulance's arrival had of course brought the rest of the family on the run. The inspector had assured them all there was nothing they could do. Mrs. Hogarth was in good hands now. "It would seem she might have been having symptoms for a while," he told Frederick. "Miss Kate told me she complained of indigestion. People often confuse heart symptoms with digestive problems."

Frederick had seemed very concerned with Mrs. Hogarth's comfort, assuring her he would come to see her later to make certain she had everything she needed. Watching his upright, military figure as he escorted the litter as far as the front door, then returned to shepherd everyone back to the drawing room, Kate couldn't accept the suspicions that had begun gnawing at her thoughts.

She became aware that the inspector and Andrew were looking at her, evidently waiting for her to say something. She looked back at them blankly.

"You had something you wanted to tell me, lassie?" the inspector asked.

Kate took a deep breath. "Uncle Frederick lied to all of us," she blurted out. "He told us he was in failing health. But his doctor says that isn't so. I met the doctor in Allercott a little while ago. He told me Uncle Frederick could live a long time."

"I'm no sure I see..."

Kate leaned forward. "If all the potential heirs believed Frederick was going to die soon, there would be a sense of urgency to getting him to change his will. It would make it seem more likely that one of us would kill Harry so we could inherit. If we'd known Uncle Frederick might live another ten or twenty years, the urgency wouldn't be there and our motivation wouldn't be as strong."

"He did keep repeating that one of the potential heirs must be responsible," the inspector murmured. He glanced at Andrew. "It was the colonel himself told me about those reports you had."

Andrew stared at him. "Was he just being truthful, or putting the others in a bad light?"

"Take your choice," the inspector said.

"*You* believed it was one of the heirs, didn't you?"

"Aye, for a while. Until it seemed the colonel himself might have been the target. I'm still inclined to think that. If Frederick was with his brothers, maybe someone's been waiting a chance for revenge. Not Mrs. Hogarth, but someone with a grudge because of the killing.''

"Something's bothering me here," Andrew said. "I've kept quiet because of client confidentiality, but now it seems necessary to tell you that Frederick never did change his will to make Harry the beneficiary. Perhaps he intended to, but he didn't even though he told everyone Harry was to inherit.''

"Who does benefit?" the inspector asked.

"After the disposition of the house, a generous allocation to Hilary and a few minor legacies, the rest goes to Robbie, Sikander, Elaine and Kate. Equal shares.''

Kate stared at Andrew. "Lottie wasn't going to get anything, anyway?''

"Not a penny." Andrew paused. "Frederick had an alibi for the time of Harry's murder," he pointed out. "He was in his study. He heard Robbie playing the piano. Robbie confirmed that he was playing at the time.''

"Robbie plays a lot," Kate said softly. "You'd be fairly safe assuming that Robbie was playing at any time.''

There was a silence. Then the inspector touched a large envelope that was lying on the desk in front of him. "Here is another puzzle for us," he said. "This was delivered to the station by the postman a couple of days ago. Addressed to me. No return address. However, as this is the only murder investigation I'm involved in..." Without completing the sentence, he reached into the envelope and pulled out a pair of dark blue socks that had been folded together.

"Why would anyone send you socks?" Andrew asked.

"A verra good question.''

All three of them gazed at the socks in fascination. And then the inspector laid the envelope down and Kate caught her breath. The address had been printed, but there was a certain angularity to the letters and a flourish to the final strokes. "That's Sikander's writing," she said abruptly. "I saw it once when he wrote down a book title for Joss."

The inspector's hazel eyes came up to meet hers, gleaming with satisfaction. "Well done, lassie," he said, then dispatched a constable immediately in search of Sikander.

There was no telltale blush to give the handsome young Indian man away when he caught sight of the socks lying on the desk. But the muscle in his cheek jerked spasmodically and his eyes blinked rapidly behind his glasses.

"Why did you send these to me?" the inspector demanded without preamble.

Sikander swallowed convulsively, then took a deep breath and squared his shoulders, standing straight as a soldier awaiting his own execution. "It appeared to me they might have some significance," he said in his singsong voice.

"And what made you think that?" the inspector asked patiently.

Sikander swallowed again. "It was when I was practicing yoga in the courtyard after tea on the day before Harry's body was found."

"The day he was killed then."

"I suppose that is so."

"What did you see?" The inspector's voice was very calm, but he was sitting on the edge of his seat.

Sikander hesitated, his eyes shifting sideways in a hunted way. "It was foggy, you understand. But when I rose to enter the house, I saw these socks, lying beside a container of flowers. I picked them up. They were wet."

It took Kate a minute to realize the significance of what Sikander had said. "Our feet got wet when we waded in the river to pull Harry's body out," she told the inspector excitedly.

"Mine, too, whilst I was looking around the area," he said.

Kate looked at the socks again. "The murderer's could have got wet when he . . ."

"Pulled him in," the inspector finished for her. "He removed them perhaps before walking across the meadow."

"And accidentally dropped them in the courtyard on his way into the house," Andrew added.

"You're saying 'he,'" Kate commented. "Are you sure . . ."

"They're men's socks, lassie."

"I wear men's socks sometimes, with my sneakers," she pointed out.

"Did you see who dropped them?" the inspector demanded of Sikander.

Sikander pushed his glasses into place on his nose and shook his head violently. "I saw no one. Only the socks. I dried them in my bathroom. I did not know what to do. Then I had the idea of sending them to you anonymously. I was afraid, you see, afraid that if . . . the person knew I had found the socks, I would be in danger. Like Lottie. I did wrong to keep them, I know. But I was afraid, you see, so very afraid."

He was afraid now. His slender body was trembling, his hands twisting each other spasmodically. Surely, Kate thought, if he had seen *only* the socks, he would have no cause for alarm. But if he knew who had dropped them. . . .

"What we need here is the Spanish Inquisition," the inspector muttered, obviously frustrated. He fixed Sikander with his most accusing stare. "I will put it to you, Mr. Balraj, that you saw the owner of these socks entering the house and saw him drop them. Possibly that person did not see you in the mist, or thought that you were in some kind of trance, practicing your yoga. It was perhaps just a curi-

osity at that time, as you did not know Harry Wainwright
was dead. But you had witnessed some strangely furtive
behavior and thought there might be some advantage in
keeping the socks.''

He was right on the money, Kate felt sure. His mouth
hanging open, Sikander was looking at him in a startled
way, as if he were a soothsayer of some kind.

"I put it to you that after you found out about the murder, you held on to those socks thinking that you would
bring them out at a strategic moment," the inspector continued. "You were perhaps thinking you might demand
payment from the person who owned the socks."

Sikander's head was again moving from side to side in
obvious agitation. "I saw nobody," he insisted, and no
matter how the inspector alternately cajoled and threatened him, he stuck to his denial.

Finally the inspector let him go, cautioning him in no
uncertain terms that he was to say nothing about this interview to anyone.

"It isn't enough," the inspector said after the door was
safely closed again. "I mean as far as the murders are concerned. We have no proof the colonel is responsible, even
if the socks turn out to be his."

"We could be wrong altogether," Andrew agreed. "I
cannot imagine Frederick killing anyone."

"He did in the war," the inspector murmured. "It's
perhaps easier to kill if you've done it before." He shook
his head. "I wish Mrs. Hogarth could have managed to tell
us how Miss Gillian died. I'm curious as to whether her
death pertains to the rest of it. If she was murdered . . ."

A thought came to Kate like a ray of light between
clouds, bringing hope with it. "Maybe Gillian's death was
the Wainwright secret rather than Dennis Riley's death,"
she said slowly. "Maybe Harry had found out about her

death. Or maybe Uncle Frederick was there when Dennis was killed and someone just found out about it and is out for revenge. And in the fog mistook Harry for Frederick. Maybe the inspector was right in his theory about Frederick being the intended victim.''

"Frederick lied about his health,'' Andrew pointed out.

"Perhaps that could be explained,'' Kate said. Then she sat up very straight. An image had shot into her mind with astonishing clarity. The attic. Andrew lifting down the photograph album, setting some folders aside.

Standing up, she headed toward the door. ''There's something I have to check into,'' she said over her shoulder. "Don't go anywhere. I'll be right back.''

Chapter Thirteen

Kate was halfway up the attic stairs, when she realized she hadn't yet told Inspector Erskine about the Stevenson page or Jocelyn's "fuzzy thing." Which had also had some connection with the attic. Suddenly nervous, she entered the attic cautiously, looking around carefully once she'd switched on the overhead light.

There was still no sign of a human presence, dead or alive. Letting out a long breath, she made her way to the bureau where Andrew had found the photo album. The album was still there; so were the manila folders, stamped—just as she'd remembered—medical records. Going through them carefully, straining to read the cramped handwriting in the dim light, she discovered they had been written up by a Dr. Grainger. An earlier physician who had retired and passed on the records to the family?

There was a chart for each Wainwright: Robert, Elizabeth, their sons—their only daughter, Gillian. Her scalp tightening, Kate seized the folder and sat down on the floor, unable to resist a peek before taking it downstairs.

Gillian had evidently been a healthy child and teenager, with few bouts of illness and only a couple of minor accidents. Until February 1934, when she had miscarried, in her sixth month of pregnancy, a stillborn baby girl. Gillian had been pregnant. Probably the Wainwright brothers had known that.

Counting, Kate reckoned Gillian had been two months pregnant when Dennis was killed. Reading on, she discovered that Gillian had died two days after the miscarriage.

No wonder Elizabeth Wainwright had died later that same year. Of a broken heart, Bennett Coby had said. First her sons had killed her daughter's lover. Then they had been banished from their home. And her daughter had died after giving birth to a dead child. How much could a mother bear?

Overwhelmed by the dimension of the tragedy that had befallen her family so many years ago, Kate squatted on the attic floor, staring dazedly at the record of Gillian's death. Gillian had been ill throughout her pregnancy, it appeared. Which was hardly surprising, considering that she had witnessed her brothers beating her lover to death.

It was very still in the attic. Yet not as still as it had been. It seemed as if something had changed, as though there had been a disturbance of air—a movement of some kind. And now Kate could feel a prickling in the back of her neck, as though someone was looking at her, watching her.

Turning quickly, she took in a great gasp of air. Frederick Wainwright, straight and soldierly in his tweed jacket and well-pressed gray flannels, stood a few feet away, looking directly at her. In his right hand, held straight down at his side, was the gun she had last seen on the dining-room sideboard.

"What have you found, Kate?" he asked quietly.

Swallowing hard, Kate got awkwardly to her feet, clutching the folder in front of her as though for protection. "Gillian's medical records," she said, her voice rasping.

"Gilly died," he said sadly. "There was no heart left in her, no wish to live. She just…gave up. The baby must have known it and given up, too. My brothers were to blame."

"I know."

He nodded solemnly. "Mrs. Hogarth. I saw you watching me when I went with her to the door. I guessed she had told you about Dennis." He lifted the gun and looked at it, then at her. "You've been asking an awful lot of questions, Kate, my dear."

"You did those things to me, didn't you?" Kate asked, trying to keep her voice steady. "You put the Stevenson page in my room, destroyed my film."

"'I feel very strongly about putting questions,'" he quoted softly. "Rather apt, don't you think?" He sighed. "I even told you to your face to stop asking questions, remember, but you wouldn't. I saw you in the grounds from time to time, overheard you on other occasions. Always asking questions."

His voice was heavy with sadness and there was a look in his blue eyes she had never seen there before. A look that was not quite sane. Her heart was beating irregularly, rapidly, frantic as a wild bird trying to escape confinement.

She took a long deep breath. *Speak calmly,* she instructed herself. *Don't make any sudden movements. Don't raise your voice.* "You weren't involved in the killing of Dennis Riley, were you, Uncle Frederick?" she asked.

He shook his head. "I tried to stop my brothers, but they were like madmen—drunk, all of them—furious that Gillian had lowered herself to having an affair with a farm worker."

"You were there then."

"I was there. But I had no part in it. I loved Gilly. I grieved when she died as much as my mother did. My poor mother. It was their fault—Will and George and Charles and Alexander. I hated them for it. And for the whispers."

"People guessed who'd killed Dennis Riley?"

"And took it for granted that I was one of them." He shrugged, lowering the gun again, to Kate's relief. "After a while, they forgot about it all. Except for Peter."

Kate frowned. "Peter?"

"My father's brother." He sighed heavily. "Harry's father."

A tingling sensation began at the back of Kate's neck and traveled down her spine, causing her whole body to tremble. "Harry's *father* knew about Riley's murder?"

"And left a written record when he died six months ago." A distinct note of suppressed fury had come into his voice now, and the off-balance expression was more pronounced in his eyes.

"Harry discovered the Wainwright secret among his father's papers after he died?"

He laughed in a brittle way that froze Kate's breath in her throat. "Sounds terribly melodramatic, calling it the 'Wainwright secret,' don't you think?"

"That's what Lottie called it."

His blue eyes seemed even brighter than usual in the dim attic light. "Lottie. Yes. Her father—my brother George—talked too much, also. They resented me—all of them, because I was innocent and my father knew it. So I could stay home and inherit the bulk of the fortune. It didn't occur to any of them that mine was not the happiest of lives, living with my tyrant of a father after his other sons had been banished in disgrace, and especially after his beloved daughter died."

"You were saying that Harry discovered the secret—about Dennis Riley's death." Should she edge closer to him, try to get around him as they talked, make a dash for the attic stairs?

As though he'd read her thoughts, he lifted the gun again, not in a threatening way, but just a little, as though to remind her he was holding it. As if she could forget.

"I take it Harry was blackmailing you?" she said as evenly as she could manage.

"Of course. He wanted everything. Peter, you see, had always resented the fact that Robert had inherited the larger share of James's fortune. And Peter was a gambler, so much of his inheritance had passed through his hands."

He laughed in a way that had no mirth to it, and once again Kate's blood ran cold. Her heart was still pounding erratically. A voice was screaming in her brain, saying this couldn't be happening. But it *was* happening, and she had to find a way out of it.

It was not a good time to remember Jocelyn's "fuzzy thing" and the person with a bloody head lying on the attic floor. Joss hadn't known if the body was that of a man or a woman.

Keep him talking, she commanded herself again. Surely Andrew and the inspector would soon realize she'd been gone for a while. Why the hell hadn't she told them where she was going? How much time had passed, anyway? Probably not much. It seemed an eternity.

Gripping the folder so tightly that her fingers hurt, she asked, "Harry threatened to expose the secret?"

"To the newspapers. How could I prove I was innocent? My mother and brothers and sister were dead. Mrs. Hogarth knew only what my father had told her—and he was dead."

"But surely, even if Harry had talked, after so many years . . ."

"The title!" His voice was suddenly intense, high-pitched. "Any breath of scandal, no matter how old, would have meant death to my chances of getting the title. And I was determined to have it. Neither of them was able to get it, not Grandfather James, nor my father, Robert. But I was going to walk up the Grand Staircase at Buckingham Palace and through the East Gallery to the Ball Room. I was going to kneel in front of my sovereign so that she could touch my shoulders with a sword. I was going to be Sir Frederick Wainwright, more than the sum of my father and grandfather put together. More than my brothers."

"And Harry threatened to ruin that." She made her voice sympathetic, though she felt increasingly nauseated. At any minute Frederick could decide to raise the gun and shoot her dead. No matter that it wasn't a smart or logical thing to do.

"You didn't want to pay Harry?" she asked.

"I did pay him," he answered. "I paid him for six months and he wanted more—he wanted me to make him my heir. So I told him I had altered my will in his favor. But I had no intention of letting my money go to Harry Wainwright. That's why I invited the whole family here, hoping one of them might take matters into their own hands." He laughed again. "Harry was very frightened when they came. He wasn't a sensitive man, but even he could feel their resentment. They wanted him out of the way, he told me that evening."

"By the river?" If only she had a tape recorder. Would her word be acceptable in court? She had no idea. She wasn't even sure Frederick would let her live to go to court.

"By the river," Frederick agreed. "He insisted I meet him there, out of earshot of the family. He was afraid they would turn on him. I must make it clear that if anything happened to him, none of them would inherit. He went on and on dreaming up various ways I could ensure his safety. Before long we were shouting at each other. But then I realized it was possible the others *could* be blamed if anything happened to him. I had taken my gun along in case he turned nasty, but my brain seemed very cool all at once and I saw that was not the way, the gun might be traced to me. At the same time I saw the walking stick he'd brought along. He'd leaned it against one of the beech trees. When he turned away from me for a moment I picked it up and struck him with it. He wasn't dead, but I was afraid if I hit him again there would be too much blood and I'd get some on me, so I simply dragged him into the river and waited until he died."

Kate shuddered. "You took the cane, the walking stick, back to the house?"

"After cleaning the blood off it, yes. I cleaned it very carefully. If Lottie hadn't seen Harry carrying it, no one would have known it was the murder weapon."

"Inspector Erskine knew," Kate said carefully. "There were fragments of the wood—stinkwood—in Harry's head wound."

He brushed his mustache with careful fingers, smiling wryly. "I didn't know." He looked quite normal for a second—so much like her grandfather that she felt old awe and respect welling up. But Grandfather Will had been a murderer, too.

"Why did you kill Lottie?" Kate asked.

"She guessed I'd killed Harry," he said promptly. Why was he so willing to confess. Because the pressures that caused a person to commit murder also made it necessary to tell someone—anyone—about it? And because he wasn't going to let her live to repeat any of it. But surely he couldn't expect to get away with killing someone in his own attic with his own gun.

Unless he were to say he mistook her for an intruder, the mysterious murderer showing up again.

On that thought, she swallowed hard and tried to tighten the muscles in her legs to stop them from trembling. Frederick was still talking. She must pay attention, watch for any opportunity to escape.

"Lottie was as sly as her father used to be," he said. "Snooping around, remembering that the cane Harry used was back in the stand the following day, using it herself later to deliberately provoke a reaction. She wasn't going to tell the police, she assured me. All I had to do was give her enough money to keep her winery going. It was the same story as Harry's. Give, give, give, then give some more. She brought the walking stick with her and I took it from her and hit her with it. Then I took it far out in the woods and hid it, and joined the others for the trip to Windsor."

"You didn't burn it in the fireplace, then."

"That would have been stupid. Anyone might have seen me doing it."

Anyone might have seen him walking into the woods with the cane, Kate thought, but didn't say—obviously no one *had* seen him, just as no one had seen him strike Lottie or Harry. Only Sikander had seen anything at all.

"She pointed it at me," Frederick said, evidently referring to Lottie and the walking stick. "Jabbed it at me, making those awful remarks she always made, in that peculiar Australian slang." He shook his head. "I was surrounded by stupid people," he said wearily. "Harry, Lottie—Hilary and Bennett and their puppy love." He grimaced. "I put Amy Sanderham up to letting the police know about their juvenile antics. That gave me some satisfaction."

No wonder he hadn't wanted Hilary to talk to Mrs. Sanderham ever again.

Kate froze. He had lifted the gun again and was pointing it at her. Now he glanced from it to her as though deciding how much distance was between them.

"Inspector Erskine's still in the library with Andrew," Kate said hurriedly. "He's waiting for me. I'd better go."

"I don't think so, Kate," Frederick said.

"But he knows you killed Harry and Lottie. Dr. Carlton said you hadn't been in for your annual physical. He said you lied when you told us you were dying."

He shook his head. "Silly thing for me to say, I suppose. Thought it would divert suspicion."

"Andrew told the inspector you'd never altered your will in Harry's favor," Kate went on desperately. "Sikander sent him your socks."

The gun wavered. "My socks?"

"You dropped them in the courtyard. Sikander *saw* you." This was no courtroom; she didn't have to worry about corroborating evidence.

He was holding the gun very steadily now.

"Kate!" Andrew called up the stairs. "Are you up there?"

Frederick half turned his head and Kate hurried toward him while he was distracted. But as she was about to pass him, he whirled and pointed the gun at her again. Her heart was beating like a trip-hammer, but she kept her voice deliberately calm. "Andrew's looking for me. I'd better go to him."

He shook his head. "I can't allow you to do that, Kate."

"You won't shoot me, Uncle Frederick," Kate said firmly. "You're very fond of me. And there's been enough killing in the Wainwright family. It has to stop. The inspector knows everything. You can't get away with any more deaths."

With that, she brushed past him and walked steadily to the doorway, her back held stiffly in expectation of the bullet she was almost sure he was going to fire.

But he let her go.

As she hurtled down the attic stairs she called out, "Get down—he's got a gun."

And as Andrew grabbed her and pulled her around the corner into the hall, the gun fired, the sound not nearly as loud as she might have expected, but unmistakable. For one split second, Kate thought Frederick had fired at her or Andrew, but then she realized, as she saw the horror in Andrew's upward glance, that Frederick had fired the gun at himself.

Below them on the stairs, footsteps sounded, coming up. A second later the inspector and two of his men passed them, Erskine glancing at her as if to make sure she was all right.

Then Hilary appeared on the lower landing, Bennett close behind her.

"Stay where you are," Andrew called down.

Her strained white face looked up at them. "It's Frederick, isn't it?" she said faintly.

"Yes," Kate said. How gaunt Hilary looked, she thought. As though she had suddenly aged ten or fifteen years.

Behind them on the attic stairs, the inspector appeared, looking down at them. "Colonel Wainwright is dead," he announced.

Chapter Fourteen

Kate and Andrew and Jocelyn had their final breakfast with what was left of the Wainwright family in the drawing room. Since Frederick's suicide and the subsequent horror of yet another inquest and funeral, no one had wanted to eat in the formal dining room with its memories of Frederick looking so distinguished at the table's head, Lottie making her colorful remarks from the sidelines, Roger, in his former role of Emory, stammering in response. Roger had left a week ago, flying thankfully back to Australia.

Kate liked the cluttered Victorian drawing room with its ticking clocks and the morning sun streaming in to strike gold from picture frames. But in spite of the cheerful ambience, the people gathered at the round table seemed very subdued. It would be a long time before those present would get over the events of the past month.

As Kate served herself at a side table, Bennett stood up, looking as if he were about to make a speech. Which he was, it turned out.

"I think you should all know that I'm staying on until Farrington Hall is turned over to the National Trust. Afterward Hilary will be coming home with me."

Neither Robbie nor Elaine seemed surprised, so Kate guessed he must have discussed the subject with them beforehand. Actually, they were both looking quite pleased, which seemed to bode well for Hilary's future.

"We haven't made any long-term decisions yet," Bennett added. "But I'm sure you'll agree a complete change of life-style will be the best thing in the world for her."

Apparently Hilary didn't object to Bennett's newfound take charge manner. As he sat down beside her, she smiled at him, an edge of relief showing in her eyes. During the two weeks since Frederick's death, she had seemed mostly bewildered and confused, but now, evidently, she was beginning to recover.

"Imagine," Kate murmured to Andrew as he joined her at the buffet, "if they end up getting married, Hilary will be Robbie and Elaine's stepmother."

Picking up a fat sausage with a pair of tongs, Andrew laughed softly. "I don't imagine they'll be a problem to her for long, do you?" He hesitated, glancing over his shoulder. Conversation had become general and no one was paying particular attention to them. "As soon as Frederick's will is proved, Elaine will get the beauty salon she's always wanted, and Robbie will build his acoustically perfect house."

"And make love to beautiful women," Kate added.

"Not such a bad fate."

"I'm going to stay in England," Sikander said to Kate as she took her seat at the table. Behind his spectacles his dark eyes were glowing with pleasure. "Aunt Hilary has invited me to stay here with her until I can arrange things."

"I have to ask you, Sikander," Kate said softly, first checking to make sure nobody was listening. "*Did* you see Uncle Frederick when he dropped his socks in the courtyard?"

He choked and reached for a glass of juice, then swallowed almost the whole glass in a single gulp. "A crumb of toast caught in my throat," he explained, which Kate found hard to believe. "What was it you wanted to know?"

Kate looked at him directly. His eyes shifted. "Ah, yes. I remember. Frederick. But you were there, Kate, when I told the inspector I saw no one."

"I was there," she agreed. "But I think you lied."

He swallowed convulsively again, then straightened his bow tie and bowed his head slightly. "You will remember the story I told you about the holy man who ate pages of the Bible and was poisoned when he reached a colored illustration?"

"You were afraid Uncle Frederick would kill you, as he killed Lottie?"

The giveaway muscle in his cheek was jerking uncontrollably. "I am going to buy a country house," he said carefully.

He wasn't going to answer her question, obviously. Cautious to the end, he wasn't going to take any chances on getting in trouble for withholding information. "Okay, Sikander," she murmured. "Let's just leave it that I'm pretty sure you did see him, but you were afraid to tell anyone."

"It is my ambition to become an English gentleman," he said stiffly, still not giving an inch. "I hope to find a house just like Farrington Hall."

Apparently he had decided to ignore his religious teachings against changing his station in life.

"Good luck," Jocelyn said, coming to sit with them, a loaded plate in her hands. "Not my idea of cozy living quarters, I'm afraid." She had spoken fairly loudly and Hilary glanced up. Jocelyn looked shyly at her, blushing to the roots of her new hairstyle. "That was rude—forgive me. I didn't mean . . ."

Hilary smiled in her usual sweet manner. "It's all right, Jocelyn. I've never felt completely comfortable here myself."

Imagine forty years of not feeling comfortable, Kate thought. The things people put themselves through out of a sense of duty.

"I hope you will have a good trip back to the United States, Kate," Sikander said in his formal way. "You will be leaving London on Wednesday?"

Kate nodded absently, pondering the reason for the swift, definitely secretive glance Andrew and Jocelyn had exchanged in response to Sikander's question. Until Wednesday, she would be staying with Andrew and Jocelyn at Andrew's house in Hampstead. No one had seemed unduly surprised at this. Elaine was the only one who had commented on it, sounding envious.

What were Andrew and Jocelyn up to? Kate wondered. Surely they weren't planning a family get-together at the airport? Much as she felt a certain fondness for this family of hers, she had no desire to extend her time with them. In the future perhaps she'd be able to face seeing them again from time to time, but right now she just wanted to escape Farrington Hall and the dreadful memories associated with it.

THEY DROVE through fiendish traffic all the way to London, Jocelyn in the Rover's front seat next to her father, Kate in the back with Gray Boy curled on her lap. Kate enjoyed just looking out of the window at the unfamiliar cars and the people driving them. When they reached the city, she gazed excitedly at the crowds and the buildings, delighted to recognize the name on the Edwardian bulk of a huge department store they passed after turning left on Brompton road. Harrods.

"This is Knightsbridge, isn't it?" she said as Andrew stopped to let a small crowd surge across the street in front of them. "I thought you lived in Hampstead."

Jocelyn giggled, though Kate couldn't think what she'd said that was funny.

"I do, indeed," Andrew said.

Jocelyn giggled again. "My friend Penelope lives here," she said, turning a mischievous face to Kate.

Puzzled, Kate leaned forward between the two of them, watching as Andrew drove down a narrow street lined with tall houses built of brick and pulled to a stop beside a lamppost. "We're going to visit your friend Penelope?"

"*I'm* going to visit Penelope," Jocelyn said, reaching back to fondle Gray Boy's ears. "For four days, actually."

"And four nights," Andrew added under his breath.

All was suddenly clear. "You worked all this out without consulting me," Kate accused. "We're supposed to just drop Jocelyn off here and go on without her?"

"Yon's a smart lassie, Fishface," Andrew said to Jocelyn with a fair imitation of Inspector Erskine's Scottish burr.

"You don't mind, do you, Kate?" Jocelyn asked. She gazed at Kate with total innocence edged with a certain complicity.

Kate looked from her to Andrew, who was also gazing at her, his expression not quite as confident as usual. Her heart did a couple of riotous turns against her ribs and her breath caught somewhere deep in her throat. She truly had looked forward to spending this time with Joss and her father. After Frederick's suicide, she had felt as though she had stumbled into dark murky water that had closed over her head. Andrew's invitation to finish out her time in England at his house in Hampstead had seemed a lifeline pulling her free of the numbing weight of gloom that filled Farrington Hall.

It had never occurred to her that Andrew would finally find a way for them to be alone, something they hadn't managed very often. The prospect, however, was infinitely appealing. "No, I don't mind at all," she said faintly but sincerely, and was rewarded by one of Andrew's slow-spreading smiles that lit candles deep in his gray eyes.

Feeling stunned, Kate sat limply in the car as Jocelyn and Andrew were greeted at the front door of one of the tall houses by an attractive brunette and an excited twelve-year-old girl. The girl was appealingly plump and jolly and kept exclaiming over Joss's new haircut.

As Andrew came back to the car, Jocelyn suddenly darted in front of him, climbed in beside Kate and hugged her and Gray Boy fiercely. "I'll see you on Wednesday morning," she said.

Her smile was so radiant, there was no need for Kate to question if she minded being dropped off at her friend's house. She hugged her back. "You are going to see me off on Wednesday, then?" Kate asked. It was difficult to ignore the emptiness that wrapped around her heart at the thought of her departure. It would have been hard enough to face the loneliness that awaited her in Seattle if she hadn't met Andrew. Having known him, having loved him, how would she ever get over him? It was going to be just as hard to leave Joss.

Jocelyn's smile widened. "I'm not worried about that," she said.

Which didn't really make sense, and left Kate pondering after the girl had given her one last hug, dropped a kiss on the cat's head and raced off into her friend's house.

"Quite a conspiracy," Kate remarked with mock indignation as Andrew confidently maneuvered the Rover around a bright red double decker bus and into the traffic on Kensington Road. She was sitting beside him now. He'd insisted she and the cat move forward before they'd left Jocelyn's friend's house. "It might even be called kidnapping."

He smiled sideways at her. "I've always rather fancied the idea of throwing my woman over my shoulder and carrying her off to my lair."

Looking at his muscular physique, she grinned, unable to keep up the pretense of annoyance. "You could do it, too."

"And may yet if this traffic jam doesn't clear itself." He reached for her hand and clasped it tightly for a moment, then released it. They were both suddenly silent.

The horror and sadness of the past weeks were still with them, Andrew realized. It hovered behind them like a malignant ghost, touching their shoulders with cold, bony fingers.

"Do you think Aunt Hilary knew?" Kate asked.

Obviously her feelings were in tune with Andrew's own. He mulled over her question as he drove past Hyde Park, heading for Edgeware Road and the way out of the city. "She told you she was frightened," he said at last.

"I thought for a while she was afraid Bennett might have killed Harry, mistaking him for Frederick. But I guess that wasn't it at all."

"She could hardly live with Frederick for forty years and not realize he was...well, disturbed." Horror touched him again as he remembered Kate hurtling down the stairs to his arms. She had faced death in that attic. If Frederick had killed her... He shuddered, then forced himself to erase the image of Kate facing Frederick from his mind. One good thing about that image, though—he had known when she'd come down those stairs into his arms that he could never let her go again. Now all he had to do was convince her.

"Hilary will be all right," he assured her. "Bennett will see to that." He glanced at the cat in Kate's lap. "At least everyone's taken care of now. Hilary, Bennett, Elaine and Robbie, Sikander—even Gray Boy. When Mrs. Hogarth is fully recovered, as seems probable, she'll have her pension and her cottage in Allercott. As for Roger—well, we can only hope he'll be able to find a job when he gets back to Australia."

Kate bent over the cat again, ostensibly to pet it. "I gave him a small stake," she admitted sheepishly.

Andrew laughed heartily and she looked sideways at him, obviously ready to defend her action. "I did, too," he admitted, and her laughter joined his.

And then she looked at him directly, turning on her seat to do so, appearing very grave. "It's hard to imagine that we never suspected Frederick," she said slowly.

"I'm not so sure we didn't. Subconsciously we must have wondered. When we were risking our foolish necks asking questions of everyone in sight, we didn't ask any really meaningful ones of Frederick. And you wondered why Frederick would make Harry his heir in the first place."

"But he explained that. And you agreed. An Englishman wants an Englishman to take over for him, you said."

He felt decidedly embarrassed. "Englishmen tend to think that way, I'm afraid. I'm depending on you to save me from my own insularity."

There was a deliberate note of hope in that, but she was too engrossed at the moment to notice. At least, he hoped that was the reason she didn't question the statement.

"You wondered, too, didn't you?" she said after a moment. "You were worried about Frederick's gun."

"He said it was an old relic, probably useless, but before I covered it with the napkin I saw that it was absolutely clean and obviously recently lubricated." He sighed. "I didn't allow myself to pursue the thought, unfortunately."

"I don't understand why he would show the gun so publicly."

"Judging by what he said about it at the time, he wanted to convince us he was taking care of us, protecting us from the murderer. Misdirection—the same technique magicians use."

"But what do you think pushed him over the edge?" Kate asked. "Was it just his obsession with getting the title?"

"That and years of resentment over his brothers' behavior. And Harry's threat of exposure, of course."

"He said he was hoping one of *us* would bump Harry off," Kate murmured. "I guess he wasn't too sane even then."

He touched her hands where they lay clasped tightly on top of the big gray cat. "It's over, Kate. It's all over."

She let out a long breath and managed a smile that brought a glow to her brown eyes. He had missed that glow.

"It is over, isn't it?" she said softly.

And suddenly it was. The spectral presence Andrew had felt hovering behind them seemed to have withdrawn, as though their talking about the people and the events they had passed through had cleansed the air of the attendant bad feelings.

"On to Hampstead," Andrew said with a rush of good spirits, and as he headed up through Saint John's Wood, he led their conversation back to Jocelyn and her excitement over her new look.

"You've seemed more relaxed with her this past week," Kate said. "You haven't had that questioning look."

"Probably because my questions have been answered," he said.

It took Kate a minute to realize the significance of that. Then she turned to him with a smile that was full of joy. "You've found out you really are her father."

He let his own smile blossom as it had kept doing since he'd discovered the truth. "Not enough to convince a court of law perhaps, but enough to convince me. I rang up Jocelyn's doctor a couple of weeks ago and was told Jocelyn's blood type is O positive. So is mine, which didn't necessarily prove anything. But it was hopeful. So I finally screwed up my courage enough to consult the police surgeon and found out Harry's blood type was AB negative. There's no possibility of an AB negative type fathering an O positive child. And I *know* Harry was Olivia's only other lover at that time. So I'm the only possible candidate for fatherhood."

"I'm so glad, Andrew," Kate said, leaning closer to him and taking hold of his arm.

Lord, he wanted to kiss her.

"What if you'd found out Harry *could* have been her father," Kate added worriedly.

"She'd still have been my daughter, Kate," he said confidently. "She would never have known there was any doubt in my mind at all." He let out a sigh of contentment. "But it's rather nice to know for sure, all the same."

"Are all Englishmen addicted to understatement?" Kate asked.

"A national trait," he admitted.

Their silence now was companionable and definitely friendly. More than friendly. Andrew could feel excitement building between them as they drove closer to

Hampstead, and he was pretty sure it wasn't all emanating solely from him. Even the cat, sitting in Kate's lap, was purring like a motorboat.

"How lovely," Kate exclaimed as they drove along Hampstead High Street. "This is just as I always imagined England to be—hilly streets and little shops and pubs." There were all kinds of shops—bookstores and trendy clothes, houses painted black and white, with mullioned windows and flower boxes exuberantly overflowing with blooms of all kinds. The old-fashioned lamp standards delighted her, most of them painted in bright colors. And when they turned a couple of corners and Andrew said, "Here we are," she sighed with appreciation of the row of terraced Georgian houses washed in pastel colors and fronted with wrought-iron railings.

"We'll walk on the Heath tomorrow," Andrew promised. "There are spectacular views of London from there. I'll take you to Jack Straw's Castle, too—it's a big plush pub with Victorian overtones—and The Spaniards Inn—it goes back to the time of the highwayman Dick Turpin. And you'll have to see the poet Keats's house, of course. Pure Regency—beautiful."

"Four days," Kate said with a sigh.

"And nights," Andrew added happily.

THE INTERIOR of Andrew's house was decidedly masculine but extremely attractive, mixing traditional and contemporary styles in a way that spelled comfort to all the senses. Add a few flowers, some pretty cushions, and scatter some books around on the tables, and the place would be perfect, Kate decided as Andrew guided her through. Gray Boy was obviously satisfied with his new home. After stalking alongside Kate for a while, he found a nicely overstuffed armchair and settled happily in for an all-over bath. It had been Jocelyn, of course, who had worried what was going to happen to Gray Boy. And Hilary had decided immediately that he'd be happiest with Joss.

"Alone at last," Andrew said with great melodrama as he showed her into his bedroom. As Kate laughed, he swept her into his arms in true movie-hero style and looked down into her face, his own face sobering. "I've dreamed of this moment," he murmured. "I was afraid it was an impossible dream."

She touched his face lightly with one hand, her thumb stroking over his mouth. His arms tightened immediately, pulling her close to his body. Then his mouth was on hers, kissing her lightly at first, then more demandingly as she responded. "I'd meant to settle you in gradually," he said, his mouth touching hers. "I fully intended making tea for you, helping you unpack, letting you rest. But suddenly, darling Kate, delayed gratification doesn't seem to appeal to me."

"I can't say I'm in need of rest," Kate said.

And somewhere between kisses and caresses and long shuddering breaths they managed to pull off their clothing and land, all wound together, in the middle of Andrew's wonderfully comfortable platform bed.

After a while, Kate stopped wondering whose hands were touching where, or whose voice was muttering incoherent but decidedly happy sounds. She and Andrew seemed to move as one as they started out on a fascinating journey of discovery, without any fears of interruption or feelings of haste.

A long, lovely time later, the room stopped whirling long enough for Kate to discover that she was tightly molded against Andrew's long tough naked body, her head cradled against his shoulder. As far as she was concerned, there seemed no reason to move. She could hear a faint hum of traffic in the distance, but Andrew's street was as quiet as a country lane. Not far away was a whole new world waiting for her to explore it. They would explore it together over the next four days. Four days. Only four days.

"We do that rather well, don't we?" Andrew said, still making understatements.

"We do, indeed," Kate agreed.

He leaned his head back and regarded her solemnly. "Is this the proper time to tell you what I've done?"

"Only if it's good news," she said. "I'm in too terrific a mood to want anything else."

"That's just it," he said doubtfully. "I'm not sure if you'll look upon it as good news or not."

She felt a sudden chill. "I think you'd better tell me."

He swallowed visibly. "Here we go then. I've put wheels in motion so you can stay in England. It's an amazing amount of red tape, of course, but the immigration officials I spoke with assure me it can be done. At the very least, they'll make it possible for you to stay on long enough for us to be married, which will simplify the whole immigration process."

Kate stared at him, speechless for all of ten seconds. Then she was abruptly furious. "Not once did you even hint at marriage," she said hotly. "I was sure you were just going to let me go at the end of my four-day stay. I wasn't even sure you'd drive me to the airport. I seriously considered hanging on to my rented car so I could drive myself."

She was sitting up very straight now. "You just took it for granted I would marry you, didn't you?" she demanded. "You even discussed it with Jocelyn, obviously—she said she wasn't going to worry about me going back to the States. But you didn't see fit to share any of your plans with me. Of all the overconfident, high-handed, arrogant..." Words failed her.

"Adorable?" Andrew supplied.

"That was the worst proposal I've ever heard of," she said. "It sounded more like a statement of personal intent."

"But it was a proposal," he said humbly. His eyes searched her face. Suddenly he didn't feel quite as confident. "You're not really angry, are you?" he asked. "I do agree with you that I'm an arrogant Englishman, taking far too much for granted. But I can be retrained, just as my father was. And I do think you love me. You do, don't you?"

She kept her face straight and an alarmed note came into his voice. "I can do this properly—truly I can. I will."

All at once he was dragging her over to the edge of his bed, while he sank to his knees on the plush cream-colored carpet and bowed his head. "You're a student of body language," he said. "What does this pose mean?"

"Humility," she said, laughing.

He raised his head, smiling at her, making all her hormones rush to positions of readiness. "You see how rapidly I can learn?" he asked. Then his face sobered. "I love you, Kate," he said solemnly. "I love you for your wit and your kind nature and your beautiful body, and not at all for your soon-to-be-acquired inheritance. Dare I hope you love me?" He made a lordly gesture. "You may answer yes or no."

"Yes," she said, touching his cheek with gentle fingers. "I love you, Andrew Bradford."

His smile blazed warmth into his eyes, turning them to silver. "Then will you please marry me, darling beautiful Kate?" he asked, then touched her lips with one finger. "Don't answer straightaway. Let me say my piece first." He took a deep breath and raised his right hand. "I solemnly promise to take you back to Seattle as soon as you wish to take care of any necessary packing and moving. I promise further to go with you to visit Seattle anytime you are homesick. And I promise to help you get started in London with your own photography business, of whatever nature you decide."

He straighened up so that his face was level with hers, kissed her lightly and then held her face gently between his hands. "And I also promise to love you always with the slightly demented, always fervent love of a man who has been starved of the stuff for years."

Kate thought she would never tire of watching that slow smile spread across his wonderfully strong face. "There's a postscript from Jocelyn, in case you need convincing," he added. "She said to tell you she's sorry you didn't get quite the family you came to England looking for, but hopes you'll accept the two of us as a substitute."

"May I speak now?" Kate asked, putting a hand each side of his face. His dear face.

"Only if you're going to say 'I will,'" he said firmly.

"I will," Kate said.

Following the success of **WITH THIS RING**,
Harlequin cordially invites you to enjoy the
romance of the wedding season with

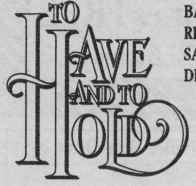 **BARBARA BRETTON**
RITA CLAY ESTRADA
SANDRA JAMES
DEBBIE MACOMBER

A collection of romantic stories that celebrate the joy,
excitement, and mishaps of planning that special day
by these four award-winning Harlequin authors.

**Available in April at your favorite Harlequin
retail outlets.**

THTH

Take 4 bestselling love stories FREE

Plus get a FREE surprise gift!

® Harlequin®

JANELLE TAYLOR

Valley of Fire

HARLEQUIN IS PROUD TO PRESENT *VALLEY OF FIRE* BY JANELLE TAYLOR—AUTHOR OF TWENTY-TWO BOOKS, INCLUDING SIX *NEW YORK TIMES* BESTSELLERS

VALLEY OF FIRE—the warm and passionate story of Kathy Alexander, a famous romance author, and Steven Winngate, entrepreneur and owner of the magazine that intended to expose the real Kathy ''Brandy'' Alexander to her fans.

Don't miss VALLEY OF FIRE, available in May.

FREE GIFT OFFER

To receive your free gift, send us the specified number of proofs-of-purchase from any specially marked Free Gift Offer Harlequin or Silhouette book with the Free Gift Certificate properly completed, plus a check or money order (do not send cash) to cover postage and handling payable to Harlequin/Silhouette Free Gift Promotion Offer. We will send you the specified gift.

FREE GIFT CERTIFICATE

ITEM	A. GOLD TONE EARRINGS	B. GOLD TONE BRACELET	C. GOLD TONE NECKLACE
# of proofs-of-purchase required	3	6	9
Postage and Handling	$1.75	$2.25	$2.75
Check one	☐	☐	☐

Name: _____

Address: _____

City: _____ State: _____ Zip Code: _____

Mail this certificate, specified number of proofs-of-purchase and a check or money order for postage and handling to: HARLEQUIN/SILHOUETTE FREE GIFT OFFER 1992, P.O. Box 9057, Buffalo, NY 14269-9057. Requests must be received by July 31, 1992.

PLUS—Every time you submit a completed certificate with the correct number of proofs-of-purchase, you are automatically entered in our MILLION DOLLAR SWEEPSTAKES! No purchase or obligation necessary to enter. See below for alternate means of entry and how to obtain complete sweepstakes rules.

MILLION DOLLAR SWEEPSTAKES
NO PURCHASE OR OBLIGATION NECESSARY TO ENTER

To enter, hand-print (mechanical reproductions are not acceptable) your name and address on a 3"x5" card and mail to Million Dollar Sweepstakes 6097, c/o either P.O. Box 9056, Buffalo, NY 14269-9056 or P.O. Box 621, Fort Erie, Ontario L2A 5X3. Limit: one entry per envelope. Entries must be sent via 1st-class mail. For eligibility, entries must be received no later than March 31, 1994. No liability is assumed for printing errors, lost, late or misdirected entries.

Sweepstakes is open to persons 18 years of age or older. All applicable laws and regulations apply. Sweepstakes offer void wherever prohibited by law. Prizewinners will be determined no later than May 1994. Chances of winning are determined by the number of entries distributed and received. For a copy of the Official Rules governing this sweepstakes offer, send a self-addressed, stamped envelope (WA residents need not affix return postage) to: Million Dollar Sweepstakes Rules, P.O. Box 4733, Blair, NE 68009.

✂ HI1U

ONE PROOF-OF-PURCHASE
To collect your fabulous FREE GIFT you must include the necessary FREE GIFT proofs-of-purchase with a properly completed offer certificate.

(See center insert for details)